PRETTY LIKE AN UGLY GIRL

CLAYTON LINDEMUTH

PRETTY LIKE AN UGLY GIRL

Clayton Lindemuth
Hardgrave Enterprises
SAINT CHARLES, MISSOURI

PRETTY LIKE AN UGLY GIRL/Clayton Lindemuth

ISBN-13: 978-1728762753

FOR THE FOLKS ON THE RED MEAT LIT STREET TEAM.
YOU ROCK.
THANKS FOR ALL THE HELP.

EVERY TREE THAT DOES NOT BEAR GOOD FRUIT IS CUT DOWN AND THROWN INTO THE FIRE. THEREFORE BY THEIR FRUITS YOU WILL KNOW THEM.

— MATHEW 7:19-20

ON THAT DAY MANY WILL SAY TO ME, 'LORD, LORD, DID WE NOT PROPHESY IN YOUR NAME, AND CAST OUT DEMONS IN YOUR NAME, AND DO MANY MIGHTY WORKS IN YOUR NAME?' AND THEN WILL I DECLARE TO THEM, 'I NEVER KNEW YOU; DEPART FROM ME, YOU WORKERS OF LAWLESSNESS.'

— MATTHEW 7: 22-23

CHAPTER 1

C ephus Graves sat in the passenger seat of a white Isuzu refrigerated box truck. The driver, his brother Finch, crowded up on a rusted Mitsubishi Trooper blocking the passing lane. A semi chugged along to their right. After nine hours of windshield time, Cephus looked forward to getting home. They had another long leg of driving tomorrow.

"Back off a little," Cephus said. "You have to be smarter than the other asshole. You get up on him, he'll just go slower 'cause he already knows you're pissed. Lot of people, that's their aim."

"I want to get home. I stink."

"Roll down the window."

"I have a headache."

"You are a headache."

The brothers made the trip every month, starting at the family homestead outside of Williams, Arizona, following Interstate 40 east to Flagstaff, Interstate 17 to Phoenix, and Interstate 10 most of the way to Sierra Vista. There they filled the truck with meat and returned the same day to Williams. The second day they drove nine hours from Williams to Salt Lake City, exchanged the meat for money, holed up at a motel, and returned to Williams the following day.

If it wouldn't have impugned their mother's virtue, Cephus and Finch could have believed they came from different fathers. Cephus, the baby of three brothers, was golden. In high school, he learned calculus because it took no effort. He spurned sports, theater, group activities, always preferring to speak for his own schedule. He tore things apart and rebuilt them. Traded for better. Talking came easily and his winsome smile, easier. He would soon follow in the footsteps of his oldest brother, Wayman, and expand the family business into new territory.

Finch, the middle son of Luke and Caroline Graves, was the black sheep. By age twenty-five, he'd already been thrice sequestered to rehab for chemical dependency, each time at a more promising, and more costly facility. He learned the yoga and the psychobabble. How to cook vegetarian. How to challenge the addiction by rooting out the deep neurosis that made him feel the need to change his mental state with drugs or alcohol, and to address it by other, more life affirming and healthful means.

Each time he came home clean, Finch quickly found his way back dirty.

His place in the family business was tenuous. The third time Luke and Caroline entered him into rehab, Luke said to her at the dinner table, *You love the family dog—but put him down when you have to. All we know about him, it's past due.*

Since then Finch had resumed his old habits. All-nighters at bars followed by poor decision making while at work, creating more risk than he was worth.

To Cephus, it was just a matter of time until his brother didn't show up to work one day.

"I ain't getting in trouble. I don't go out rabble rousing. I'm not the one with a felony record. Let's have a little fair play. All I'm asking."

It was true. Finch's older brother Wayman had spent three years in jail. But not for wild ways and stupidity. He'd taken the fall for another when, at his father's request, he moved to Salt Lake City to begin expanding the family operation. Wayman had been hit with a first strike possession-with-intent charge, and Luke had felt guilty for putting his son out on his own too early. Luke hired the best criminal defense attorney but drew a fire and brimstone judge. Wayman and Luke felt the mere three-year sentence, out of a possible and more-likely fifteen, was a blessing from providence. Because of the hard lesson, they played the game tighter, took fewer chances, and did their best to make sure Cephus learned from their mistakes.

Professional criminality was different from criminal recklessness. A mature human being calculated risks, took precautions, put insurance in place. A professional knew sometimes bad breaks happened. It wasn't like they took the field unopposed every day. Cops, DEA, ATF, FBI—there was no end to the agencies and resources dedicated to curbing their economic freedom. Even if the so-called good guys were corrupt and incompetent—what was the saying? A blind squirrel finds a nut once in a while. Law enforcement won every now and again. So what? A pro didn't leave the game. A pro took calculated risks that sometimes went against him. It wasn't dumb; it was smart because the occasional three year stint in the pen meant nothing compared to the bank made the rest of the time —especially when the pro decided to play it so tight, that shit never happened again.

Finch, however, didn't limit his criminality to the work his father required of him. He supplemented it with lifestyle criminality as well. Stupid shit. Shoplifting. Bar fights. Selling X to college girls.

They took Interstate 40 west at Flagstaff. Cephus let his eyes drift to the buildings and lights for the short stretch where Flagstaff was visible from the road.

He closed his eyes and rested his head against the seatback. Thought about a girl he'd met at the bar the other night—

Finch swerved hard. Cephus grabbed the door. A loud clunk sounded, and the vehicle bounced like it had run over an I-beam. A tire exploded and hissed. The truck shook. The vehicle pulled right.

"Don't brake," Cephus said. "Coast."

Finch locked his arms and white knuckled the steering wheel. He sat back in his seat and removed his foot from the gas. The Isuzu slowed.

Cephus reached to the console and hit the hazard light button.

"Just drift over to the edge."

"Shit. Wow."

"What the hell was that?" Cephus said.

"I—I barely saw it. Looked like an axle."

"An axle? Like, the whole thing?"

"What it looked like."

"Nah. Can't be."

Finch pulled over. Cephus ran back and discovered the object was a drive shaft. He waved an oncoming car to the other lane and dragged the hazard ten feet from the road. From the double thump, Cephus surmised they'd hit it with both right front and dually rears. The front blew.

Cephus trotted back to the truck.

"There's an exit in a mile or so. Drive on the berm until we get there."

"Won't that ruin the rim?"

"Yeah, but we've got *meat*, and I don't want a state trooper stopping to be helpful."

"Dad'll be pissed about the rim."

Cephus shook his head. "Drive. It's about being exposed, dumbass."

The blown-out tire shredded and, after what seemed like ten minutes of thwacking and thumping, fell off the rim.

Metal on concrete.

"Thought you said a mile. It's been at least five."

"Cool Pines is up ahead. Just keep going."

They arrived at the exit. Finch turned.

"Okay, here. Up ahead it comes to a T. We can pull over on the flat and change the tire out of the way."

Finch drove onto red volcanic dirt. The sign said: FIRE DANGER *MODERATE* TODAY!

Beyond a wooden ranch style fence, several hundred acres of flatland grass and sporadic evergreens vied for moisture, before giving way to forests and scattered mountains.

Stepping out of the truck, Cephus smelled wood smoke. He studied the tree line, surveyed a half circle for light or visual smoke. The air was still—it could be coming from anywhere. Cephus leaned a .308 rifle he used for hunting deer against the side of the truck.

Finch exited the Isuzu NQR refrigerated box. It hadn't come with a spare tire, and in the meat business, they couldn't afford to wait all day for a repair or tow truck. They'd built a contingency box in the back of the truck, toward the cab. It held anything they'd need in an emergency, spare front tire and jack, torque wrench, flares, triangles, blankets, candles.

Pick and shovel.

Finch unlocked the back door, removed the lock, and rotated the latch.

"Hold up," Cephus said.

"What's to think about?"

The door flew open. A black-haired boy bounded out of the back, shouldered Finch backward, and launched himself down the road at a sprint. He cut to the left, dove to the ground, and crawled under the barbed wire.

Now running in the open, he headed straight away from the truck. Cephus looked inside. The boy's handcuff hung on the wall rail used for binding loads, like in a U-Haul. The loop that should have held his wrist dangled open. Cephus studied the girls. "Show me your wrists! Hold them up!" He held up his arm and grabbed the closest girl, lifted hers. The others stared at him, and slowly lifted their wrists. They were all handcuffed.

Cephus stepped to the right front tire. Lifted the .308, wrapped the sling around his left arm, and lowered the rifle. He assumed an unsupported standing position, at an angle toward the rear. He glanced around for any oncoming traffic. It was dusk. Nothing, anywhere.

The boy's red jacket was easy to spot. Cephus lowered his eye to the scope and found the picture. He aligned the cross hairs on the boy's back. Elevated for distance—the little shit was quick.

Cephus switched off the safety.

"Any traffic Finch?"

"No. None."

Cephus fired.

A girl shrieked.

The boy tumbled.

Cephus peered over the riflescope. From his left field of vision darted a coyote—no, it was a white dog. He picked it up in the scope's cross hairs. This was a challenge, a dog running full bore. He led by two lengths and pulled the trigger. The animal rolled.

Cephus slung his rifle and turned to Finch. "Stupid cock. Why'd you open the door?"

"Like that was my fault."

"It's not about fault. It's about not doing shit until you're prepared."

Cephus turned to where the Mexican boy lay. His jacket would be easily visible from the road. Might be visible even from Interstate 40.

"We've got to bury him," Cephus said.

"You shot him," Finch said.

"I'm not leaving you here with the meat and the truck. Go."

Cephus stared at his older brother.

"I'll fix the flat," Cephus said. "Move, dammit!"

Finch climbed inside the truck and grabbed a shovel secured inside the emergency box.

CHAPTER 2

L and out here's so dry you can stretch out with yer feet on a log and don't get yer back wet. Fire burn low and slow, keep the coals ready to cook. Got the butane stove but ain't learned to use it.

Mountains dropped all over. Climb one and gander full circle; they's everywhere. Just like a flat, and somebody with a big ass bucket dropped a mountain here and there, no rhyme or reason, 'cept mebbe he was walking northeast and kept changing bucket hands. They boil up outta nothing, rest the land smooth. Uncanny.

Accourse, time you get the top it's good as drinking a half gallon a hooch. They's no air up there. Glad I done it, but once is nice and twice make the fool.

Now I's back, got the feet elevated and the blood rushing back the brain. This's what I wanted, all them years writing letters to Ruth. Got a space to lay down under never ending sky, and Ruth's a half day walk away. Slip in when I want—so to speak.

Almost wasn't so.

We drove two women yammering and three kids a-crying all the way from east to west. Noise and deceit. Women don't know better. It's how they think, crooked paths, can't get to the kernel 'less they whittle at it from sixteen directions. Each time it looks and feels like deceit—'cause they don't even know theyselves what they think till they say it the third time. Damndest thing. They manage to eat and comb they hair and do all the things a body got to do, but shit if I know how. Women minds don't work right.

7

So we split up.

Mae got on a red wig and Elton John sunglasses and I throw on the suit. We go to five banks. Split the gold 'tween ten deposit boxes. Traded some for walking cash. That, and I found a leather belt at the outfitters. Got pockets for cigarettes and phones and all whatnot, sit the small yer back. Filled 'em with ten-pound specie, so if the banks confiscate the boxes, I ain't destitute.

Now the women's at the hotel and I's under the sky. Got the waterproof backpack. Down sleeping bag. Cook stove. Water purifier with the hand pump and ceramic innards. Pouches of backpacker food, all you do is boil water and pour. Salty like you dragged yer tongue on a deer lick.

Peace, quiet. I's set up like a king, for equipment. Tactical knife with a nub for breaking glass and a slot for cutting parachute cord. I bought parachute cord so's to have something to cut. Plastic coated topographical map, whole top half Arizona. Karabiners. Cargo pants. New boots and wool socks. Compass. Fishing line. Snakebite kit.

Got a spoon with nubs like a fork. Hippies come up with that.

Got a small jug likker too, but it been two days silence with no women and kids, and I don't take a pull but when the mood strike. I don't hardly remember I got it, and when I do, I's so damn thirsty I drink water first. After that, they's no room for the likker. Too much 'sploring to do.

I set up camp two hundred yard from the road where Mae and Ruth cut me loose. Said they'd be back for me in two week. I'd use the time to let my brain get used to peace, and they'd use it to not have to deal with a ornery cuss likes to shoot people. I give each the kids a peck and a hug to the women. They drop me off and here I am. Walked two hundred yard, said shit, I's here; Joe let's pitch the tent. Ain't moved camp; just been scouting about with this as home base.

Way off comes a rifle *crack!* and echo like from a deer rifle. Hear 'em all the time back home. 'Cept we's too close the road for legit hunters.

Stinky Joe sets out at a dead run.

"No! Joe! C'mon back here."

He been sniffing and chasing every animal you can imagine—pronghorn cave wall animals live out here. I grab my new binoculars. Light getting low.

They's a white van, maybe a refrigerated truck, fella in a standing position with the rifle. Scan left to where he look—clump of red in a pile, got legs and black hair. Back to the fella got the rifle. He faces left and right, naked eye. Sees Joe and pull up the rifle.

"Ah, hell no!"

I drag Smith out for duty, but time I got him level, they's another shot and Stinky Joe rolls in dust.

Holster Smith. I couldn't hit land from here let alone a man.

Joe's a pile of white. He kicks and wiggles. I picture the man shot him—inside fifteen minute he'll be upside down from a oak, skinned from the ankles. Put his head in a bucket and keep his mouth above the blood line and his nose below.

Feel like I's Job and God decided to write a book. It ain't ordinarily possible a man can go through so much travails with his canines.

I swallow back stomach acid and set off on legs still wobbly from the mountain climb.

Twenty yard in, I's working a good stomp. I'll get there 'fore they change the tire and, if not, fill the cab with holes.

Dusk come fast out west, was already on us before the commotion. Now I want a little light, seems they ain't a minute of day left. I stalk the truck. Another fella walks out a ways, climbs over a wood fence. I stop next a evergreen and look him over with binoculars. This ain't the fella shot Joe. This one's a white boy with dreadlock hair.

Look'im over. He ain't armed—'cept a shovel.

He cut toward the shot body with the red jacket.

Now I got a good angle, I see the other fella works a jack at the front right tire. It's an Isuzu box, white with the refrigerator unit above the flat nosed cab. Side of the van's got a picture of a eight foot T-bone. A smoking black brand in the meat says GRAVES MEATS.

Guess in Arizona they brand the meat, not the hide.

I think through what I see.

These boys got a flat, pull way off the interstate to fix it, and shoot a man run off for the mountains. Is these boys the famous *coyotes*, smuggle illegals so they can beg work at the Home Depot parking lot?

I's close enough to mostly read the front plate with the field glasses, though dark is near on us and the letters don't resolve. ACP 1288.

Mebbe. The last three could be any damn thing.

I look back to Stinky Joe and can't see his white coat nowhere. Search back and forth with the mountain for reference, but I moved since I last saw him. I still got the better elevation but he's nowhere.

Dreadlocks boy with the shovel sets about digging beside the body of the fella that run. I keep my peace for the moment—but just the moment. Man with the shovel be easy take down. I'll get the one with the rifle first.

Gander all around so they's no surprises when I come out shooting, and a knee-high ghost lopes 'tween scrub and pine toward camp.

Stinky Joe's alive.

I let the blood drop from boil to simmer. I saw the man shoot the blackhair and saw him shoot my dog. Seems like a right-thinking man'd do something about him.

But I slip back to camp.

Mebbe this ain't my fight. Be nice to go a couple week without trouble. And I shoot these pricks, I gotta break camp.

SIT ON A ROCK. Ain't right, grown man weepy on a dog. But Stinky Joe ain't a dog so much as noble creature. He'll shake to pieces wanting a belly rub, and when danger come he'll piss hisself then jump out the window to save you. Noble creature—and that's why he's man's best friend. He'll sleep beside and fight beside you. Eat anything you give him. Nasty ass old Burger King. He'll answer back but won't start too many conversations of his own. Near perfect animal.

Now I got it all: got my solitude and big sky; a woman stops talking when I poker; got the daughter you'd dream of, level headed and carries a forty-five; got the three grandbabies. I got it all and when I think I lose my dog, I weep.

Must be all the killing. Ain't a month since I come home to see Fred with a hole where his eye was. And a fortnight removed from the butchery I done with the wood alcohol. And then with guns and a firecracker.

All a man wants is a world without the evil that calls his own to match.

Found Stinky Joe at camp. Pet him while he shook hisself tired. Had blood on his coat but I let him curl up on my sleeping bag anyhow. Rubbed him up and down and that rifle bullet grazed the top his neck, a slice out the skin and a nick of bone I felt with my fingers. Musta been the shock of bullet on bone dropped him. I love him till he growl, then sit myself outside on a rock.

The meat truck drove off long ago, and it's dark enough I need a fire to see.

I think on what I saw and what my stake is with the body they left out there. Some Mexican come into the country and got shot by the man brought him. Don't know I's the one responsible to solve that crime.

But that body out there—I saw him in the dirt, and he didn't seem the size as the man with the shovel.

I sit and ponder what I got and don't got to do, and the moon come up silver and big. Outside my little copse of evergreen shadows, the landscape lights up, and I can almost see the messed-up earth where Dreadlocks buried him.

"Stay in the tent, you hear?"

You should stay too ...

"Don't I know it, Joe."

Don't get reckless on me.

I look at him. He bury his head in the sleeping bag and I cover the rest him too. I don't know why we got to have such a evil world. I don't know.

Smith at my hip but it's just a cold lonely night, now the killers 've left. I can't do nothing even if I see what I don't want. I can't call in what I saw. Can't involve myself. And no matter what I do this man with the red jacket's dead. I ain't fixing that. So why in hell I strut out in the moonlight to dig his ass up?

I get to the pile of dirt and rocks and can't hardly believe the depths of stupidity. Dreadlocks had the shovel but didn't dig a hole. He scooped up dirt and drizzle it on top. Good wind'd blow the body clean.

Half his shoulder's out. I grab under and lift, roll him face up.

Ain't but a ten-twelve-year-old boy. Eyes open. Mouth open.

Am I your problem to solve, or not?

"That's fine English. And I don't know."

CHAPTER 3

M ae sipped beer from a frosty mug at a bar in Flagstaff, Arizona. At eight in the evening on Friday, the place was already crawling with college guys. It wasn't her scene. She'd seen a poor female dog once, licked and slobbered on by a male that wouldn't leave her alone. He just kept licking her. The female had looked up at her, and they'd shared a moment. Being in the college bar, Mae felt like that. Every five seconds, some guy whose sack had barely descended and fuzzed over ogled her, offered to buy her a drink, used a dumb ass line.

"If a charming, intelligent fellow was to successfully get into your underwear, what would he say?"

"I don't know. But he'd use first person, you pretentious bitch."

He returned to his frat buddies and the next came up. This one, red hair with dimples.

"Are your legs tired?"

She said nothing.

He lifted his eyebrows. Exhaled. Recovered with a broad smile. "Because you've been running through—"

"C'mere. You see this?"

She angled her purse toward him. Inside, the chrome of a .45.

"Piss off, okay? Just leave."

One more swallow of the house-brewed chocolate stout, and she'd find a joint with some gray ponytail dudes.

Glancing across the bar, she noticed the red headed man-child gesticulating to the others, his face painted red with apparent alarm.

Whatever.

Mae drank chocolate stout.

After serving shotgun with Baer Creighton driving a pristine 1982 Chevy station wagon he bought with gold specie from a white-haired widow who kept saying, *Mmm, if I was twenty years younger,* Mae had no doubt why Baer had spent his life alone.

He was intolerable. Compassionate. Giving. Yes. Every thousand miles or so. The rest of the time, *evil this, lyin' that.*

Nonstop.

He passed a semi in Oklahoma and said, "That's an evil sombitch in there."

"How you know?"

"He look at me."

"You need meditation or something. Hypnotherapy."

"Aromatherapy," Ruth said.

"That wouldn't make him smell better, Ma."

"Well, maybe it wouldn't be so stuffy in here. Would you lower the back window a hair? Joseph must have farted again. I hope."

Tulsa. The next exit was Tulsa. What would be wrong with her asking Baer to drop her off at Tulsa? Find a Hardee's or something ...

But she'd stuck it out, knowing ultimately, her life and her kids' lives would be better with Baer Creighton in them.

Looking at it that way, their lives would be impossibly bad without him.

If he just wasn't so intolerable.

"Why are you so gosh darned judgmental all the time?"

"I ain't judgmental. Just discerning."

They'd get to Flagstaff, the town Baer kept musing about, and then go back to the way things were.

Separate.

Mostly. Until he needed something.

Until *she* needed something.

Face it, you weren't doing so hot when he was your uncle. You needed him a hell of a lot more than he needed you.

"Excuse me, miss, I see you sitting all alone, got these kids bothering you all the time."

Mae looked up. Swallowed. Fifty-something white dude with sun baked skin and a voice like crushed limestone.

"Want me to sit here so they fuck off?"

"Uh, that would be perfect."

"What's your name?"

"Mae."

"Pretty." He waived. A woman with an apron came. "I'll have ginger ale. Mae—care for another chocolate porter?"

"Sure."

He nodded at the woman. She spun. From the corner of her sight, Mae noticed the red-haired boy approach the bar. He spoke to the bartender, nodded toward Mae.

Crushed-limestone-man pulled back a stool. They were heavy, the legs made from small trees that barely had the bark removed before being dipped in varnish. He dragged the chair with one hand like it was on wheels. Sat.

"I don't get out much," he said, "but I haven't seen you before."

"But you know the house chocolate porter on sight."

"Well, I still haven't seen you before."

"Enough about me. What's your name?"

The beer wench returned with two fresh mugs, one sparkling, the other black with foam rolling over the top. The man peeled a twenty from a money clip.

"Thanks, Nat. Say, you running for governor?"

Bullshit! Get up and leave. This is a routine. He throws around the money, she says the line. He practices—

"No interest whatsoever."

"You ought to. Clean this state up."

"Thank you, but I'm a private sector guy."

The beer wench looked at him too long, then turned.

"So you're not running for governor—Nat, is it? That your real name?" Mae said. "You don't expect me to buy any of this, just because you're an older guy, right? What, you set up the routine with the beer girl before coming over to save me?"

Nat regarded her. Someone broke a rack on the pool table behind her. Mae jumped. Gritted her teeth.

"Tell you what, I made a mistake, but I'll salvage this for both of us. Take my ginger ale over there and let you enjoy the evening. Pleasant to meet you, Mae."

Bullshit. He's playing mind games. He won't leave.

Nat walked to a table across the bar, sat looking away from her to the sidewalk beyond the window. He sipped his ginger ale.

"Excuse me miss. You have to leave, or we're calling the cops."

Mae turned. The bartender stood beside her, and beside him, a man built like a barn.

"What?"

"We have a report you're carrying a firearm. I should have called the cops already, but you're apparently not from around here. You have to leave now, or I'm making the call."

"Well, that's a bunch of bullshit."

"Mike, stand here; don't let her move, unless it's out the door."

The bartender turned and halted. Nat Cinder stood behind him.

"Nat?"

"Hey, George, I know this girl. She causing trouble?"

"She brought a firearm into the establishment. Now she's being pissy about it. I'm calling the cops."

"Mind if I go to work on her?"

"You got one minute."

Nat stepped between the George and the barn. "Mae, give me the gun. You'll get it back."

Mae extracted the .45. In handing it to Nat, she swung the business end past George.

"Whoa, easy. Don't point that thing unless you want to shoot it."

"Who says I don't want to shoot it."

Nat eased the gun from her hand, released the magazine, pulled back the slide, and held the pistol so the ejected bullet landed on the table. He slipped it into the magazine.

"George, is it all right with you if I lock this in my vehicle and the lady and I stay here and talk a while?

George nodded, closed his eyes.

"George?"

"Okay. Miss, you can't ever bring that in here again. Next time I or my staff sees you, we're going to check. Got it?"

Mae nodded.

Nat walked around the bouncer and Mae followed him outside. He pulled a key fob from his pocket and a Ram truck flashed its lights. He opened the driver side door, pulled a metal case from below the seat, tethered to the seat frame by a quarter inch steel cable.

"So this is what I had in mind. We'll stow you piece in here. I'll let you hang onto the key, and when we're done chatting, you get your gun back."

"Good."

He opened the metal box, pulled the pistol that was already in it out, and jammed it under his jacket into his pants at his back.

He placed her gun in the box, locked it. Closed and locked the Ram, then gave Mae the key to the box.

"Wait a minute. Now you're going to carry your gun into the bar?"

"Uh-huh. Difference is, no one sees mine until I'm ready to use it."

She followed him back inside the bar. He stood at her table a moment, nodded. "All right. Glad I could help." He headed back to his table and ginger ale.

Mae finished her existing mug of porter, wondered how many calories she'd just dumped in the trunk, and stood. She grabbed the mug Nat had bought. Walked across the bar. Drank half and sat down next to him.

"Excuse me. I seen some of these boys kissin' other boys. You want me to sit here and keep 'em away? Long as I don't give you any more shit? Or better yet, how about this? I'm sorry. I'm a dumb ass. I've had my guard up for— well, not long enough, to tell the truth, but—"

"Have a seat, Mae. Glad for the company."

CHAPTER 4

Cephus set about the evening's work. Mentioning a woman in Flagstaff, Finch took off the moment they arrived at the house, before their father came out to greet them. Luke Graves stood at the entrance from the garage to the house. He looked around as if expecting to see Finch.

"What brought you in late?"

Cephus explained about the drive shaft, flat tire, runaway boy, and having no recourse but to shoot him. Luke nodded. The logic was sound.

"Your brother say where he took off to?"

"A female obligation."

Luke was silent. After a moment staring at the far end of the garage, he smiled as if whatever troubled him found resolution. "Let's get a look at this truck."

Father and son inspected the Isuzu's rear tires. Luke pointed to a gash in the sidewall of the driver's side inner tire. Some operators might trust it not to blow for the remainder of the journey.

"We take zero chances," Luke said.

They'd have to deflate the tire, remove it from the vehicle, and replace it with another kept at the garage for just such exigencies.

On the monthly run from Sierra Vista to Salt Lake City, Cephus and Finch always stopped at the family homestead for the night and unloaded the meat into a specially constructed basement under the garage. Windowless and bare, a wide storage area hid its entrance. The chamber's only accoutrements were a toilet, sink, ten double mattresses on the floor, and ten wool blankets. Luke considered it safer than either trying to make the drive from Sierra Vista to Salt Lake City straight through, or staying at a hotel and leaving the cargo in the truck overnight.

"You unload the meat, and I'll get things together for the tire change."

Half expecting another person to leap from the truck, Cephus unlatched the back door and eased it open. The girls were still handcuffed in place.

Cephus smelled something wretched—then he saw it. In the twenty-minute drive between where Cephus put on the front spare tire and where they arrived at port for the night, one of the girls had placed a pile of defecate in the middle of the truck bed.

Cephus saw flecks of green chili.

He observed each girl in turn. None met his gaze. One softly snored.

This had never happened before.

First, meat was warned about the nine-hour drive to ensure they made their best use of the toilet before getting on the truck.

Second, none had ever taken a serious issue with traveling in handcuffs before. They weren't prisoners. Exactly. At this point in their journey, they were closing in on the payoff and hoping for a better future. They'd been recruited throughout Central America and promised transportation to the land of opportunity and jobs. They all wanted to come—even if they weren't fully aware what their eventual jobs would be, they had to be able to guess. The girls were all pretty. Some were stunners. The boys were effete.

It wasn't rocket science.

And the business of pairing worker with work, or dreamer with dream—was virtuous. His father had explained the principles dozens of times.

Two factors made their work noble.

First, these boys and girls weren't even people. Latin Americans all belonged to a sub-class. The way you could tell was what happened when you left them to their own devices. Now, you could transplant a few into America here and there, and they'd do fine. They'd blend right in with the other trash —white, black, brown, yellow, red. Every race produced rabble. But, when you looked at what happened when they ran everything themselves, you saw how profoundly inferior they were. All Latin American countries were shitholes. The people were unintelligent, lazy, and corrupt. They baked those attributes into their way of doing business, their politics, everything about their societies. It was nothing against them. They were what they were.

God gave a man eyes for a reason.

Luke explained it this way: If you bred a German shepherd with a pug, the result would be a dog, but damn sure not a German shepherd. Pugs are okay, but next to a German shepherd, well, you see the difference.

"Why would you mate a German shepherd with a pug?"

"Why would a white man screw a darkie? He has a dick. That's why. You get what I mean, right?"

The second factor making their work noble was that the kids they brought to Salt Lake City would live in the United States. If you're going to suck and fuck for a living, it's best to do it where they teach hygiene in elementary school and most homes can afford soap and running water.

"That's how to think of it," Luke had said to Cephus when he was still in high school and the new part of the family meat business was taking off. "We take them from where they live in fields, where they're subject to misery, labor, drug dependency, and exploitation. Instead of that, we bring them into the house. They get clean, warm and dry, and we get money. Win—win."

But this group had a couple rebels. First was the boy who'd figured out how to pry open his handcuffs.

The second was the girl who defecated on the floor.

The dirtiness wouldn't be an issue. They washed the truck in bleach after every run. It was a meat truck.

But the attitude ...

Some deals you didn't take, because beyond the immediate profit, lurked unintended consequences. A boy who'd bolt from the truck at first opportunity? That was a future risk in a dozen ways.

Just like a girl who'd try to make a statement by leaving a pile of shit on the floor.

Were she to live and enter their employment arrangement at Salt Lake City, she might pay for herself and then some. But she would be difficult to control. She would sow seeds of disorder and resentment one by one, or inspire wider revolt. She could harm their business's reputation with their clientele. And the greatest risk: she could escape and bring back law enforcement.

The limited loss of the cost of acquiring her—a few grand—compared to the tens or hundreds of thousands of dollars harm she could potentially cause, made culling the risk the only smart move.

"One of the girls crapped on the floor," Cephus told his father.

Luke came to the door and looked inside. He led Cephus away from the back of the truck. "Whichever girl did that, she'll be a problem later. Find her. Take her out to the other and make sure they're never found."

"Yep."

Cephus entered the back of the Isuzu. All the girls pretended to sleep. The defecate was as close to dead center as possible, as if someone had drawn lines corner to corner and placed the pile on the X. It could have been any of them.

All the girls had a single hand cuffed to a wood slat located on the wall one foot from the floor. None—even the girls closest the center—could have gotten her rear end to the center of the truck.

The pile, which had flattened upon impact, had not rolled. It landed where it now rested. There were no smudges, nor were there other traces elsewhere on the truck bed or walls.

Cephus concluded one of the girls had messed into her hand and tossed it to the center.

Water was unavailable in the back of the truck, and no amount of spit could wash a hand clean. He grabbed the first girl's wrist, inspected her open hand, then brought it to his nose. Cephus went to the second girl. The third ...

The sixth girl resisted when he grasped her arm. She held her hand closed, and when he pried it open, shoved it flat into his face. Cephus responded by instinct, clubbing her with his hand so quickly it was like a slap, except the impact was mostly at the palm of his hand. The blow stunned her.

This was the girl. He smelled her hand to be sure.

She was pretty in the face, but skinny and undeveloped elsewhere. A kid.

He knew what he had to do.

However ...

Cephus had never killed a girl.

Something deep in his biology revolted at the thought. He'd look at himself differently if he crossed that line.

That wasn't a bad thing. Just a thing.

His older brother Wayman would kill her and not be put off by the work. He wouldn't enjoy it, necessarily, but he would find sufficient satisfaction in knowing he fulfilled his duty with intelligence and dedication. Just like Cephus imagined a utility worker might come home after a ten-hour day and feel good about restoring the power, plugging the leak, whatever they did. There's pride in doing a dirty job well.

Wayman had crossed the line so long ago, he seemed comfortable with the depth of his criminality. He was pro, nothing squeamish about him. Cephus looked forward to seeing him the next day. Wayman ran a tight operation and always took pains to explain his processes and strategies, so his little brother could someday run his own shop and not make the same mistakes.

Cephus unlocked the emergency box at the front of the truck. He removed a twenty-foot quarter inch steel cable with a loop at each end. He brought one to the farthest girl, unlocked her handcuff from the wall rail, and fastened it to the loop. He locked another girl to the opposite loop. One by one, he secured the rest to the cable.

Except the one who shat.

He led the string of girls from the Isuzu, down a ramp, to a wire storage cage set up to partially hide the basement entrance. After unlocking the cage, he led the girls inside, down the steps, and to the basement. He uncuffed each, dragged the cable outside with him, then locked them in.

Standing at the door, Cephus listened. Heard nothing. The drug was marvelous at shutting down the girls' brains.

Except when they didn't take it.

Cephus washed his hands and face in a sink at the side of the garage near the entry to the house. He would do as his father required. This was exactly the kind of obedience and level headed thinking his father needed to witness before entrusting him with the next level of responsibility.

The easiest kill would be to choke her. No blood. Tiny struggle. She was small and had one arm bound. It would be an easy task.

But then he'd have to carry her body everywhere, including a couple hundred yards from the road to the body of the boy he'd shot earlier. People's sphincters released when they died, and the thought of carrying the girl's unwashed and newly soiled ass a few inches from his head …

Be a whole lot easier if he let her walk. She'd enjoy it more too.

Cephus forced the girl to lie on her belly with her arm held up by handcuff to the rail. He removed it and snapped it to her other wrist, behind her back.

He lifted her to a standing position. She kept her eyes downward, but when he stepped in front, her glare flashed hatred and she spat in his face. It came out as a dry-mouthed spatter, almost nothing. Cephus backed away, shook his head.

Beating her would do no good, and her resistance would end soon enough anyway. He wiped his face with the bottom of his untucked flannel shirt and steered the girl to the doorway and down the ramp.

The next problem was transportation. He could take her in the bed of his pickup truck, but she could easily make herself visible, even handcuffed to a tie down. He could put her up front, but not if she was going to shit all over his leather seats. The only thing he could think of was to give her a good beating. That almost turned his stomach. He could do his duty if he kept it clinical, but hearing her whimper or cry out would go straight to his weakness. Sometimes it was hard to remember these girls weren't really girls, the way he was taught to think of them.

He decided to use duct tape.

His father worked at replacing the near-blown inner tire. Luke gave an approving nod as Cephus manhandled the girl to the cement garage floor, rolled the tape around her ankles several passes, and then right up to her knees, so she had no ability to separate her legs.

"Get her mouth too," Luke said. "She gives you any trouble at all, just squeeze her nose. She'll get compliant."

Cephus covered her mouth with tape.

She writhed and kicked when he threw her head first onto the back seat of his extended cab F-150. On the drive, though she had no voice, she repeatedly kicked with both her taped legs against the door.

Cephus pulled over on the highway, opened the back door, and slammed the bottom of his fist to her forehead. She stopped kicking.

Arriving, Cephus drove up and down the road parallel the highway until deciding there was no one around. He turned and parked where he'd changed the front tire on the Isuzu.

He opened the back door, pulled out the girl, and tied a rope to her hand-cuffed hands in case she bolted. Then he cut the duct tape between her legs and ripped it from her skin.

The temperature had plummeted after nightfall, heading from the seventies straight down to something more like snow weather. The girl wore shorts and a thin shirt, the same she'd worn in Sierra Vista, and probably in Mexico. The rest of the girls would be given additional clothing in the morning, and a wardrobe suitable to their profession at Salt Lake City. They wouldn't need anything else because they'd never leave, except on to the next city.

The girl shivered.

"It'll be over soon," Cephus said, though none of them ever spoke English.

Instead of bringing his .308 rifle, for this job Cephus carried a Sig Sauer P226 chambered in a .40 S&W. It was an expensive gun preferred by law enforcement for its superior ergonomics and reliability. Cephus owned it because it came with a shit ton of cool factor.

He withdrew the pistol from his hip holster and showed it to her. "You work with me, I'll make this fast and easy. Cause any trouble, it's going to take a long time and you'll go through a lot of pain. *Comprende?*"

He grasped her upper arm and guided her to the fence. She bent over to pass between the rails, but with her hands locked behind her back, she couldn't grab a rail to balance herself, and couldn't lift her leg between the horizontal fence slats. Cephus supported her shoulders, and thought what an irony, how she trusted him to not let her fall on her face now, knowing in five minutes he'd blow a hole through it.

On the other side of the fence, they walked into the hundred-acre flatland. A distant mountain rose black against the moon-gray sky. Again, Cephus smelled wood smoke.

After several minutes of back-and-forth searching, he found the red-jacketed boy.

"Dammit Finch!"

The body was completed exposed. Finch had apparently scraped the shovel to the ground a few times and called it quits.

"That's the kind of shit right there—"

"Want somethin' done right, gotta do it yer own damn self."

Cephus spun but the source of the voice was darkness.

"Got ya in the moon, asshole."

The voice came from low.

"Let the boy go."

Cephus saw a flash.

CHAPTER 5

Driving to Flagstaff, Finch Graves threw up in his mouth and choked it back down. He pulled a bottle of water from the center console of his Mustang. Gargled water and tried to swallow the burn out of his throat. It didn't work.

The drugs and alcohol charade was wearing thin. He didn't crave excess by nature, as some did. Truth was, he hated being stoned or drunk. However, years earlier, when the family first made the foray from being the town butcher to the town brothel, *from one meat to another* as his father said, Finch had stayed out partying one night. The next day he arrived late for work, and found his father made an allowance for him. Luke wasn't pleased, but accepted the explanation that Finch was incapacitated due to alcohol.

All night drinking served two functions. On one hand, he missed a lot of work. On the other, he coped with the self-loathing created by the work he didn't escape.

The strategy became successful, if unsustainable. The more he drank, smoked pot, and let himself go, the less Luke and Cephus expected from him. He carried less responsibility and figured small in their plans, if at all.

On the downside, Finch saw his lack of reliability was wearing thin, and his body was telling him he couldn't abuse it forever.

He needed out soon. He *wanted* out now. Tonight.

He swerved into the parking lot of a realtor located next to an outfitter. Flagstaff was full of tourist shit. They came to see the natural wonders, the red rocks of Sedona, the San Francisco Peaks, the volcano cones and Cinder Lake, and canyon after canyon. Elk. They came for the clean air.

But no one saw the raw, human reality hidden between, behind, and underneath the landscape. The misery that passed through—very often in a meat truck.

Finch parked next to a Chevy Impala and waited. He watched the cars that had been behind him to make sure none followed, or pulled over up ahead. Satisfied his brother or father had not had him tailed, Finch powered down the window.

The Impala window descended. Inside sat a woman with hair pulled tight in a ponytail, maybe a little too high on the head for a woman her age. It made her face brittle.

Finch noticed things like that. Finch noticed everything.

"Oh Christ, I gotta talk. I need out. I gotta get out."

"Get in the car."

He exited the Mustang and climbed into the Impala "Got your text," she said. "What's going on?"

"I finally saw it. I finally have what you need."

"What's that?"

Finch unzipped his jacket. Pulled his shirt from his pants and up to his chest. "Take it."

"Is the run over?"

"No."

"Then put your shirt down."

The device looked like a circular band-aid, an inch and a half wide with a slightly thicker pad in the center. It recorded only when sound amplitude was high enough for the microphone to catch conversations at the preset desired volume. The battery lasted days, and the memory chip held up to fifteen hours of talk.

Finch lowered his shirt.

"It's the same deal, right? I'm coming clean. I've got no part of this. I'm giving you everything."

"The deal hasn't changed." The woman looked away from him and then back, a move he interpreted as saying, *Spit it out.*

"Cephus shot a man tonight."

She adjusted her weight in the seat. "One of the kids?"

Finch nodded. "A boy."

"How did it happen?"

"I—I wanted to help him escape. All of them. I thought if I gave him a key —I was going to open the door to the back of the truck at a gas station. We usually fill the tanks at the same station, at the end of the run. They'd all get out and there'd be nothing Cephus could do to get them back."

"That would have been really dumb. We'd have no case, and your father would bury you in the desert. What were you thinking?"

"About the kids. Each of them. They're all lost!"

"Calm down, tell your story."

"Well, it didn't work. We hit something on the road and had a flat. When I opened the back door of the truck to get the jack and spare, the kid who had the key bolted. And it was just the one. He didn't help any of the girls. He just took off."

"So ..."

"Cephus shot him with his rifle. It was off the Cool Pines exit, close to Williams. Then he sent me out to bury him."

"Did you?"

"Yes. But barely. I piled some dirt on top, but he'll be easy to find."

"Okay. And you're sure he was dead?"

"One hundred percent dead."

"That could be useful, but here's the problem. We don't have what we need. Not even close."

"What the hell are you talking about? My brother murdered a kid. I'll say it in court. He shot him in the back. The kid was maybe fifteen. He was running for his life."

"And that'll be helpful. We might be able to bargain with it. Your brother gets a reduced sentence, maybe, for giving us what he knows about the Salt Lake City operation. It's something to keep in our back pocket. And to make it work we'd need your testimony, and the murder weapon with fingerprints. That and the matching bullet, it'd be air tight."

"So what's the problem?"

She smiled at him—the dumb kid getting the remedial lesson.

"That's not the case we want. We don't have a team deployed here and at Salt Lake City so we can grab one guy for murder. We want your father and both your brothers. And we want them to roll on everyone else. Their contacts on both sides, the supply chain and the distribution chain. Who does your father buy from in Mexico? Who does he sell to after the girls leave Salt Lake City? Who are the clients? We want *everything*. Not some murder rap on a single guy. That's not the FBI. Without everything, we don't even put a dent in it."

Finch shook his head. Sniffed. "Yeah, while you're dicking around, another truckload of kids gets shipped to the city."

Finch stared at her. Agent Lou Rivers regarded him with unperturbed composure.

"You need to get us more. You're completing the trip tomorrow?"

"Uh. Yeah."

"Okay. You're going to keep wearing the device. Get your brother and father to discuss their contacts. Business arrangements. We need more than criminality on their parts. We could put them away right now and it would do no good because the system would stay in place. If you want to really save these kids—and all the ones who will come after them—you have to let the bigger case unfold. We're making a big omelet. You have to bust a few eggs."

Finch stared at her. Wondered.

He exited the car. Closed the door.

Finch didn't keep track of the numbers, but given how few they shipped to the next shop in Denver, Colorado, he guessed up to half of the kids they brought in from Mexico died of overdose or were killed for attempting to escape. All within maybe six months of entering the country.

Finch sat in his Mustang with his eyes closed. FBI Agent Lou Rivers fired her Impala's engine and pulled away.

I'm going to hell for this.

We're all going to hell for this.

CHAPTER 6

Getting easier to shoot people. Right situation presents, I don't think on it more 'n a second. Even all my life seeing liars and cheats, never woulda guessed how many pure wretched souls is out there. Cursed, murderous, evil ass souls. This one stands frozen in the flash of Smith & Wesson. Even with my voice coming low he's looking high when the bullet pops off the back his head.

He come out to do in another blackhair. Now he on his back, feet pointing at the dead Mexican. His face reflect the moonlight and his glare make it colder.

I'll leave him where he lay.

Blackhair takes off, stumbles and lands on his face; got no hands, and rope strung behind him. I step on it.

"Hold on, dipshit. You'll freeze dressed like that. And you got cuffs on."

I holster Smith and from my other side fish out my Leatherman tool. Got a couple varieties of awl and if I jam 'em in the handcuffs, or pry on the fold, I'll bust em loose somehow.

"You wanna take off into the hills and that's fine as water. But you's liable to freeze to death with no clothes and yer hands locked behind yer back. Stop bein' so cussed stupid and let me free you."

Boy squirms, tries to get to his feet with no hands. I grab his shoulders and square him on his knees.

"Stay like this a minute till I get these cuffs off."

He obey, like he senses my words is true even if he don't ken their mean-ing. I pick at the handcuffs in the hole and have no success. So I switch to the heaviest Leatherman tool I got, a flathead screwdriver built wide and thick. I look for a place to pry and find none.

Last I figger it must be a ratchet inside that holds em. You can always jam a ratchet. But it makes things worse before they's better. I go back to the awl tool and feed it in the hole. Damn near impossible to see. I got to spin the boy for the best moonlight over my shoulder.

"Gotta squeeze the cuffs tighter on you. Hold on."

I push in the awl and the cuff arm at the same time. The awl rides up in 'tween the teeth and the shebang looses. I peel it off his wrist.

"All right, that's one. Get the other off in no time."

The boy's still, save the shivering. I'll give him my coat when I get off the second.

Only take a minute now I'm smooth. I pull the cuff off his other wrist and he pops away, spins, and goes to a fight stance.

I back off a step.

"Fuck boy. Easy. You's loose now."

He looks like the dead boy, pretty like an ugly girl. Maybe queer.

"Hold on. I see you's set to take off. Here." I peel off my jacket and toss it. He's got on a t-shirt and shorts, some kinda thin sandals. Seeing the feet, I wish I kept the jacket 'cause with no more'n that he's good as dead anyway.

"I'll take you back to camp. Got a fire. Food. You can take the sleeping bag. Got a dog and the whole shebang. Taker easy. You be all right."

Still crouching low he backs off, turns for a glance at what he's walking into. But keeps his wary eyes on me. Steps silent and low and, in seconds, he's no more'n a flash of gray on black night, smaller and smaller. He's set off at a run.

Mebbe come light I'll look his body and get my jacket back.

Shame.

I think on how evil work. See it everywhere, every one of us. 'Ventually it's the first we expect, we seen it so much. Survival is keeping the guard up. Get in a bind and help come along, we got no way to trust it. Helluva predicament for the soul of man.

Back at camp, I smell the smoke but don't see the embers. I'll leave it die off complete. Start cold in the morning.

I stop at the tent door 'fore unzipping it and listen to Stinky Joe snore. Mebbe he forgot his fear of the gunshots, having a bullet cut part his bone out, flipping him midair. Mebbe he dream he's in a pasture eating cow pies or some other dog delicacy.

But I bet his dreamland's dark as the one I walk in. Got the dead Mexican boy two hundred yard off and the other set to freeze to death and can't trust the fella that'd save him.

I go inside and don't got the heart to move him. He's curled up and somehow wiggled hisself inside the sleeping bag. Stinky Joe's a Carolina dog, not quite got an arctic coat of fur; I shoulda got him a wool blanket at the outfitter. I get him out the bag he'll snuggle agin me, and he'll have part the sleeping mat. But I's troubled anyhow and leave him the king size to himself.

Grab a liter jug of shine and a wool undershirt from the backpack. Get 'em both to work.

I sit at the stone circle and when I got heat in the belly and the moon's about passed out the sky, I get a shiver up the back says it's time for fire. I think on that boy and how about now he's prolly making a bed out leaves, freezing. Some point, he'll get so cold he don't shake no more. Then sleep.

Real sleep.

Poke around the coals till I spot the red, just a couple ember here and there. Bunch 'em together so they can cooperate and add some pinecone I gathered for this very purpose. Twigs, sticks, logs. Got the whole party built, and all I need's the spark make it dance.

I get down and blow.

Old lungs only carry so much air and after two puffs the coals glow brighter but I need resuscitation. I wait on it. Fill up on air and blow. A couple more and I'll have flame. Inhale deep and huff so long I got the dizzy on.

They's feet behind me.

Lightning quick.

Up on me and something knock my shoulder, bounce off the noggin. I fall part to the pit. My shoulder took most the blow so I got my wits back quick. I'm on my feet with Smith ready and randy, but it's the blackhair boy.

He shake. Go to his knees. Violent body wiggles. Head bobbin', shoulders, knees, the whole works in a giant nonstop shiver.

"Helluva way you got, askin' help."

I get on my knees and blow one more time like the dumbass I am, and flame curl up about a pinecone. In a minute it flares up big, and that excites the other pinecones and soon it's an orgy down there, flames licking and lashing. Pure ass chemical fornication. Make a man wanna visit Ruth about six minute.

Side my noggin aches when I stand. Wonder if that little shit busted something in my head. Good thing about that is you don't know 'less yer dead, so they's no use to worry on it.

"C'mon up here and get warm."

The boy convulses. Tries to knee walk forward but falls over. Never see shakes like that—not on account the cold.

This little fucker tricking me?

I touch his elbow. Feel the muscles vibrate under the skin. Seem real enough.

No good asking. He don't know the language, won't show no red or give me the juice. But I ask anyway.

"Boy, why don't you come up by the fire?"

I connect with his eyes and get the feeling something in my world is a touch off center. Something ain't lining up right.

"C'mere."

I get behind him. Lift the lower shoulder and get under the arms and across.

"The fuck?"

Them's *tits*.

Pretty boy an ugly girl.

I lift her just same. Get up close the fire. "Hold on a second."

Unzip the tent. "Joe, we got company. That's good work on yer part, keepin' watch and all, so I don't get clubbed on the head. Much appreciate the diligence. Now get up out the sack. Get up, puppydog. Got a girl out here like to freeze to death."

I lift the top part the bag. Joe stretches long and sighs hard.

"Joe, lessgo." I cuff his ass gentle. He see it time to wake up and get a move on.

While Joe find his motivation, I fetch both spare wool socks.

Carrying the bag, I feel along for Joe's blood and it's all dry. I unzip the whole bag and the Mexican girl found my sitting log. The flames is tall and bright. Now I worry on who's looking for light in the woods. She stand and I put the bag open on the log so she can step in it. Cover her shoulders and she grabs the flaps and wraps herself. I feel in along her lower legs and undo the shoe buckles on her feet, slip on them inch-thick wool socks. Then open the flaps to put em on her hands. She only shakes occasional. Her eyes follow my every move and now we got some light she ain't so ugly as in the dark, and if they's ever a place it's better to look good, it's the light.

She ain't got the hood part the mummy bag over her head. I get behind and lift it up, settle it down over her. She shake again, and I think on what she saw and come through. Mebbe that was her fella back there, dead. Mebbe she was too much trouble and they saw fit to leave her there too. Cuffed and tied with the rope, had the tape on her mouth. Expected to die. And born to look like a boy at night. Whole world agin her.

From behind, I put my arms around her arms and get up close the sleeping bag and figger if some warm gets through that's good, and if some kindness finds it way in, mebbe for this girl that's better.

CHAPTER 7

Wayman Graves wore denim and flannel. A tight beard and long, straight hair. He looked every bit of his family's history: rancher, meat cutter, businessman. They'd turned their talent for cutting animals into steaks into a thriving business; then, learning another venture lay within easy reach, built upon existing infrastructure and satisfied other, more basic appetites.

Wayman's father Luke didn't want to shit in his own back yard, and sent his son to Salt Lake City.

After a year attempting to liaise a relationship between his father and local operators, he served a three-year stint for possession with intent to distribute. They were at a party. Police closed off the exits. In a misguided stab at proving nobility of character, Wayman took the rap for a man who promised to make a key introduction.

While imprisoned Wayman had the good fortune to meet an optimistic stoic. The seventy-year-old former refrigerator and coolant specialist had hacked his cheating wife to pieces. Coming from a butchering background, Wayman spoke his language.

The man explained his life philosophy to Wayman:

You wave your arms around the house and it's hot, right? The refrigerator doesn't turn hot into cold somehow. It pumps out the hot, and what's left is cold. So you feel the hot, but in between is the cold. It was there all the time, but you didn't know. Prison is like that. Pump out the bad and you find the good.

The philosophy kept Wayman grounded in an optimism that suited him. There was always something good to take from the situation.

Upon his release from prison, he learned the man he'd taken the fall for had succumbed to the next sting and went to prison anyway. Further, the man's boss wasn't inspired by Wayman's loyalty—said it looked more like stupidity.

He'd gone to prison for nothing but the optimism it taught him.

Wayman pumped out the bad and found the worthwhile. Eliminate from mind everything he didn't have, and he was left with what he *did* have: a father who could supply cash and girls from Mexico. Wayman enjoyed nightlife and had a talent for fast, profitable decisions. Best of all, Salt Lake City—like every sizable city—had a large male population that wanted to have sex with kids.

Luke and Wayman's original goal was to use their capacity to transport meat from the Mexican border to also traffic kids. Buy them low, sell them high. Unable to connect with buyers, Wayman became the buyer. Vertical integration, upstream, no less.

Within a year, Wayman opened *The Butcher Shop* Restaurant and Nightclub, each with a separate entrance. On the left was the restaurant, which served few sides but every imaginable kind of meat. On the right side, a pulsing, pounding, flesh market of a nightclub. In the highly secured apartments above, prostitution, and more.

The Butcher Shop was the first building block of an empire constructed in Wayman's mind. He'd chosen it first because it would serve two vital purposes. Being an often-cash business, the restaurant and nightclub allowed him to launder money. More important, it was a surreptitious marketing system that put him in contact with the kind of men who would value the exotic menu of services deeper in Wayman's portfolio.

Drugs, of course. Not participating in the drug trade left easy money on the table. But drugs were never going to be a large profit center. Too much risk. Too many unsophisticated, violent competitors.

Prostitution, of course. Very early in Wayman's vision, prostitution had been the main profit center. But that was when his vision was still comparatively small, when all he wanted was a little lucre.

With his father's refining wisdom, Wayman quickly saw regular old prostitution was not the most exclusive, high priced, highly sought-after service he could provide.

Child prostitution was where it was at.

As Luke had taught him, business was always supply and demand. There's no end to the people who eat meat, right? A lot of demand. But there's no end to the people who feed them meat. When supply equals demand, you're a slave, not a business man. But when demand is great and supply is short, you're king. For the long term, the only way to assure limited supply is if someone limits it for you. For that, you need a cartel. Like the doctors and dentists. The unions. Every trade organization that puts up barriers to entry. The beautiful unintended consequence of the police state is that everything considered a vice is of limited supply. So that's the true capitalist's revenge on big government types. They help us make more money by restricting supply. All we need is the balls to start a business.

But was there a market, Wayman wanted to know. Screwing kids was kind of sick.

Luke had said, you're missing the point. You're not supplying the kid. You're supplying the safety.

"Any pedophile could find a kid and screw it—if he knew he could get away with it. What did the movie director Roman Polanski say? *Judges want to fuck young girls. Juries want to fuck young girls. Everyone wants to fuck young girls.* But there are a lot of newbies out there, a lot of guys who would do it if they thought they could get away with it, but don't even try because they fear the risks. Remove the risk, you own the market."

Wayman and his father turned wealth into riches. A monthly truckload of girls and boys from all over Latin America fed their machine. The meat truck arrived at The Butcher Shop kitchen every week. Every fourth week, it carried a different kind of meat. The girls were escorted to the upper apartment levels. They signed contracts that had no legal power. They showered, put on new clothes, and visited with a doctor whose payment was first stab at his pick of the new girls.

Then they met their new daily taskmaster, a nineteen-year-old *chica* who'd risen from the ranks and taken the bubble gum name Amy, who told them the length and quality of their lives from this point forward depended on their willingness to embrace every form of sexual corruption or deviancy presented them.

BUSINESS WAS VERY good until a banker choked a girl to death while singing *Back Door Man* loud enough other patrons complained.

Then business got exceptionally good.

The banker pumped her corpse with Wayman at the door, providing Wayman enough time to see the upside. The girl was young, relatively new, with many months left before she washed out. She was pretty, docile, and seemed to take to the life. She had unnaturally large breasts for a kid. In short, she was a prize.

Wayman thought on his feet.

The inherent contract in all pay for pedophilia schemes was anonymity and silence. You pay to fuck our kids, and you move along when it's done with a rebar-reinforced concrete assurance it'll never come back to haunt you.

But, in an inspired moment Wayman understood the product was potentially much larger. It wasn't just the extraordinary number of men who wanted to have sex with kids and get away with it.

It was the number of them who would pay an extreme sum to kill one.

He'd test his theory. Right then. Although several cameras already monitored the rooms , Wayman pulled out his phone and took video of the banker pumping the dead girl. Her arm hung limp from the bed.

"What the hell?"

Wayman came up and lifted the girls head, took video of her rolled back eyes.

He turned and captured the man's face. Stopped recording and said, "Come see me when you're done."

Wayman closed the door behind himself and stationed a lieutenant to wait.

A half hour later, the man arrived at Wayman's office. Three-piece suit, gray hair, glasses. Pudgy belly accustomed to pheasant and twenty-year scotch.

"Sit."

The man did. "I was assured absolute privacy and I demand that video. I absolutely—"

"Fine. No worries. But … that girl was worth at least seventy thousand to me, what she'd bring in. Docile, big tits. Still fresh. Plus the fifteen I'd sell her for. So you've cost me a lot. Shit happens, I understand. But you also subjected me to a new risk, outside of what we bargained for. Now I have to eliminate her body and sanitize a room you turned into a murder scene. Last, you dropped this mess in my lap unprepared. You're making me scramble, and in this business, that's not comfortable. We're at a hundred fifty thousand. That's the price of the video."

"I anticipated this conversation—but not your number. She's a Mexican, for Christ's sake."

"I'm not a religious man, but you didn't kill her for Christ's sake. Here's my final word. You coerced my involvement in both a crime and a business transaction. You threatened my freedom and robbed me of property. I don't think you understand how antagonizing that is."

Wayman looked at the lieutenant standing by the closed door. The man stepped forward.

"It'll take time. I have to move some things around. No one has that kind of liquidity."

"How much time do you need?"

With that, Wayman established a new product line.

He was surprised how quickly other patrons began asking about the service. In the space of two years, it became his largest profit center. He dedicated the entire fifth floor: covered each room with linoleum, replaced the furniture with racks, cages, tables, and other devices obtained through S & M outlets. Installed special lighting, video cameras, the works.

Soon, the other services took second place. He abandoned the drug business and phased out adult-aged prostitution.

A final refinement to the business came with the pricing. As word spread, Wayman realized the risk he was taking demanded a tremendous premium. He needed to fully vet every client. That created costs. But more than that, the value wasn't in the girl. It was like *goodwill*. The intangible value created by a brand.

Thinking the first man's willingness to pay $150,000 might be fluke, Wayman had originally set the price at $50,000. Since then, he'd increased that number again and again, and so far hadn't located the price point that would slow demand.

CHAPTER 8

Never sleep so terrible in my life. Barely any mat 'tween me and the ground. Got all my spare clothes on but I only ever use the one I wear and the one I wash. Girl's in the bag and I try to get close. Don't want in the bag with some girl kid. Once she got the shiver off, they's no need to be so close. So I freeze one side and flip so I freeze the other, back and forth, till I's ready to go rebuild the fire and crawl in it.

I step out the tent with my bottle. Drink and whiz. Look Ma, no hands. Wander 'round to make the blood percolate and mebbe thaw out my left half. 'Spect at some point whoever keeps track the fella I shot's gonna wanna know why he ain't showed up for work. They was two fellas at the meat truck when they shot the boy, and only one come back to kill the girl. That other fella—he know his partner didn't come home.

I mosey off, let the mind puzzle it. Boy jumped out the truck, they shot him. Next they bring a girl.

Was she in back the truck, earlier? Was she part the trouble the boy was in?

My original think on it was the refrigerated Isuzu hauled illegals come up from Mexico to look construction work. If so, where the girl come from? She with the crew? Or was I wrong on the whole thing? Mebbe they's only two Mexicans and they didn't have nothing to do with one another.

Or here's a thought. Mebbe I killed the good guy. Who the hell knows? I take a pull off the bottle, help me think. Nah, they's kids. Nobody ought shoot kids. Wait till they grow up.

Been walking a wide circle, all the way 'round a massive flat plain with scrub and pine here and there, grass and dirt the rest. I come clockwise on the road, then up on the truck of the fella I took off his head. Another F-150.

How much the world's metal got FORD stamped on it?

Now I's close the vehicle I got the nerves on. Look for headlights ahead or behind and even the highway's down to nothing. Must be close four five a.m., from the gray in the east. Got no gloves on, so I try the handle with my sleeve over my finger. Door pop open. Light go on. Half expect another kid or something, but nope.

Look around. Climb up in the seat. Open the glove box and pull out a plastic folder. Got a business card from the dealership. Sheet a paper the length of three peckers with the sales and lease numbers. On and on it goes.

Inside a plastic glove is an insurance card. Name and address.

Fucker's name was Cephus A. Graves.

Cephus.

Fuckin' Cephus.

Like the horse?

Whoever named that boy sealed his fate. Someone was gonna shoot him.

I tuck the insurance card in my pocket and make sure I ain't touched nothing else. Give the likely places a rub down anyhow.

Have to admit the truck seat's fine. Been days without upholstery and truth told the drive from east to west accustom my ass and back to the accoutrements of fine living: cushions.

Still, any second someone could come along and wonder why I's in this truck. I get out, close the door. Wipe it off and head for camp.

Almost time to make coffee.

'Cept at some point they come back and mebbe they bring the search party. These boys from last night wasn't running they own operation. Not with the fella with dreadlocks being half the brains. The other couldn't have enough to make up the difference.

I come up on camp easy and get the lay, like old days in North Cackalacky. Overheard some Flagstaff hippy with the rainbow t-shirt call it that.

No smoke from the pit. No snoring from the tent. No nothing.

I unzip the tent flap.

Joe eyeball me, cold on the nylon floor.

Girl's gone. Everything in the tent's gone save Stinky Joe.

"Joe—what the hell'd you say to her?"

She just run off.

"With everydamnthing?"

See for yourself.
"Ahhhhhh. Fuck."

CHAPTER 9

While Luke Graves changed the tire on the Isuzu, his wife, Caroline, drove to the Williams Taco Bell and bought enough burritos to feed the guests. She returned at midnight. Luke carried the fast food bags to the basement and unlocked it. Caroline followed. A dim light was always on. He flipped the main light switch and recessed fluorescent lights illuminated the basement. The girls moaned.

Next, with a bottle of Equate sleeping pills tucked in his pocket, Luke carried a case of bottled water from the garage to the basement, and placed it on a fold-out table constructed of plywood and two by fours. Caroline organized piles for distribution: two burritos, three sleeping pills, two bottles of water per girl.

In their language, she told the girls to form in line. Luke and Caroline waited as each followed a procedure that was for them in its second iteration. They took the pills, drank enough water to get them down, opened their mouths to show the pills were swallowed, then took their meals.

They would be awake for a few hours at most. The recommended dosage of sleeping pill was one or two for an adult. During their transport from the border of Mexico to Salt Lake City, each roughly eighty-pound girl took six per day. The drug left them barely coherent.

When the line passed, Luke folded and locked the table. Caroline told the girls they would resume their travels in the morning. They locked the girls in the basement and Caroline went inside the house to prepare for bed.

Luke returned to the garage and sat on a folding lawn chair with the bay door open. The tire was fixed. He looked from his watch to the night sky and wondered why a simple job was taking Cephus so much time. His son had a long day ahead of him. There was no way he went to town for a drink or stopped at some woman's for a quick poke. Cephus had the right priorities. He was the most responsible twenty-six-year-old Luke had ever seen. Pure ambition, had his head on right. Could think through complicated moral questions, pick apart the tripe big government and big business overlords used to manipulate the masses, and make decisions based on his family's interests. Most people never learned those skills—that's why they were slaves to the state. The fact that Cephus had taken Luke's lessons to heart so young made him special.

So where the hell was he?

And where the hell was Finch?

Luke stood, shivered, and dragged the lawn chair deeper into the garage where he'd be directly under the glowing heater. Thinking better of it, he replaced the lawn chair with a lounge from the front deck. He turned off the garage light and stretched out. Let his eyes close, and told himself he'd rouse when Cephus's headlights arrived.

Instead, the sound of Finch's Mustang wheels on the gravel driveway woke Luke at dawn. Like the girls he drugged, he stretched and inhaled a sigh before cognizance came upon him.

Cephus's truck was not in the driveway. Luke lifted himself from the lounge and went to the door for an unobstructed look outside.

Finch exited his car.

"Where's Cephus?" Finch said.

"Was about to ask the same. You see him last night?"

"Nah. Cephus don't party."

"Yeah. So where the hell is he?" Luke went into the garage and found his cell phone on the tool table. It was dead.

"You got your cell? Give him a shout. See what the hell he's doing."

Finch dialed his brother. Put it on speaker phone and entered the garage. Voice mail picked up after four rings.

"Text him."

Finch half smiled. He texted to Cephus the same message Cephus texted him on a near daily basis. "WTFAU?"

Luke went inside the house and wove his belt through a holster with a .357 pistol in it. He also grabbed a .30-30 Winchester, a beat-up lever action brush gun he'd inherited from his father. Luke had a lot of pretty rifles with glassy stocks and perfect bluing. The Winchester was not one of them.

Caroline had made coffee. Luke filled two mugs, figuring after a night of intoxication Finch probably needed it worse than him. At the garage he grabbed a shovel. Put the rifle on the window rack, lifted the rear seat, and placed the shovel across the crew cab's cargo space.

"Get in. Where'd you leave the body?"

"Cool Pines exit."

Luke gassed the RAM truck. "If something happened to Cephus while you were off smoking dope, I'm going to leave you there with him."

CHAPTER 10

F inch read the clock on his father's RAM truck dashboard. 6:31. They traveled east on Interstate 40, the sun exactly ahead, glaring the sleepiness out of their brains. The temperature on the truck's dash read twenty-eight degrees.

Finch looked over at his father, behind the wheel. Bristling mustache. Weathered cowboy hat. Wrinkled face. He looked worse than his fifty-some years, staring ahead like a man bent on murder.

Finch thought of the recording device on his chest—the futility of recording a conversation no one would ever hear.

He'd long known his probable lifespan was short.

He was twenty-eight, and the problem was, he didn't want to die. He saw the movies where the war hero jumps on a grenade. He couldn't fathom it. Or people jumping out the windows on 9/11. To Finch, deciding to die earlier than what fate demanded was insanity, not courage. He wanted every breath of life, and nothing was scary enough or important enough to make him want less of it. His life wasn't terrific, but it was all he had. He dreaded the moment when his consciousness would go forever black. A universe without his awareness of it was an indescribably terrible and horrific thing.

And yet when he thought about the suffering of other people, he empathized. When he gave one of the captives a key to the handcuffs, he knew Luke would probably end up handling him the same way he handled all his problems.

Permanently.

He also knew that in perpetrating the fraud of being a drug and alcohol addict, he was skirting a line with terrible things on the other side. For a man fearful of death, conscience kept him in intimate proximity.

"It's this one," he said, looking ahead to the exit.

Luke blinked, held his eyes closed.

Finch watched the road.

"Left after the exit?" Luke said.

"Yes. Up to the T."

"Where'd you go last night?"

"Charley's."

"Got a girl there or something?"

"Several. None in particular."

"Get any sleep?"

"Enough."

"Good. Because the run to Salt Lake's happening today, one way or another."

Luke took the exit and Finch lowered the window a couple inches.

Luke raised the window from the control on his door panel. "If you want to change the temperature, adjust the air flow from the dash. Too early for noise."

"I'll wait."

In a moment the truck crossed the bridge over Interstate 40 and, ahead, Finch saw Cephus's truck parked very close to where they'd parked the refrigerated truck.

"There it is," Luke said. He accelerated, braked, swung behind it.

Finch said, "We pulled in right along here, same as you are. It was the right front tire and we wanted the whole truck on the level. This is about where we were parked."

Luke exited, leaving the Winchester and shovel in the cab. He got up close to Cephus's truck and looked in the back and front windows.

"He in there?" Finch said.

Luke climbed into the bed of the truck and with the higher elevation, looked a full circle. He stared a long time facing the direction where Cephus had shot the boy in the red jacket. The sun was to his right front. He shielded his eyes with his hand.

"Ah Christ Jesus. No."

Luke opened the tailgate from inside the bed and sat on it. He slumped, lowered his head, removed his hat. He pulled the .357 from his gun belt and held it in both his hands.

Finch crossed between slats in the wood fence and trotted toward where he'd buried the Mexican boy.

Had the FBI sent someone out to investigate? Had agent Lou Rivers come out herself, and surprised Cephus? Finch tried to imagine the timing of it. Without knowing when Cephus returned to the location, it was impossible.

What could he say? Someone had seen the body from Interstate 40—at night? How could he explain it?

He saw the red jacket and a mound beside it.

Cephus.

Finch stopped walking, wondering if Luke would make the shot clean. Part of him wanted to stand still so he didn't get winged. But another part of him considered taking off like a rabbit, a zig zag pattern that would make it difficult for a rifleman at two hundred yards.

Finch looked back.

Luke still sat on the truck's open tailgate.

As Finch watched, Luke jumped to his feet, raised the .357 into the air as if aimed at heaven, screamed and fired five shots, fast as the revolver cylinder could spin. Finch didn't know a revolver could shoot so fast—like a single continuous sound. After the blast ended, Luke's wail continued until it turned into a cry and died.

Finch stood at his dead brother's feet and turned at the crunch of his father's long strides across the gravel. Finch again thought of running, but it would be an admission of guilt. He couldn't run far enough. He had no way to support himself. He had to grit out the moment and hope for the best.

Maybe the FBI had the whole area under surveillance this moment, and he was safe ...

Finch studied Cephus, waiting for Luke to arrive. When footsteps neared he said, "They got him, Dad."

"Who got him?"

"I don't know. He's shot in the forehead. And that isn't how I left the other one. He was covered head to toe. Totally invisible."

Luke knelt by Cephus's head.

"Who'd he bring out here?" Finch said.

"Just a girl." Luke rolled Cephus and nodded at the back of his head. "No way. That skinny girl couldn't lift the gun that did this."

Luke rested Cephus again on his back. Stood. "You smell that?"

"What?"

"Wood smoke?"

"I guess. But it's faint. Could be from anywhere."

"You walk out that way last night?"

Finch looked toward the trees another hundred-some yards to their left.

"No."

"Run back to the truck and grab my rifle."

"You think—"

"Go!"

Finch took off.

CHAPTER 11

L uke kicked the dead Mexican's head, bringing the top of his boot up under the boy's chin, again and again, until neck meat ripped and exposed jagged flesh and bone. The body hadn't frozen over night, but was long past bleeding. Very little blood transferred to Luke's boot.

He wanted more.

Seeing Finch arrive at the truck and grab the rifle, Luke returned to desecrating the Mexican. Partly jumping, he brought his heel down on the boy's head, but it glanced off the side. He lost his footing and landed on his tailbone and right elbow, bringing sharp pain to both places.

He jumped back to his feet and pulled his pistol.

"Dad—that isn't good thinking."

Finch had arrived with the rifle. Luke let the sting in his elbow fade. He opened his revolver and replaced the cartridges he shot on the bed of the truck. Put away the wheelgun.

"Chamber one."

"What?"

"Put one in the barrel."

Finch worked the lever action. "I didn't hear you."

"Closest woods is that way."

"There was a dog yesterday, come to think of it. A white dog. Cephus shot it somewhere over this direction."

"I hope some hillbilly didn't kill Cephus over a dog."

They walked, each careful choosing his steps. Luke motioned to his left. "Get a little distance between us."

Finch shifted.

They crossed the terrain. Luke stopped. "Hold up. Got a boot print here." He searched the area for another, and stepped forward. Halted, again shuffled forward. He craned his neck, searched farther ahead, then again at ground level.

"Dad, see up there? It's a tent."

"That's where he was headed. Okay. No more talk. I'll come in from the right, you stay lower on the left. Watch for my signal. When I tell you to stop, don't move, say anything, nothing. We clear?"

Finch nodded. "Got it. You think he's still asleep after the five rounds you shot off?"

Luke regarded his son. "No, I was thinking maybe we wouldn't let him know we were right on top of him."

They continued forward with the distance between them widening. At the edge of the wood, Luke motioned for Finch to stop. A bright yellow backpacker's tent had been pitched ten yards into the thin forest, located under the protective girth of a massive ponderosa pine. A few yards away was a fire circle with ashes and no smoke. Luke studied the woods beyond: more ponderosa; deciduous trees, bare of leaves; and Douglas fir growing dense like clumps of Christmas trees.

Seeing no motion, no color out of place save the yellow tent, Luke made a fist signal to Finch, telling him not to move, then eased toward the tent. He stepped under the ponderosa's wide ceiling.

"You in there?" he said. "Come on out. Want to talk with you, get your take on what you saw last night. That's all."

Luke waited.

"Not here to give you any trouble. Come on out the tent."

He motioned Finch to approach.

"My boy's missing and—"

Luke squatted and lifted a corner of the tent where a spike held it to the ground. He pulled the spike, then stood and lifted the whole corner of the tent.

"Nothing inside," he said. Luke stepped to the front and unzipped it. "Empty."

"Someone run off without his tent," Finch said. "Maybe after all the shooting?"

"Ease the fuck up." Luke held his son's stare. "I'll shoot when I damn well want."

Luke paced the campsite with his gaze directed at the ground, seeking anything the camp's occupant might have left that would provide a clue.

"Maybe we could take that tent into Babbitt's and see who bought it," Finch said. "I know they sell that kind."

"Yeah. Tear it down."

Luke stood at the ponderosa trunk, unzipped his fly, and urinated. "We're going to bury Cephus today. If anyone ever asks, say he ran off and we haven't seen him. No body, no crime. No link to us."

"But how will they ever catch who shot him?"

"Who the fuck's *they*? All these years, you haven't learned shit. The state doesn't exist to protect you or give you justice. It exists to do the opposite. And if you haven't learned that yet, just get out of my sight. You're an embarrassment."

"Okay."

"Wait you fucking prick. We bury Cephus today, then take the rest of the girls to Salt Lake. I had big plans for your brother. You aren't big enough to fill them, but I'm giving you one chance to pull your shit together. From this moment, you're either one hundred percent dedicated, or you're out. Which is it?"

Finch breathed in.

CHAPTER 12

W e bury Cephus, then take rest the girls to Salt Lake. I had big plans for your brother. You ain't big enough to fill 'em. So you gotta decide. From right now on, you's either one hundred percent in, or you's out. Which it gonna be?

Okeydokey. That feller's the daddy I just killed his son. Other with the dreadlocks is getting called out. Time to be a man, son. That mean you gotta shoot Mexicans run from the truck. Then take blackhair girls out to shoot in the head.

Fuckin' devil.

I's up in the ponderosa, got to stay on the backside like a gray squirrel—but can't jump limb to limb like the tree rat. They come 'round back and look up, I's in trouble. Got Smith ready for a quick hello.

Told Stinky Joe to stay put down by the crick. He hear voices and we'll see if he listen.

The old man giving orders turns away from Dreadlocks and parks his thumbs on his belt. Dreadlocks pulls the stakes on my tent and stretches it flat. Folds and rolls like he's familiar with the concept. He put the roll under his arm, and though I'd like if he forget the Winchester leaned agin the dead birch tree, he grab it and they walk off together into the morning sun.

But I saw that young feller's face when his daddy looked off. Boy and his daddy ain't on the same page.

Mebbe.

I stay in the tree while they cross to the fella I shot dead last night. Old man hoists him over the shoulder, and as he walks, the body flexes some at the back; he start off like a board but time they get him through the wood slat fence he's folded at the middle. Daddy got his head next his dead son's ass—I bet he ready to hunt somebody down and kill him.

That be me.

Dreadlocks comes back with a shovel to the Mexican with the red jacket. Sets about covering the body agin. They think they's gonna seal this up. Hide the boy. Bury they own, proper, with mother crying and words from a black book—cause they doing the Lord's work. Then they drive a truck of girls to Salt Lake City.

But that dead Mexican got a voice they ain't yet heard.

Mine.

I got the insurance card with name and address. I want the connection that'll put me in Salt Lake City with that meat truck.

Take stock the full situation.

Girl left with all my things. I's underdressed for the weather. Got the gold on my back but that don't keep a fella warm. Little snipe took my booze too. I got a knife, Smith, bullets, and a dog. Mebbe fifteen-thirty mile from Flagstaff.

Don't know if I can get there while they's any stores still open. So I either spend another night in the cold, visit Mae and the grandkids, or poke Ruth.

She won't let me in without I poker.

Dad and Dreadlocks enter different trucks and drive off. They head up the interstate westbound.

You coming down?

"Ah, I was lookin' the other way. Didn't see you, Joe."

I coulda been a grizzly bear.

"You wish. You's barely a dog."

Joe look down. Away.

"Ah, I didn't mean it. Joshin' ya."

I climb down and keep from busting my nuts on a saddle or breaking a leg on the fall. Get the ground under me, and I wish I had some that salty back-packer food that girl stole. How the hell she carry the whole pack I dunno. But she been in a scrape, and I don't give a shit about the bag. Money'll buy more. Still think she liable to freeze to death if she don't get to town, and problem is, they ain't many folk'll take in a kid girl from Mexico without wanting something back. She run off from the only help she was liable to find.

Ground level, I get a good look all the way 'round and head back the dead Mexican. Un-bury him again. That father feller did the boy's head wrong. Smashed in and pert near broke off. Thought I'd put him roadside, but if I take the body I's not sure the head'd tag along. And now I look at him, my resolve is strong but the stomach is weak. Mebbe I'll just leave him in the open with the red; make a call from a pay phone ...

"Come on, Joe. We got a long ass walk."

I think on it while trudging east. Follow a road runs parallel the highway. I'll go cross country if it ends.

No likker, no cabbage. Situation hopeless.

But the morning sun burns plenty warm and time we cross a mile two I gotta unbutton the top my shirt and let the heat go. Now and again a truck roll by and I get the goose bumps each time, 'cause the bad guy I shot drove a Ford F-150, and his daddy drove the Dodge Ram, and it just so happens out west, they got a law every man woman child got to drive a truck. So each time I look and see what's coming, I wonder if it's time to pull Smith.

Now the tires come behind me, and I turn 'cause they slow to a crawl. Look back.

"Going to Flagstaff?"

"What's it yer business?"

Man don't glow or give me the juice, but that don't mean a damn thing, lately.

"Well, I'm going to Flagstaff and don't mind giving a lift to an asshole and his dog. Hop in if you want to get there today."

I stop. He stops the truck. Fella either seventy-year-old, or a hard, hard fifty. Short hair like the military. Got a TRIUMPH ROCKET III sticker on the back his truck cab. I think that's the one carried Neil Armstrong to the moon. Not sure. Next the Triumph sticker is a yellow one, got the coiled snake and DON'T TREAD ON ME.

He see my gun and don't care. Must be on account his gun. All in all, he's offering and it'd almost be impolite—

"Look fella, it's an easy call. You want a ride, hop in. Otherwise, I'm late for breakfast."

Fucky fucky. Bacon, eggs. Lordamighty.

"C'mon Stinky Joe, get up in the truck."

I come 'round the side and open the king cab back door. Joe jumps, misses. I grab his ass and lift him. Put him in the back seat. They's dirt and all kinda grief there already.

"Stinky Joe," the feller says. "That's some truth in advertising."

I climb in the front. Stretch my hand. He look at it, then me, and I look at it, and he say, "Looks like blood."

"You law?"

"I'm about the farthest thing from law as you'll meet. But before I want that blood on my hand, where'd it come from?"

Guess I'll just shoot him if he don't like the truth. But truth is, a man'd fly the Gadsden flag is likely as fair and dignified as man is capable, given his universal predilection for lies, deceit, and thuggery. I'll speak truth and if anything go wrong, I got the grizzly bear in the back seat to protect me.

And Smith, accourse.

"They's a dead Mexican boy back the road a ways. Fella shot him last night. Then he shot Joe. You can see the crease on his neck. Hit bone. Prick. So when the fella shot the Mexican come back with a girl to shoot, I got the drop. But this ain't his blood. I never touched him. Just shot him. Anyhow, the girl took off half nekkid and two three hours later come to my camp shakin' so bad she could hardly clock me with a log. I put her in the sleepin' bag to warm up, took a walk, and time I come back she stole all I got save Stinky Joe and Mister Smith & Wesson. So now I's set on findin' the fella with the fella shot the Mexican—he and his father gonna truck a bunch more blackhair kids to Salt Lake City. I figger they's sex slaves. Ima track down the two fellas and kill 'em. Is all."

"Oh."

I still got my hand out, and if this feller don't shake it quick I'll shoot him on principle. But his head starts to noddin' and last he say, "But which person's blood is that?"

"I guess it's the Mexican. I dug him up so the law could see his red jacket when I call it in."

He shifts in his seat so he can get his right hand at a good angle to shake mine.

"Name Creighton," I say. And wonder if the name mean anything.

"Cinder."

Now we met and shook.

"So you're set on some vigilante justice," he say.

"What I seen, it don't get done otherwise."

He park on the road next a joint with a lotta glass and blue and white curtains.

"You want breakfast?"

"I doubt they could break a maple leaf."

"I got it."

"We 'preciate ya."

"Leave the window down for the dog. Maybe it'll stink less when I drive home."

CHAPTER 13

We go inside and feels like I stepped back to 1969. Long hair and braids, men in socks and sandals. Damn near giggle at 'em. And they's a couple old-timers too, prize they whiskers and boots. Veins in the hands. Sound is clinking silver and porcelain; smell is fried meat and seared taters. Mouth drool; ribs shake hands and slap asses.

"This good for you?" He opens his arm at a table.

I drag the wood chair and plant my ass. He does same. Flips over the newspaper someone left on the table.

"So this crew you're after, you ever run across them before?"

"Nah."

"You know anything about them?"

"Just the truck said Graves Meats, and the picture had the brand on the meat. Like they eat beefsteaks with *Graves Meats* seared on 'em."

"They don't brand meat where you come from?"

Suspect he's asking what part the country cooks up critters like me. Cut the chase. "North Cackalackee, as you people say it."

"That meat truck belongs to Luke Graves. His family goes back a hundred years. The meat business, maybe two thirds that. You saw his truck?"

"Meat truck had a flat. Mexican jumps out the back. Fella shot him, fixed the tire. Other fella with dreadlocks went out with a shovel but didn't hardly sprinkle any dirt on the dead man. Then they drove off. What's your name agin?"

Cinder looks up. "Cinder. Nat."

"Uh-huh. Well, I dunno if they own the truck or stole it, but when they come back, I was in the tree and they said they'd finish the run to Salt Lake City once they bury they boy."

Waitress clears her throat. She got a little cushion for the pushin' and her face is like Jackie Kennedy. "Start you boys off with coffee?"

Cinder nod.

I do too.

"Then I want a mess a eggs and meat. Don't care which but if its pork you cook the shit out it. And I need some scraps for Joe. He's my dog in the truck out there."

I look back from her pretty face and see Cinder wrinkle his brow and shrug. Oh, I get it. *Fuck y'all, I's from Flagstaff.* High and mighty. Let's see how the Cinderman order his eggs.

"How 'bout you, Nat?" she say. "Two eggs over easy on top a stack of buckwheat? Home fries and ham?"

He smile like each hand found a titty.

She throws the hip and her whole bottom quiver. "Saw you in the paper this morning."

"I knew I'd regret it," Cinder say.

"No, you come off real good. People say you're running for governor. I'll be right back with your food."

"You politician?"

"Not a law man. Not a politician. Retired businessman with some libertarian friends who like to raise hell."

"Uh-huh. Well, way I see it, that truck had the blackhair they shot. Then they come back with the girl, and next mornin' they say they'll take the rest to Salt Lake. So I figger two things. They got the home base somewheres nearby. And they got a bunch more blackhair kids on the meat truck. If they's ready to kill 'em so easy, them kids ain't there on they own accord. Way I figger."

"You talk pretty loud, being in public."

They ain't no one near. But he's saying I don't yet know who he is. And that's truth. But he don't know I can spot a liar most times, 'cept the ones don't know they's fulla shit.

Jackie Kennedy come back with mugs and coffee. Fills the first with the second. Put a tin of cream on the table. I top mine off. Cinder keep his black. The waitress wiggles to the hippy with the sandals, and I get a charge of juice off her. They ain't ready yet and she goes the next table. I get another jolt.

Each time she meets someone she amps up the deceit. But not when she talk to ole Nat Cinder.

"That waitress used to date one of the Graves brothers. I don't recall which. And the old timer you see behind me, back on the wall with the apple-sauce for sale? He worked at Graves Meats most of his life. He's a meatcutter. You look close you'll see he's missing an index finger. He takes a pension from the Graves Meat company, and I bet the way he'd see it, a man about to dick that company is a man about to dick his retirement. Graves Meats employs folks from all over Flag, Sedona, Prescott. Supplies Phoenix, Tucson, Yuma, the whole state. Beyond. And the family homestead is in Williams. Which is just another exit down the Highway from where I picked you up. So maybe we ought to talk about how cold it is, for so early in November. Save the real conversation for the sidewalk."

"It is cold, I'll grant you that. And a dry cold. You people don't have humidity at all. Got a nosebleed on yer mountain." I feel I got to adjust my underwear but now I's self-conscious. Got to running my mouth and who knows if I just kick started myself some trouble. "Well, Mister Cinder, you spend yer life in Flagstaff? What's your story?"

"No story. Just a regular cowpoke. Got a ranch. A couple head."

I never in my life struggle for conversation 'cause mostly I don't give a shit. But this man's buying my eggs and meat, so I keep at it. "What you think my story?"

He grin.

"You smoke?"

"Nah."

"After breakfast."

He look up and Jackie Kennedy got a plate in her hand and another on her arm. She swoop in like a hawk, arms wide and ass on a glide, and 'fore I know it ham and bacon smells up my nose; got the near-runny eggs on the side, toast, jam; Flagstaff is heaven.

Cinder's got a stack of cakes varnished in syrup and egg. Slice of ham like a ribeye. Home fries in cubes, browned all 'round. I could eat my plate and his.

"Say, here's a subject you might find suitable. Where can a fella trade a maple leaf for the paper money, and not get robbed?"

"What kind of weight are you looking to trade?"

"Just a coin."

Cinder pulls one of them cellular-style telephones from his coat. Works it with his fingers. "Gold's at eight seventy-four. I'll give you eight hundred even."

"Shit. May as well toss it on the sidewalk."

"You can do that. Or you might counter offer."

Cinder grin at me, and I don't know exactly how much of this feller I'll tolerate. Maybe get some egg and meat in me 'fore I get about the business.

I chew a whole piece a bacon and same time chop ham with the fork. Mince eggs to a sloppy pile and mix in the ham, scoop the mess on toast. I's done with two egg, ham, bacon, two toast, in thirteen second. Gulp a full mug of coffee. So hungry I could eat baked beans from a dead cowboy's ass. But druther have another plate of ham 'n eggs. Maybe some of them flapjacks.

"All right, I'll take yer eight hundred. I got to get another plate." I reach around my back and spin the money belt so's the pocket I need is in front. Pull out a maple leaf and land it on the table.

He don't speak and we cross looks a long minute. Cinder reach to his ass and come out with a billfold. Peel off seven Franklins and two Grants. They's a shit ton more inside them leather folds. And he prolly seen the rest my gold pouch sparkle. Oh, Baer Creighton a *moneyed* man.

"How come a man with the Gadsden flag on his truck likes so damn much fiat paper?"

"Same reason you'll take a shitty deal to trade out of it. You can't buy breakfast with a maple leaf."

I slide the coin 'tween the plate, ketchup and syrup. Leave it. He pick it up. Flip it.

"You gonna bite the damn thing?"

He folds the bills and reaches 'em to me. I counted when he counted so I take 'em without fuss.

"Let me freshen that coffee." Jackie Kennedy pours black, and I grab the tin for the white. She fills Cinder's mug and scoots off. "Hold up. I wannanother plate. Same's the first, 'cept with them flapjacks."

She bobbles her head like she never see a hungry man, scoots off.

More folks come in the door. Fella smiles all the time and his woman walk in six inch steps and studies the hillbillies and hippies.

"Here's the deal," says I. "Mister Cinder. I got the uncanny feelin' you think I's fulla shit. But I's the least likely liar you ever met, and my life's worked out so all I give a shit about is when I see a little blackhair girl 'bout to get shot, I wanna tear down the whole ghetto that sprung the prick with the gun. So what you know 'bout Graves Meat? Top to bottom."

Cinder chomps on his last fork of egg and pancake. Stabs his last ham and adds it to the mix. Being polite, he don't talk while he chew. Finally swallows his last. Waves to Jackie. She comes.

Touches his shoulder.

"One check—I'll take it. And bring a to-go box for my friend's second order."

She go away and Cinder lets the silence at our table push out on the jabbering folks 'round us.

Cinder says, "I've things to attend, but I want to be on the same page with you, and this isn't the place. You have a place to stay? What's your situation?"

"I've a couple family people in the hotel. Got in last week. Still lookin' the lay."

He nods. Reaches his buzzing phone. "Excuse me." He fondles his machine and talk to it. "Hey Chuck, I'm in a meeting, but we need to talk. Hit me back in a half hour. Good? All right."

I pick my fingernails. Listen to the woman walks in six-inch steps. "It's so quaint. So common. Delightful."

Here a week and I hate the tourists.

Cinder hear her too. Narrow eye smile.

He sign a paper and I take my box. Now it been a minute I don't care to eat, so much. Make Stinky Joe happy. Just same I open the box and eat the bacon.

We step to the side walk. I open the truck door.

"Get on down, puppydog."

Joe jumps to the cement. I rest the open clamshell on the sidewalk and he get about business.

Cinder say, "Here's what maybe you don't know. That meat truck comes up from Sierra Vista. Luke Graves's sons—including the one you shot—take trips down there once a month. They make deliveries in Phoenix and Tucson on the way down. Maybe other places farther south. Then they meet members of MS-13. You heard of them?"

"Nah."

"They're a gang. Mara Salvatrucha. They do all the shit you'd think a gang does, but more like a terrorist group. Drugs, murder for hire; they shot up a bus in Honduras full of women and kids to protest the death penalty. Killed twenty-eight. They're all through Latin America and the US. Luke Graves and his sons get their girls from MS-13."

"Where does the MS get the kids?"

"Kidnapping, some. Recruitment. Promises. Then there's the orphanages. Lot of kids with no parents down there. Different kind of violence."

"You sayin' Luke Graves is tied with nasty people, and I tangle with him it's same as them."

"That's right. You see someone with tattoos all over, neck, arms, hands, even on the face, they're likely fighting for the other side, and they fight hard."

He don't need know 'bout my skill or the twenty some bodies I piled up the last month. Truth is I's got the taste for it. Feel like it maybe purifies the soul. Live a life of petty persecutions, little jolts a juice every time someone say a lie. Get the rage bottled up 'cause you can't do nothing. And one day you see they's plenty you can do.

Plenty.

Cinder say, "What's your plan?"

"How you know so much 'bout Graves and this MS group?"

Cinder lean to the truck front fender. Cross his arms. "I got tangled up in a little fiasco last year—one of those situations where you take a stand on principle, though you don't care for the people you're standing with. I'm an alcoholic. I got clean in the process, and you might say I started looking a little deeper at things. Illegal immigration. MS-13. The kids. All of it. I'm used to being ... involved. And I haven't yet decided what to do about it. But for the gangs, you don't solve a weed problem with a lawn mower. You do it with napalm and a bulldozer. Burn them out and bury them."

I look up and down the street and kinda see things come together. I got no business. No home. Wanted by every law organization in the United Police States of America. Retired by dint of standing up for myself. I got a daughter and three grandbabies and though I love 'em, we's far past living in a single home and sitting down for dinner at six. And Ruth is Ruth is Ruth. Couldn't live without her for thirty year—'cept I did. Now she reveal the mystery behind the curtain, I like the curtain. I's set in my ways and she in hers. We poke and tussle 'cause we got body parts made for it. But rest the time I make her howl and she drive me batshit. Sum of the whole is I got strings but no ties.

Mexican girl with the backpack? She'll run out food and have no means. In a month she'll be camping in three feet snow. Suspect she didn't learn snow skills in Mexico, and she'll meet up with the dead blackhair on the other side soon.

Feel like so far I danced around it without being straight with the man. I's done pretending. Done living in the woods 'cause they's nasty people telling lies all over. Though it's just me I only got one way to see it. Time to call the evil man to account—where ever I find him.

"Cinder, the man I shot was evil and the clan that come for him too. They got more kids, and all around is people who got a good clue and don't care. Now, if all this was in the paper they'd be outrage and fury. People'd put down they paper and drink they sweet tea satisfied they outrage is enough. So if a man like me—got no permanent attachments—don't take it up a notch and do something, them kids'll keep comin' in and getting shot. An used for whatever else they bring 'em for. You don't gotta guess 'bout that. So my intentions is to hunt down them men and kill 'em."

Cinder pushes off the truck fender. Offers his hand for another shake. "I'm interested in your work. I'll keep an eye out. Maybe I'll see you in here for breakfast one day soon."

I shake his hand. No juice, no red.

We'll see.

Old-timer from the breakfast come out the door, walks sidey sidey like a mousetrap caught his balls. But he don't seem to mind like I would.

"Cinder!"

Old-timer takes Cinder's paw in his then covers it with the other, shaking his arm and pulling close. "Don't mean to interrupt, Nat, but I hope you run."

CHAPTER 14

A in't a block two from breakfast to the hotel and they's a good chance
Mae's still in bed. So I rap on Ruth's door, and she open it wearing
granny glasses with chains about her neck. Quilted pajama gown.

"You get them glasses at the pawn?"

"No these are new." She uglies up her face. "I hope you're here for a bath."

I grab the newspaper on the floor by the door. Sit on the desk chair. Joe
slink in and take cover in the cubby tween sofa and wall. Ruth close the door
behind him and slide the lock.

"I was about to go in the bathroom. Take a shower."

"Don't let me stop you." I read the paper.

"I don't have time for frisky business this morning," she say.

"Good 'cause I can't pop a woody for granny glasses and quilted jammies."

"I'm saying I don't want to have sex this time around, Baer, and you're not
going to trick me."

"My pencil outta lead."

"So no busting in the shower again."

"Shit, woman, give a man peace."

She close the door and I hear the lock. Old gal's like a sawmill opened up
and need a steady feed a timber.

Rustle through the newspaper and see the fuss about Nat Cinder.

Is Nathan Cinder Running?

71

. . .

You know him as the Arizona recluse millionaire who brought down Democrat governor Virginia Rentier. With Rentier's former chief of staff already in prison and state attorney general possibly close to indicting Rentier on charges of conspiracy, racketeering, and obstruction of justice, you might say Nat Cinder achieved all he set out to achieve.

Now Arizona wants to know, is Nat Cinder running for governor?

I joined him for breakfast in Flagstaff recently for a wide-ranging discussion.

FC: We have to start off with the big question. Your name keeps coming up among well-placed Republicans as the front runner, should you decide to run for governor. Will you?

NC: Decide? There's nothing to decide. No interest whatsoever.

FC: The rumor mill has it that you're meeting privately with all the right people.

NC: I guess to tell each one that I'm not interested. Arizonans have for too many years been mistreated by the career politician. I understand that and believe it. It's time for someone with a different background to step up. But as I've already explained to a lot of people, I haven't yet felt called to be that person.

FC: Sounds like a lot of wiggle room. So what's been happening in the last year? Obviously, your testimony put former governor Rentier's chief of staff, Mick Patterson behind bars. If Virginia Rentier is charged, your test—

NC: I need to stop you right there. Both my attorney and the state prosecutor have advised me not to discuss those matters.

FC: So it's been a year. What other interests have you turned your advocacy toward?

NC: Well, as you know, we have a border problem, and that's been leading to a lot of other problems. Regardless of what side a person takes, we can all agree the immigration process is broken, and the result affects all of us. We have a class of people coming into the country illegally, and that's one set of issues. But another problem is far more troubling to me personally. We also have a set of people—very young people—orphans, kidnapping victims, runaways, being brought here against their will. I'm talking about human trafficking. And what distinguishes this problem from the others is that this group is the only one where they aren't their own agents.

FC: What do you mean by that?

NC: Well, they're not making their own decisions. They're the most disenfranchised of all. To my mind, if a society doesn't protect its kids, it has no reason to exist. It has failed. These kids are stolen, brought to the United States, and sold throughout the country as sex slaves. That's the issue I've been investigating for my, as you put it, advocacy.

FC: What a horrifying problem. What can be done about it?

NC: A lot of things. Obviously, a more secure border would raise the cost of getting these kids to the markets that are buying them. I don't mean to sound cold, but even though this is a moral issue, I believe the solution is economic. All human action is economic. If you want to reduce an activity, you tax it—meaning you stress it. Well, you can't impose financial taxes directly, but you can create the same financial impediments through law enforcement. Secure borders would limit the routes available to bring these kids in. Every market requires a certain level of activity to flourish. Just like the stock market. If suddenly there were no sellers, the price would skyrocket, inventory would crash, then the market would close because buyers come to markets to buy. Literally, the market would starve. So on one side, you attack the problem by closing off the supply.

FC: Is that possible? Aren't there other sources of children for what you call the markets?

NC: There are, and I want to be clear about one thing. Human trafficking isn't a crime against borders. It's a crime against people. It means trafficking in people, or selling people. Transportation of the victims is not what identifies the crime. It just so happens we have tremendous numbers of children coming into the country in this manner, and they have no voice. That's what strikes me as so important about the issue. Now the other part of solving the problem is limiting demand. We can't do as much about that in Arizona because most of the children brought through our state have other destinations. Some wind up here, but most go to Las Vegas and Los Angeles. Then second tier destinations are Seattle, Saint Louis and Chicago. That's why, so far, my work has been into the supply part of the problem.

FC: Wouldn't a cynic just say you're trying to find yet another way to justify closing the borders, and that you're really just aligning yourself with the hardliners in your party, but in a way more palatable for the more centrist voter?

NC: Who the hell has time for cynics? I don't affiliate with a political party. I have rece—

"HEY."

"Hey yerself."

I look up. She nekkid.

"You want a little mud for your turtle?"

No, I want a gurgle of Wild Turkey and a nap. A bath in a cool brook with a couple wood nymphs slobbin the knobbin. A bowl of boiled cabbage and that razor sharp cheddar out Vermont. Smoke from cherry wood. But looking up from the paper and seeing Ruth in the window sunlight, it ain't like she's got leprosy.

"Turtle need a bath 'fore it get muddy."

She pull me from the chair and show me the way.

CHAPTER 15

Wayman started his day at noon. He kept an apartment adjacent his office, which overlooked the nightclub dance floor through mirrored glass. His bedroom also had a glass wall looking down on the dance floor. When a woman saw the room, she assumed things about his character. She expected coke on a mirror. A candy jar full of X.

Wayman didn't party often, and when he did, he remained stone sober.

He lived square in the middle of every possible kind of excess. Alcohol. Drugs. Sex. Violence. He learned early the only way to survive was to associate fear with pleasure. He governed the chaos with rules and, like his father, enforced them instantly, without hesitation or remorse.

Wayman never slept while the club was open or in a room with a door that wasn't locked.

Never spent the night with the same woman twice, and when she entered his room, she did so nude, and carried nothing with her.

And last, when the party was over, the woman had to leave. No sleepovers.

Except last night.

Claudia.

Wayman opened his eyes and his first thought was to touch her again. She was his first conquest in a month and he'd exhausted himself on her, almost mad for her perfume and softness.

Eight weeks ago, he'd noticed she drank water all night. She danced and laughed with her friends, batted away men, and left at midnight. Designated driver, he'd thought.

The following week, same strawberry blond girl, same water on the rocks. He'd sent a guard to invite her to the balcony. He'd spoken with her there. She was twenty-nine, a doctor of anthropology, and by far, the most enticing creature Wayman had ever seen. Not in the club.

In his life.

He led her by the hand toward the office. She shook her head. "I don't go off with strange men."

"Me? Strange?"

"Men I don't know. Or men I do know, for that matter."

Wayman had nodded, seeking words and not conceiving them. The dance music was too loud. The pulsing lights, annoying. He wasn't frustrated so much as surprised, and not by her. Other women had rejected him—diehard lesbians. Not his fault.

This one didn't frustrate him. And she didn't surprise him. She made him surprised with himself.

He felt something different toward her, that he had not felt toward other women. He watched her walk away from the door, back to her dancing friends on the balcony.

She had a nice backside, but another thought rose to the top of his mind.

Child bearing hips.

And her skin ...

European stock.

One of the many necessary corollaries of existing so high up the food chain was how tiny others appeared. The men who served him were his inferiors. All but one, Asger Erickson, were order takers, not thinkers and doers. The women Wayman slept with were barely more human than the ones he bought and sold. Sex was mechanical, temporal.

Seven weeks ago, when Claudia walked away, he'd entered his office alone, taken a notepad and pen, and returned to her while she danced.

He took her hand, put his mouth to her ear, and said, "Dinner and a movie?"

"Okay."

He took her out as frequently as she would allow, until finally last night she joined him in bed.

Instead of following his rules, her clothes were in a pile on the sofa and she lingered half awake and half sleeping with him all morning, until now.

He wanted her again, and he wanted her elsewhere. In a house, with a back yard and a pool. With a family room. Christmas tree and presents ...

"I have to work," he said.

"What time is it?" Claudia said.

"Eleven fifty-three."

"I thought so."

He squinted at her.

"Approximately."

He watched her slip into her clothes. "Where I come from, what we did last night means we're gettin' hitched."

She smiled. "I didn't think a nightclub owner would be the marrying kind." She threw her purse strap over her shoulder. "Can you show me out? I have to get ready for a class I teach."

"Sure."

Wayman put on a robe. "Seriously, though. I'm going to marry you."

"If you think that's how to propose to this girl, I've made a mistake."

He led her from his bedroom to the adjoining office. She halted.

"Who's that?"

On the other side of the glass wall stood Asger Erickson, at post and awaiting his boss.

"Asger. You might call him my right-hand man."

"He looks like a body guard."

"That too."

"I don't want him to see me."

"Why?"

"Because I don't shack up." She smiled. "Isn't there another exit?"

"Just a minute. Wait in the bedroom."

Wayman knelt. Twisted a lock placed frustratingly at the metal base of the glass door.

"Asger, please wait for me in the elevator."

When Asger entered the elevator, Wayman motioned to Claudia.

He led her across the balcony, down the stairs, across the dance floor, and to the nightclub's main entrance. On the cement step ,he reached for her hand but she pecked him on the cheek.

"I have to go. I need time to get cleaned up, and I'm going to be late."

He took her face in both his hands and kissed her, hard.

She returned his force.

The kiss broke and she left him there, again watching her form, but now relishing the secret knowledge he had of it.

He wanted to take her places and tell her stuff. Listen to her stuff. Intoxicate himself on her.

A block away, Claudia stopped walking. She turned to him. Wayman looked both ways. The street bustled with noon traffic, foot and vehicle. He stepped toward her in his robe and bare feet. She came back toward him with short, quick steps, and thirty feet away, put her hands at her mouth. "You have to ask my father!"

"Yeah?"

"Next week! He'll be here next week."

She blew him a kiss, turned around, and jogged toward her car.

CHAPTER 16

L uke Graves drove Interstate-40 west in Cephus's F-150 with Cephus lengthwise in the bed. He powered down both front windows and the bracing wind buffeted his face and tossed his hair. His ears grew numb and his eyes wet. He felt their redness. The sting.

He'd taught Cephus better than that. He'd taught him to always be thinking ahead, anticipating surprises. Life was hard enough dealing with the known threats. You also had to know where to look for the unknowns.

As a boy Cephus displayed abundant charm and cunning. Loyalty. When it became apparent Cephus was a thousand-fold superior to his older brother Finch, like an archer bent for distance, Luke had taken special pains to aim Cephus high. Make him perfect. That's what you do with an Albert Einstein. A Mozart.

So how the hell did he take a taped girl out for a quick bullet to the head and manage to get shot in the face? The girl couldn't have done it. Cephus didn't shoot himself.

An angel of God didn't do it.

The only way it happened was treachery. Someone in blind, ready to kill in an instant, didn't give him a fighting chance.

Luke wondered what sort of man had stayed in that yellow tent. Probably some darkie wandering across the state, left from LA, looking for New York. Some spic. A Zionist. It had to be one of the inferior races—a test from God, to prepare him for the coming wars.

Another thought lurked in the corner of his mind, just out of the light. It had been there for years, and Luke had never brought it forward ... *Absalom*. The son who excelled his father, King David, in every way, and turned on him ...

Had Cephus's murder spared Luke a future agony? Was it conceivable? Could God be somehow protecting Luke?

Luke exited the highway and a half mile farther, turned on his long driveway. He saw his log cabin framed against the rugged hills behind it. What would he say to Caroline?

How do you make it sound natural? Something as outrageous as the glorious Cephus being dead.

Butchers know the lifetime odds of a band saw taking a finger are pretty high. Men of every physical occupation know someday it'll be the back, the joints, the lungs, or, if the work is just miserable, the liver. He'd long before made his peace. Every occupation enjoyed its hazards, and his work carried a higher kind.

But he'd always assumed it would be Finch.

How the hell had it been Cephus? How could a young man as gifted as Cephus be surprised by a nobody, head shot in a field, with almost nothing around him? What kind of lapsed thinking allowed an accident like that?

Luke pulled up to the garage and sat in the driveway with the engine running.

Finch, driving Luke's truck, pulled to his right and remained in the cab.

From the side, Luke saw the log cabin's front door open. Caroline ran out wearing her yoga outfit, barefoot on the stone sidewalk, her face drawn tight. She floated across the gravel and syllables came from her mouth. They formed no words but spoke grief. Luke opened the truck door. Caroline must have looked out the second-floor window.

She climbed over the rear wheel and threw her leg over the bed wall. She went to her knees, took Cephus's hand, but turned away from the cold stare of his face, with the extra hole in his forehead.

Luke went into the house and used the bathroom. Splashed water into his eyes. Filled a mug with coffee and heavy cream, drank a long pull of the stale elixir, then returned to the truck. He said, "I found him like that. He was out doing work, and someone left him, out in the open."

"Why?"

Luke shook his head.

Kneeling on the rough bed liner, Caroline rested her head on Cephus's chest, draped her hands over his shoulders, and wept.

Luke removed his jacket and gave it to Caroline. She lifted herself and put her arms through the sleeves.

"Don't you worry," Luke said. "I'm going to track down whoever did it."

Caroline sat in the bed. She held Cephus's hand. "He's so cold."

"It must have happened last night."

"Was it a Mexican?"

"I don't know."

"We should kill all of them. Bring them up here one by one, let them see what they've done. Kill them with a knife, so they die slow. I want those animals to know why."

"Suspect it was a darkie, hiding. I don't know who, but I will, and he's going to suffer. I promise you that."

"No," Caroline said. "Bring him to me. You chose the path of this family. You owe me that."

Luke nodded. Looked off.

"It'll be a few days. But I will." Luke called to Finch, still sitting in the other truck cab. "Open the garage door."

He took Caroline's hand as she climbed over the tailgate, then carried her to the house like he did on their wedding day, and set her down inside.

"We'll have a service this afternoon. I'm going to take him to the shelter."

"The bone room?"

"That's what it's for."

"I—"

"Never expected to use it this soon." He put his hand on her shoulder. "I'll be back for you in a bit. Don't come up on your own. We put out new hazards. Cephus ... He was good at that."

She nodded, and Luke turned away.

He stopped. Looked back. "Call Pastor Sowell. I want to send my boy right. You understand?"

CHAPTER 17

Wayman found Asger Erickson in the elevator, his foot holding the door open. As he'd told Claudia, Asger was more than a bodyguard. The beefy blond Norseman was skilled in martial arts and held an MBA from Brigham Young.

"Come on," he said. Back at his office, Wayman prepared a cup of coffee in a Keurig machine.

He sipped, noticed the delicate scent of Claudia on his hand. Smiled inwardly. Business was good. Profit was astronomical. He loved where he lived. What he wore. What he ate. Everything was perfect. And now, this one little super nova of emotion. This curiosity.

He held out his mug. "Coffee?"

"No thank you, sir."

"What's up?"

"Last night's client—Mister Naganori. He's still at it."

Wayman blinked. "Did she give him a problem?"

"No. He wanted it to be slow, but she's taking more time than he thought. I asked if he needed assistance—"

"You shouldn't have done that. Not this guy."

The client was a Japanese bond trader worth a couple billion. He would resent the implication he didn't know how to kill a woman. Respect, appearances, meant everything. And a billion dollars made the relationship worth preserving.

But also worth renegotiating.

"Where do things stand?"

"I left him about forty minutes ago. He's aware the room was supposed to have been vacated by four a.m. He said he would address you about my behavior."

"Yeah. Wait here a minute."

Wayman returned to his room, pulled on jeans and a white t-shirt. Slipped boots over bare feet and tucked a .38 at his back.

"Come on."

Asger followed to the elevator. They rode in silence. Exited on the sixth floor.

"Thirteen," Asger said.

Wayman hesitated before knocking. The room was sound proof, but he thought he heard something. A woman, maybe. He rapped. The door did not open. He stepped back. Asger unlocked it with an old-fashioned metal key.

The gray-haired billionaire sat naked in a plush leather chair, his body streaked in blood. He looked up, as if roused from sleep. Smiled with the side of his mouth.

Wayman looked at the bed. The girl's arms and feet were bound to the bed posts. Long slices opened her body, here and there, random. A gash split her thigh. Another exposed white nubs of rib. One breast removed. Her face was battered and for a split second, Wayman felt something for her: he was glad she was gone.

"You were supposed to be out of here by four. My people have a schedule. It's hard to sanitize a room, and it's time-sensitive. It's why these things were agreed upon before your visit."

The Japanese man nodded.

"You have not followed our agreement. With respect, we must renegotiate."

The man blinked. Nodded almost imperceptibly.

"Another fifty."

Again the same nod.

The girl coughed. Wayman spun. Her lungs rattled like they were soaked in blood. She moaned. He closed his eyes and opened them before turning back to the man.

Wayman's cell phone vibrated. He looked at it. Luke.

"Cut deeper," Wayman said to Naganori, and left the room.

In the hall with the door closed behind him he answered, "Yeah."

"Can I get a sitrep?"

"All clear, here," Wayman said.

"Good. Be safe. See you tonight. Oh, and that thing we talked about. It's now."

Wayman ended the call. He turned. "Open the door."

Asger opened it. Wayman pushed inside. The man still sat on the chair.

"Change of situation. If you want to finish her, do it right now."

"We already renegotiated."

"Fair enough." Wayman walked to the end table beside Naganori, lifted a knife with a six-inch blade, and drove it into the girl's heart. He turned to Asger. "Escort Mister Naganori to his changing room, then the airport. Plan B."

WAYMAN FINISHED the coffee he'd made earlier, went into his apartment, and took a quick shower.

The phone call from Luke hadn't meant the end was nigh. But it was the first time either Wayman or Luke had made the coded call. Reflecting on his response, Wayman might have over-reacted.

When Luke called, he wasn't asking for a situation report, but was using code to give one. Things on his end were fishy. The call signaled a low-level alert. Something unknown was wrong, and there might be a risk to the whole operation. Bottom line: keep your eyes open and initiate no new risk.

What about when you're in the middle of risk?

Finish it and hunker down.

Easier said than done when you've got a mangled corpse to deal with.

Plus, he had another guest due to arrive in six hours, this one from Florida. The man was probably boarding his flight right now.

"Shit."

Although Wayman used no written contracts, he was explicit with each client. The rules were absolute, and due to the risk he took for his clients, the rules could change at a moment's notice. If he gave the abort call, turn around, don't call us, we'll call you. Your date will be rescheduled or your money returned.

The man due this evening had given Wayman business worth a cool half million over the last three years—not counting several clients Wayman suspected the man had referred. He was bona-fide serial. Alienating him at this late moment ...

Wayman's instincts clashed. He avoided all chance-based risk. If it felt like gambling, Wayman was out. He took calculated risks, always where the payoff was extraordinary and the risk of something going wrong was tiny and mitigated.

However ... if it had been Wayman who'd paid a hundred grand, boarded an airplane, and was this moment lusting about satisfying his deepest need, he'd be pissed if he got the *abort* phone call.

Along with Wayman's deep aversion to risk-taking, his second most deeply held instinct was to take care of the customer. It wasn't some smarmy bullshit like the customer was always right. His customers got off on murdering kids. They weren't always right. They were sociopaths. Wayman took care of them because it made the best business sense.

Confidence mattered.

His clients had to be able to trust he'd disappear the evidence. They knew they were placing their lives in Wayman's hands. Some men were reckless enough to do so without much thought, but most were not. Most of his clients would never have the guts to act out their lusts without Wayman's careful protection, and his protection included not just who he was, but the soundness of his entire operation. Every detail had to inspire confidence. Men who killed in Wayman's habitat had to have absolute faith their actions would never come back on them, and nothing was more harmful to Wayman being held in ultimate esteem than having to cancel an appointment. It was like saying, *I don't have my shit together. Something surprised me. I wasn't ready for it.*

And given how rapidly word had spread when he'd added the last item to the menu, Wayman had little doubt that if he canceled the evening's appointment with the man from Florida, other clients would desert him as well.

Despite his warring instincts, the business demanded he carry on.

Wayman picked up his cell phone and powered the screen. Should he call Luke and find out what the hell was up?

No. He'd wait. The second part of the call meant not only was Luke coming personally this evening with the load, but the plans they'd discussed for Finch were under way.

That was good. Because he had a room full of blood that needed to be cleaned.

But that meant Cephus was sitting this one out. Had the old man finally decided to let him open up his own shop?

The computer desktop finally came to life. He opened a video program, clicked the link *Room 13,* and his second monitor opened a window with four camera feeds showing the girl Wayman had stabbed, the chair—where minutes ago, Naganori sat naked—and the bathroom where Wayman had washed his prints from the knife.

It was Naganori's first time with Wayman, and his only security video of him. At a minimum, Wayman had to delete the final act. Would the video hold coercive value with just the old man torturing the girl? Enough to keep?

Wayman decided to keep it. He opened the editing function, rolled back the time bar and found his first entry into the room. He deleted everything after that point.

He backed up the file to his external hard disk, then saved it again to a micro SD card, wrote *Naganori* on it, and unlocked his desk drawer. He withdrew a nylon wallet filled with plastic sleeves, each holding three slots. He flipped to the second to last and pushed the SD card into the slot.

Five openings remained. He'd need a new wallet soon.

CHAPTER 18

Two hours later, Luke Graves was back at the cabin, dressed and ready for the makeshift service. He'd taken Cephus to the ossuary and prepared him best he could, which amounted to wiping the blood off his face and cleaning the hair that remained on the back of his head.

His brain had worked partly out the hole. The bullet had blasted a lot of it through the back, and what remained was pulverized. It had congealed with blood over night, but vibration in the truck bed had worked some loose, and when Luke moved Cephus to the trailer hitched to his four-wheeler, a clump fell out of his skull.

Luke thought of getting a shovel, then picked it up with his hand. He placed the brain matter beside Cephus's head, and while he thought about stuffing it back inside the skull, he also wondered which part of Cephus—if it worked that way—he'd just touched.

Was it his wit? The part that gave him the perfect smart-ass rejoinder? The part that told him when to wink at a girl? The part that made him loyal?

It occurred to Luke there wasn't a single thing about his son that wasn't good.

Luke held his bloody hand up, studied it, and then pushed it aloft, palm skyward, for God to see what innocent blood looked like.

"There will be weeping, and gnashing of teeth," he said.

He squeezed his eyes tight. Wiped his bloody hand in the grass, then hauled his son to the shelter, cleaned him, and placed him in the ossuary.

He returned to the house, put on black jeans, black boots, and a black overcoat.

Finch, who hadn't helped and had seemed lost in soul searching, had stayed at the house. He hadn't changed clothes because, having moved to a Flagstaff apartment, he no longer kept anything at the house.

While Caroline was upstairs in a daze, preparing herself, Luke joined Finch on the sofa.

"Give any thought to what I said? About your role in the business going forward?"

Finch was quiet.

Luke wondered if he could trust a word his son said, if he had to give the first syllable so much care.

"I have," Finch said. "I've thought about what this family does, not just the first business, the, uh, meat business. But the second. Helping the young ones from down south find their way to opportunity. I ... I thought about what this family believes. About the future, and the race wars to come. And I think I know why I had such a problem with it in the past. I don't know where I got the idea, but I just never felt like I was as good as Wayman at anything. And it didn't take long until Cephus was showing me up. And I hid from it. That's what I think all my troubles have been. I'm not good enough to be part of all this, and that's why I never wanted to be."

Luke nodded, seeing how maybe Finch had a point. When he was a baby they wondered if someone had dropped him on his head—a babysitter or something, when no one was around. Finch never could think anything through. Never see what mattered. Couldn't add one truth to another. And when Cephus showed such promise early on ... Luke could understand how Finch would feel inferior.

It was true. The first thing Finch said in a long while that made any sense.

"That don't let any man off the hook, though," Luke said. "We're all responsible for who we are. What we choose to become."

"I'm not disagreeing. I'm just saying I think I know why I became what I am. Because if I just told you, Dad, I've seen the light, you'd think I was full of shit. I wanted you to know I've put some real thought into it."

Luke began to nod. "Okay, *yeah*. So ...?"

"Well, Dad ..."

Smiling, Luke stood and began to reach for Finch.

"This isn't what I want to do with my life. I don't want this. It's fine for you and Wayman, and I'm sure Mom is happy with the whole business. But I don't want to be a part of it anymore."

Luke halted.

Finch stood. He tucked his hands in his pockets.

Luke opened his mouth, then closed it. He looked out the picture window.

Finch didn't turn.

"The pastor's here," Luke said.

Pastor Sowell drove a Hyundai Sonata that made Luke wince every time he saw it. The car was old and worn out and ... made by slopes. Luke faced Finch. Clenched his teeth and smiled. "Well, you've made up your mind."

"I figured I'd help you out through this, uh, situation. And whatever you want afterward. I'm not trying to abandon the family. But you asked if I wanted it, long term. I didn't want to give you a bullshit answer. I figure I owe you more than that."

"No, I understand it all. Perfectly. We'll take the meat up this afternoon and I'll work it out with Wayman. I'm sure he's got somebody up there we can get to fill in down here, till we make permanent arrangements." Luke locked eyes with his son. "It's good to know where you stand. Tell your mother the pastor's here, and I'm going out to meet him."

PASTOR SOWELL EXITED his vehicle and approached Luke with his right hand out to shake, while the other floated to the side, ready if called into a hug.

That wasn't happening.

"Cephus was my best boy," Luke said. He looked to the hills. "Cephus was the apple. You know? And we can't bury him out in the cemetery like he died in a car accident. Because a murderer got him, and if I let the police in on it, that hamstrings my options. You understand? War's coming soon enough anyway. Hell, this is very damn likely the first shot, far as I'm concerned. This family has a vital role. And you. So I wanted you here to make sure we send off Cephus right."

Sowell, along with Graves and a few dozen others scattered over Coconino County, were regulars at the separatist meetings. They shook hands every month, and talked about the havoc being caused by Blacks and Browns. How the havoc of the under races was forcing them to prepare for war, just as soon as democracy crumbled under the weight of socialist totalitarianism and the ever-expanding police state.

Finch joined them from inside. "Ma's coming," he said. He sat on one of the four-wheelers near the pastor's car.

Sowell said, "Inviting the police to investigate Cephus's death would be tantamount to inviting them to investigate his life, and with the work he was doing for the cause, that's clearly not the Lord's will."

"Amen, pastor. A-fucking-men."

Sowell used his floating left hand to clasp Luke Graves's shoulder. He gave a quick squeeze and release, then a couple slaps.

"You don't need to say any more," Sowell said. "We need to get Cephus sent off to the Lord. He's a just and deserving soldier and the Lord's mercy is assured. We can all rejoice in that. Amen?"

"Amen."

Luke pulled a blindfold out of his pocket. "If you don't mind."

"What's this?"

"The ceremony is going to be inside our compound. When the shit hits the fan, you and the rest'll be welcome. But for now, it's location is strictly need-to-know."

"I, uh, see."

The pastor closed his eyes.

Finch said, "Just a minute. Why don't you climb aboard before you get blindfolded?"

Sowell swung his leg over the seat.

Luke wrapped the blindfold around his head, tied it off.

Luke and Caroline boarded another four-wheeler, this one with a .30-06 holstered in a leather scabbard on the side. Luke led across the back yard to a trail that zig zagged up the hill, and then partly around the side, before joining an old logging road. There, they turned left and continued a quarter mile. Between evergreens, through bare branches of deciduous trees, the view stretched across an enormous straw-gold valley set between two randomly spaced mountains, belched up from a perfectly flat plain. Far below, vehicles passed along Interstate 40.

Looking at it, Luke wondered if anyone had bothered to check on the meat in the basement. Without their morning pills, the girls might be vocal when he returned to them in an hour, to start the journey to Salt Lake City.

He'd need to keep Caroline away from them. He didn't spend fifty grand on a bunch of chicas to have his wife carve them up.

Luke swerved onto a barely discernible trail. In summer, foliage would hide it. Now it was visible. He downshifted the four-wheeler, and the machine ground slowly up the steep trail. Luke leaned forward. Caroline squeezed him. The four-wheeler crested, and Luke kept it easing forward. He stopped at a rock outcropping.

Six years ago, the rocks had been a pair of mostly-buried boulders.

He'd stood there with a representative of Longterm Family Shelters, a company from Boise, Idaho, that specialized in constructing hidden, unknown, off the grid, secret, no-fucking-way-anyone-will-ever-know-you're-there shelters for folks who could see the end was nigh and wanted a safe perch to watch it.

The rep had pointed to the rocks, and said, "This is it. Perfect camouflage."

With the man's explanation, Luke agreed to the 2.2-million-dollar price tag.

"In one sense," the rep said, "It makes a lot more sense to pay with a mortgage than to use your own money. The day comes when you need this place, no one's going to keep track of your credit score."

"But how can it be secret if I mortgage it? Wouldn't that mean an appraiser, and all that?"

"Many of our clients place a second mortgage on their existing homes. Say it's for business expansion."

Luke had done so. In the end, if he could screw a Jew banker, that was gravy.

Within weeks of that conversation, all very quietly, with no one the wiser, rough looking men from Longterm Family Shelters began to arrive. They worked all summer, under tree cover.

First they tethered the two boulders with multiple I-beams set two feet deep. Built a facade between them with a hidden door. Dug thirty feet back, straight into the hill, then down ten, and excavated a three thousand square foot concrete cave, with ten bedrooms, a kitchen, common area, command center, three bathrooms, the works. Electricity came from solar units hidden over the mountain. Water from a well, dug from inside the unit, to be maintainable and free from tampering from the outside. Equipped with state of the art electric controls, the unit also had solid state fail-safes, in the event the sun went dark. In addition to the 3,000 feet of living space, the company excavated another 2,000 feet of storage, and last, the ossuary.

He hadn't wanted it at first, but the company representative suggested all his biggest clients were going with it. The reason? When outside circumstances demand you enter one of these shelters, you never know if it's for the last time. You'll likely be with others. One of them might pass away. When that happens, you don't want to have to keep him in a bedroom, and it would be a shame to spend a couple million dollars on a shelter, and then lose it to a band of roving marauders when you open the door to bury grandma under the apple tree.

Luke had no idea how soon the ossuary would be useful.

He looked behind him and dismounted. Pastor Sowell still wore the blindfold.

In the five and a half years since the shelter had been completed, the facade had weathered, moss had grown, and the illusion was perfect. Though he knew exactly which part of the rock to reach under and press, it amazed him each time to feel the entire boulder seem to pop as if on a latch. It was an illusion. Only a doorway opened. It was six feet wide, as was the thirty-foot walkway to the chamber rooms. The door swung inward on hinges hidden in a vertical crevice.

Luke pushed open the door, turned on the lights, and drove the four-wheeler inside. Finch followed.

Luke closed and bolted the door. He pulled the bow tie behind the pastor's head and stuffed the blindfold in his pocket.

"Welcome to our future home."

Luke helped Caroline off the four-wheeler and led the party to the door at the end of the wide hall. He pushed a key into a lock located in the center of the door, a design reminiscent of old European locks. A single mechanism controlled fifteen deadbolts, each drilled four inches into the concrete wall. The action was smooth and the door drifted inward.

Luke pushed it and turned on a light, revealing stairs that descended ten feet. When everyone was on the stairs, he turned off the hall light. They waited for him to lead down the steps.

They arrived at the largest room in the shelter, the common room. Equipped with the finest electronics for surveillance of the mountainside and valley below, it also held several gaming tables, a dart board on a wall, and book shelves, as yet unpopulated. Luke still hadn't fully moved all the equipment he'd bought for it. He had a couple tons of supplies, food, clothing and water in the basement of his house. The time just never seemed to be there, with his dual meat businesses flourishing.

When it was all over, when Cephus's killer was tortured and dead, he'd make a point to finish preparing the chamber.

"Will television stations be operational, when you're using this?" Pastor Sowell said.

"That's just for nowadays, when we watch football up here. Have to stay inside and get used to it, a little. That's what Sundays are for."

Luke took Caroline's hand and led the group across the main chamber past a kitchen area—he left the light off, there—and down a hall that branched into sizable bedrooms. Each was capable of housing six men on bunks. At last they arrived at a door at the end of the hall, also equipped with a multi-deadbolt lock. The manufacturer had explained, you'll want to maintain rigorous control over what is placed in storage. In hard times, even the most trustworthy family members have difficulty with rationing supplies.

Luke pushed open the door. The empty chamber seemed vast, but was the size of a large basement, with a twelve-foot ceiling. He led them through this to a door at the far end, again locked.

Inside, a dirt cave another fifty feet long, with hollowed out thigh-high side chambers, two feet deep, six feet long, for the placement of corpses.

At the end, under the last set of LED lights, rested Cephus Graves.

CHAPTER 19

Ruth gimme a lift and drop me off 'bout two mile from the Graves house. I's re-outfitted with pack, bag and tarp, food. None of that bright yellow bullshit. Got the camouflage on everything.

Plan a three day reconnoiter. Topo map, binocular. Some point the house'll be empty. If Luke Graves takes Dreadlocks with him to the Salt Lake, it'll be just the missus to deal with. Rap her on the head if I gotta. She ain't without part in what her husband done.

Woods is mixed hardwood and conifer. Not like Carolina wood; here the land's bare under the trees and you can see uncanny far. Plus with no leaves on the maple and oak, sunlight keep the whole thing bright. Fella's exposed long way off in these wood, so I find a pine with low limbs and stretch out the tarp, lay out the bag and climb in for a lazy day. Joe nestles in tight, and I can't imagine a world more perfect. Got the pine tree scent and clean woods far as the eye can see or ear can hear. They's a crick you don't notice till the breeze is total still, and you almost gotta stop breathing to pick up the sound. No bugs. No men. No red. No juice. Mind wanders till I see dead men hanging in trees, and I know I was dreaming.

They's more killing coming.

Open the eyes and pull back the tarp.

Sun down, dusk up. Got the ambition comes with an empty belly. Roll the tarp and shove the bag in the backpack pocket. They thought of everything. Gulp water and start moving, looking shelter for the cook stove. Ahead is all flat land and trees, open like the rest. But behind, I think on that crick. It's eroded the ground and I hop down in the cut.

Daylight slow to a stop. Hang the tarp with bungee cords and stakes, shape an A with openings facing the crick banks. Oughtta keep the light low. Fire the cookstove and boil water, fill two pouches. Twist the knob and the flame die.

Total dark now. Fish in the pack for the flashlight with the red-light filter. Gimme just a tiny glow and put away the cook stove, tarp.

Fill a foldable nylon bowl with Purina for Joe. He sniff it.

I'll have some of that chicken a la king.

"Fuck you will."

Now the backpacker pouch of food is done, I open it and the steam smell like a gourmet restaurant. I spoon some out.

Said I'll have some of that.

"I treat you too good."

I dump some gravy and chicken on his chow and Stinky Joe launches in.

"You need to catch a rabbit or something. How come I got to carry all yer food?"

I wait. Stinky Joe too polite to talk while he chomps and chews. I finish the first bag of chow and start the second. Each bag's suppose to feed two people, so I eat for four.

This one's the beef stew. Wish I had a loaf bread.

You look full.

"Dark out. You can't see shit."

Still.

"Here. I hook you up. But drink lots of water. Salt in this'll last rest yer life."

I fetch his bowl. Empty. 'Nother handful of dog chow, cover it in beef stew. Pour what I don't give him down my throat like drinking out a mug. Swaller carrot and tater chunks whole.

Joe finish same time.

"Aright. We got mebbe two mile to the house. You ready?"

You know that girl stole your shit?

"Uh-huh."

She's out here.

"I know."

I mean, close.

"Well, let her follow. She won't do me no harm. Just a girl."

I rinse his empty bowl in the crick and tuck it under straps on the pack so its exposed to dry but won't flop around.

Got the waxing gibbous above, already high in the sky, so mebbe it'll set around two three in the a.m.

Joe go out sniffing. I look about the darkness for a clearing. Head there. Bust out the map, red light, and Polaris for the north heading. Rotate the map. I's north Interstate 40, headed west. Staying on the south side the hills. Put the Polaris off my right. Locate the road Ruth left me on, the hill off my right. Straight line to the Graves joint has me climbing two hills. But if I stay south and follow a course like the under wire in a bra—mebbe a big ass bra—I travel farther but less up and down.

I speculate on the size of hooties would need a bra that big.

Stinky Joe come up beside. We ease into the walk.

CHAPTER 20

Wayman stood with his back to his office desk, looking out the mirrored glass to a thin crowd on the Butcher Shop dance floor.

It was only ten. A disproportionate number of the folks at the bar and on the floor were men. Men arrived first, laid low next to the oasis that brought in the prey.

The only girls present had gotten juiced early. They'd already taken the dance floor—as if getting out of their heads was more important than going someplace specific.

Every night, the same thing. The first men came to prowl. The first women, to escape.

Wayman stared. The wild was the wild. It was an environment. Environments don't give a shit. They starve or feed you, depending on your decisions. What you're willing to take.

These last few weeks of being head over heels for Claudia ...

Could he trust her absolutely? In his line of work, that was imperative. How would he be able to find out if he could trust her, without risking everything?

No woman could be more important than business. Ever.

But thinking about a solitary life, no kids at Christmas time, gleeful around a tree, making a mess of the mashed potatoes and ham gravy ... And what about old age? If he lived that long, his path led to desolate solitude, no one to trust, no one to be generous to, no one to protect. No one to carry on his blood, his genius.

What was the use in creating wealth if you didn't have the woes and joys of family?

Self-gratification. They used to call it self abuse.

Wayman was bigger than that. Claudia had awakened him. He needed to work for something more.

He'd pondered both Luke's *sitrep* warning and his last statement, indicating Wayman needed to make Finch's life-or-death test today. If Claudia was the right woman, he wanted to know. And if she wasn't: even more so. He'd create a test for her, just the same as Finch.

Wayman's pocket vibrated, and he remembered a news headline that cell phones stored next to your nuts make it hard to get a woman pregnant. Mobility. Motility. Something.

Wayman answered.

"Five minutes," Luke said.

Wayman pressed END and, about to slip the cell into his pocket, placed it on his office desk. He stepped to the door. Turned back to the phone. Shook his head.

Grabbing it, Wayman looked down on the dance floor and saw Claudia making her way to the balcony.

"Shit. Asger—the truck'll be here in five. Go meet it for me. I'll be right behind you."

He wove between dancing girls and crossed the balcony, meeting Claudia on the top step.

"I have to attend something at the restaurant. I'll be a while. I didn't know you were coming tonight."

She took his hands. "I'll come with you."

"Sorry, I—it's a personnel matter. Someone's about to lose his job."

"Oh. Can I stay here?"

"Yeah, I'll be back in a few." He kissed her cheek. "We can visit a little, but this is a work night for me. We need to have dinner again. So we can talk about everything. You know."

"Okay. Call me."

"No, stay."

"I shouldn't have come," she said. "Call me; we'll have dinner. Set up some boundaries."

"I don't want boundaries. I just have to work."

"That's what I mean." She smiled at him, big, and Wayman smiled back.

From the balcony he entered his office, locked it behind him, exited into the second hall, took the stairs instead of the elevator.

What was he thinking? Like he'd ever find a woman he could level with.

He'd have to ask his father how he knew his mother would be okay with the business.

He walked through the Butcher Shop's kitchen and to the loading dock. Asger stood at the open garage door, looking out into the night. The truck had not yet arrived.

"You have a woman? Amy, right?"

Asger partly smiled, partly wrinkled his brow. "Amy. Others."

The Isuzu refrigerated truck pulled past, stopped, and backed toward the dock.

"All right. Double check and make sure no one's in the kitchen or anywhere, right? And after that, I'm going to have Finch work with you."

Asger hesitated. Nodded. "Yes, sir."

The truck backed against the rubber and stopped. Wayman opened the door beside the bay. In a moment, Finch jumped down from the driver side of the truck holding a newspaper. He climbed the cement steps and entered, looking like he'd partied too hard the night before.

Luke came into view around the front of the truck, appearing just as run down.

"What's wrong?"

Without answering, Luke entered. Wayman closed the door behind him.

"Finch," Luke said. "You know what to do with the meat?"

"Asger!" Wayman called. He held up his hands.

"Clear."

"Take them up," Wayman said to Finch. He turned back to Asger, still across the bay. "Help him."

Luke unlocked the truck, and Finch opened the latch, the newspaper tucked under his arm.

"What are you doing with that?" Luke said.

"Just want something to read later."

Finch made noise inside the truck as he prepared to secure the girls. Luke led Wayman a few steps.

"Your call ..." Wayman said. "What happened?"

"I don't know whether it's about the business or not. But someone shot Cephus last night."

"What?"

"He had trouble with one of the girls. He took her out and didn't come back."

They walked farther from the dock. Wayman turned and saw Finch pull the first girl, tethered by handcuff to a steel cable, across the bay.

"Shot?"

"In the face. Dead."

"What do you mean, dead? How—was it the girl, you think?"

"No way it was her. Someone in wait. We searched the area and found a tent. Whoever—"

"Where was this?"

"Off forty, before Williams. Anyhow, whoever was staying in the tent loaded up and left right before we got there."

"A tent?" Wayman rolled it over in his mind. "That doesn't fit. We've got two enemies in this business, and neither stay in tents."

"That's why I gave you the heads up. I don't know who killed him. But the other thing that doesn't add up is this: A couple hours before, Finch hit an axle on the road. When they were coming up from Sierra Vista. Blew the front tire out. They were there fixing it and, you know, to get the jack, you have to open the back. Finch opens the door and the only boy in the group jumps out and hauls ass. Cephus put him down with the .308. And he went back to the same place with the girl."

"That means it was chance. Not a sting, or something."

"Right. It was pure chance. Someone happened to be there the first time, and Cephus didn't know it. He goes back the second time, and they got him."

"Or ..."

"Say it."

"Or was it somehow planned?" Wayman said. "Someone put that axle out there for Finch to hit, and he was part of it?"

"I thought of that. But with all we know about Finch, him being a screwup, he's never actually taken real action against us. He's never fully crossed over."

"Yeah. I don't see Finch having the nuts to blow out a front tire on purpose. It's not a threat to the business. It's some asshole we have to find and put down."

"Well," Luke said, "Not so fast. What's an ordinary person going to do if he sees what I just described? Wait with a gun in case it happens again? I don't see it. Ordinary man hauls ass and hopes he wasn't seen. Self-preservation. But our guy sat there and waited. Took one shot. A head shot. At night. Who does that? Point being, you can't trust this is isolated, and has nothing to do with anything else. That's why I gave the sitrep call."

"Okay. I get it." Wayman leaned on the wall. "So, was Finch part of it or not?"

"Don't think so. But afterward I gave him the chance to get in or out and he chose out. I'm not going to have that kind of risk floating around. I want it done and over with. Tonight."

"Roger that. But do you think maybe you ought to give it another day? You just lost your son. Hell, we all knew he was the golden boy. You can't be thinking clear, whether you're right about Finch or not, your thinking isn't right."

"Decision's made."

"Let me double-check your work. I have a special situation to deal with tonight and it's perfect to figure out where Finch's head is at."

Luke exhaled hard.

"Dad. This is a decision that's worth a second opinion. He's your son, and even if you're right, what's the harm in delaying a day? Let me help you out with this one. You'll thank me one day. Even if the decision is the same, you'll thank me you didn't make it in haste."

"Fine."

"You want a room tonight?"

"Nah. I'm going to the Motel 6. Get some sleep."

Wayman rested his hand on his father's shoulder.

"I feel like I haven't slept in a long time," Luke said. "It's only been one day."

Wayman slapped his back. "Get some rest. I'll deal with Finch. One way or the other."

CHAPTER 21

F inch followed Asger through the kitchen, past a butcher room replete with a band-saw, a massive bench table suitable to butchering anything from antelope to bison, sausage grinders, bell scrapers on the wall, the works. When Wayman first opened the place, Finch had eaten there and thought it was the coolest thing in the world: an older brother with a fine restaurant and quaking nightclub, all named the Butcher Shop. Hell yeah.

But Wayman had never led him any deeper into the building. Never upstairs. Cephus had always taken the meat up, leaving Finch to practice staying in role. He'd drift over to the nightclub side and bum weed off the bartender. Make passes at the beer maids.

Now, after telling his father he wanted out, he was being led deeper inside. Was it an effort to compromise him? Like when the kingpin forces a doubted underling to make a kill? A way to make a part-out guy all-in?

Or was Luke forcing him to see what he would give up if he left the family business?

Finch led the first girl by her arm and the rest, attached by handcuff to a steel cable, followed. They were still drugged, but it was near the hour when, for the last few days, they'd had their second knock-out of the day. They were becoming more aware, and as they walked, would become less groggy.

Asger stopped, held open a door. "End of the hall. We take the stairs."

Probably too much weight for the elevators, Finch thought.

"Hey, I'm going to leave my stuff here."

Asger nodded.

107

Finch shrugged out of his jacket and piled it along with his paper on a food preparation table.

The door to the stairwell was marked. Finch opened it. "Up?"

"Up."

He led. The girls trudged.

"Stop at four," Asger said, entering the stairwell behind the last girl.

Finch thought about the building's layout, what he was familiar with. The nightclub had a separate street entrance from the restaurant. They were linked by a hallway behind the kitchen, which connected to the storage area behind the nightclub's back wall. But no customer could go from one to the other without first going back to the street.

The restaurant had a two-story ceiling. The nightclub, three. Wayman kept the remainder of the third floor as his office and residence. The fourth floor, apparently, was where the girls lived.

The fifth and sixth?

Arriving at the fourth, Finch tried the door handle. Locked. The girls stopped climbing. Asger pushed one aside and joined Finch. He unlocked the door and said, "To the right. Get them all against the wall, and wait."

"Yes sir, captain." Finch waved his arm. "Come on, girls, you heard Ragnar, let's go."

Asger held open the door.

It felt like a hospital. Linoleum floor, white walls. Except the floors were devoid of the red dots they painted on the tiles to tell you where the heart clinic was, or radiation. At the distant end of the hallway, a door opened and a young woman emerged. She walked toward them with an assurance that made Finch wonder what Asger would do when he saw one of the prostitutes had gotten loose.

"Hey, you probably want to go back to your room, missy. This doesn't concern you."

"Who the fuck are you?"

She barked in Spanish and the girls froze. She lifted the first girl's chin, studied her eyes, mouth. Squeezed a breast. Snickered.

Asger leaned against the opposite wall and crossed his arms.

To Finch she said, "You have my key?"

"What?"

She took the lead girl's hand and lifted it, displaying the handcuff. "Key." She cocked her head toward Asger. "Who is this retard?"

"Boss's brother." To Finch he said, "Meet Amy. She runs this floor."

Finch gave her the universal handcuff key.

Amy unlocked the first girl, commanded her. The girl walked to a room, opened the door, and entered. She did not close the door behind her.

Amy moved to the next girl, and the next.

The elevator dinged.

Wayman emerged into the hall but kept an arm back, holding the elevator open. He waved Finch toward him. "Asger, you too."

They all entered the carriage. Finch took it in. Wood paneling. Mirrors. Hardwood floor. He watched Wayman press the top button and noticed it said 13, even though in sequence, the floor would be the sixth.

"You've never been up here, have you," Wayman said.

"No."

"What do you think?"

"I don't know what to think. I guess I haven't seen enough."

"That's about to change. Dad told me about your conversation. He wanted me to show you a little more of how we do things. He thinks maybe you've only seen the work, and not the reward."

The elevator dinged. The door opened. Finch stepped on a burgundy carpet. Opposite the elevator, a painting that looked splotchy, like a Monet, opened the entire wall into a field of flowers. Turning, Finch saw painting after painting, each lit with a recessed fixture above. He stepped to the first.

"Is this real?"

"Yes it's a real painting. But no, it's not Jackson Pollock, if that's what you meant. It's a derivative painter."

"Who?"

"Who gives a shit? It's derivative."

Wayman led them down the hall. Even the air smelled different on this floor. It must be where all the sex happened, Finch thought. Like a high-class whorehouse, crown molding, twelve-inch baseboards, brass fixtures, and sex with kids.

Finch wanted to throw up.

Wayman put his finger to his lips. "I want you to be very quiet now. The walls were sound proofed—but years ago, when the technology wasn't perfect. I need to have them redone. Even our weight as we move across the hallway can disrupt the most sensitive people, like the man in the next room. So just be quiet, and see if you can hear anything."

Finch followed, light on his feet, a sense of dread rising as the constriction in his chest grew tighter. He didn't want to hear some kid getting molested, but he sensed that was not what Wayman wanted him to experience.

Looking behind, he saw Asger had stopped walking. Finch tried to think tactically. If he had to escape, the only ways out were the elevator and stairs, situated beyond. He'd have to pass Asger to reach either.

There were fire escapes, but with the business being a sort of prison, he doubted the windows could be opened. If something went haywire, he had no choice but to overcome both Wayman and Asger.

Wayman stopped. Finch bumped into him. Wayman put his finger in the air:

Any moment now ...

They waited.

Longer.

Wayman's eyebrows arched. He nodded.

Finch heard nothing.

Wayman tilted his head and smiled.

Faint ... the voice of a girl. Screaming.

Wayman looked down the hall where they had come from and nodded. Finch backtracked. Twenty feet retraced, Finch said, "Why did you want me to hear that?"

"Anticipation."

They walked and stopped where Asger stood beside a door. Finch looked at the number.

13.

"Some kind of joke? The floor number ... the room number?"

Wayman nodded to Asger and stepped aside. Asger unlocked the room. He pushed open the door.

"Go ahead," Wayman said. "Go inside."

Finch stepped around the corner and froze.

"What—oh, God."

Wayman pushed his shoulder. Finch backed from the door.

Inside, on the bed, a naked girl lay with a knife perpendicular in her chest. Beneath her, brilliant white sheets were slashed and soaked in blood. Red spattered the walls behind the bed, and Finch thought of the fake Jackson Pollock—here was another derivative—dribbles and splashes of red on white.

The air from the room overcame him. The smell was metallic and pungent, like feces and blood. His stomach rolled.

"That's why she was screaming, little brother."

Gashes exposed the inner parts of the girl's muscles and bones. Her thigh was open, split apart across the top, lengthwise. Her left breast amputated and placed on the night table. Her ribs exposed, like a four-inch swath of skin and bone had been peeled away.

Finch turned away. Blood rushed into his brain, and the sound was like the ocean coming in, spinning him and stealing the air from the hallway. He felt sick in the back of his throat, like he would vomit. He leaned forward and noticed footprints of blood leading to the bathroom.

Finch remembered the wire on his chest, the mission from the FBI. He remembered his father agreeing to his help, this one time, to get through the pinch without Cephus.

"Oh, wow, shit. I wasn't ready for that. Whooeee. Wow. What is this?" Finch said. "Who is she?"

"You brought her here last month."

"Who, uh, who's the *painter?*"

"His name is not important. But it is Naganori. He's a finance man from Japan. Big, big money."

Calm. You're cool with this shit. How's the weather? Fuckin A hot for this time of year, right?

"Holy shit. You, uh, don't see that every day. I think I recognize her. Oh, shit, I didn't see that coming. But you got me good. So uh, when did this happen?"

"She's been dead about twelve hours. A couple less than that."

"Some accident, huh? Wow."

"No. This is ROI. Return on Investment."

"I don't understand."

"I know, and that's the purpose of tonight's lesson. To see if you *can* understand. So here's an example of the business model. An exact replica. Give me a dollar."

As Finch stared at the dead girl his mental awareness drew to a single focus: the wire on his chest, the band-aid sized recording device.

"I'm not bullshitting. You really need to understand this, and I want to break it down for you in terms you'll grasp. Give me a dollar."

Finch extracted his wallet. "I don't have a dollar. Here's a five."

"Perfect." Wayman took it, reached into his pocket and withdrew a hundred.

"Here, take it."

"What's this?"

"Shut up. It's a C-note. Now what if every time you put a five into your business, two weeks later, it gave you back a hundred? What if it happened every time? What would you ask yourself?"

"I—"

"Yes, you do. You know *exactly* what you'd ask. How many five-dollar bills can I put in? Well, the answer is about five thousand a month, meaning, twenty-five thousand dollars a month is what you can put in. We average five clients a month right now—usually about a week apart. Each of these girls costs us five grand. Each one pays a hundred. That's a half million dollars coming back at us, every month. But we're growing. Our maximum would be about thirty a month, when you look at supply, transportation"—he waved his arms around— "the size of the factory. Our max is about thirty girls a month. So you might say, out of our complete capacity utilization—the total amount we're capable of—what we're actually doing is about *sixteen percent*. That's a lot of room to grow, little brother. A half million dollars a month is only sixteen percent of what's possible, with our present arrangement. Is it starting to sink in, Finch?"

"I had no idea."

"You thought sending T-bones and rib-eyes to every grocery in Arizona is what made the money, right?"

"Not really. I thought it was just, you know. Pedophiles. And the money ... I didn't know the business ... the kids ... was this big."

"Big isn't the word. Huge isn't the word. Not when you think of the size of the market. And it's all ours to grow into. We're making the fucking iPhone here. No one knows the size of the market, or how badly they want the product. You know there's five hundred billionaires in the United States, and a couple thousand in the world. And listen to this. There's thirty million millionaires in the world. Thirty million. Now you think about the proportion of people who want to fuck a kid, and the proportion who want to kill one, and see if you can guess the ultimate size of our market."

"I—can't guess."

"I can't either. All I know is, we'll never saturate the market. We can grow as much as we want and we'll never reach the top. The only thing that can get in our way is the bad guys. The people we can't trust."

Finch glanced at Asger, whose eyes seemed to hold nothing at all.

"So tonight, my man, you see it all. The business and the reward. Tonight you clean a room, dispose of a body, and then have a five-thousand-dollar hooker from downtown slob your knob in a hot tub. Then you'll go out and buy your first Range Rover, cash. Then you'll get a second blowjob in the front seat from the guy who sells it to you—thumb up your ass if you want. You're going to know the full experience. Buckle in. Finch. Buckle the fuck in."

Finch looked at the blood pooled on the tile floor.

"Go on," Wayman said. "This room's got to sparkle."

Asger walked down the hallway.

Finch moved farther into the room.

A moment later Asger entered pushing a mop in an empty pail on wheels.

In his other hand, a five-gallon plastic bucket filled with supplies, sponges, rags.

"Everything has to be spotless. We clean with industrial oxy cleaners, spray the room with luminol and even have the UV light built into the ceiling. We learned from the best. Our second client happened to be a former forensics cop who advises Hollywood on murder scenes and shit."

"I'm going to throw up."

"Bathroom's there," Wayman pointed. "Get it out of your system. We have a lot of work to do before you get that thumb up your ass."

"This is ... it's just going to take me a minute. I never even liked hunting. You know, gutting animals."

"You got to carry your weight. In the end, it's a good time to be a Graves."

Asger carried the mop and both buckets to the bathroom. After removing the items from the five-gallon bucket, he filled it with hot water. He also filled the mop bucket, then dumped Neutrex Oxy into the steaming water and pushed it out of the bathroom. Wayman motioned for Finch to take the handle. Asger returned to the bathroom.

"We have a process. Makes things go fast. You'll be surprised how easy it is to make a scene like this disappear. First, body goes in the bag. Then the heavy blood. We mop the floor to pick up everything red. Then we work top to bottom. Wash down the walls in oxy. They're all plastic. Clean easy. All the furniture has disposable cloth over plastic. We remove the covers, place them in the trash bag. Then oxy and water on the plastic. Then mop the floor again. We turn on the UV lights, check for anything we missed, and then the bathroom. Three of us? We're out of here in a half hour."

Wayman studied Finch.

"What?"

Finch nodded. Quirked his lips. "You could handle a lot more than thirty a month, if cleanup only takes a half hour."

Wayman half smiled. Then whole-smiled. "If we had the right people."

"Spotless," Wayman said. The UV light lit the room in a purplish glow. "You could pick up a ham sandwich off the floor and eat it."

Sweat stood on Finch's brow. He looked for any bright areas. Wayman had explained the luminol they'd sprayed would react with the iron in any blood they hadn't cleaned, and would show up as a bright area under the UV light.

The room was sanitized.

"That's good, right?" Finch said. "Now that you mention the ham sandwich, I don't think I've eaten since before we left Williams."

"We will soon fill all your appetites. But we have more work, first."

Wayman stepped around the bed, pushed a chair forward. Walked to the bathroom, with the door open against the wall, and looked behind it. "You have to observe every square inch. Because Utah is the only state in the union that executes by firing squad."

Asger left the room.

"It's good," Wayman said. "Now the girl."

They'd placed the corpse in a plastic body bag and then cleaned the bag to ensure blood hadn't contaminated the outside.

Finch turned his head. Asger had found a hospital bed somewhere. He pushed it inside.

"You've really thought things through," Finch said.

"Give me a hand," Wayman said.

Each lifted an end of the body bag and they placed it on the hospital bed.

Asger put the trash bag full of bloody bed linens on the body bag, over the girl's head.

Finch grinned, but inside tried to remember the girl, when she was alive. Maybe to give her some kind of memorial, a spiritual send off, in the moment. But all the girls' faces blended.

I'm going to hell.

Asger pushed the bed into the hallway and toward the elevator.

"We'll be down in a minute," Wayman said.

He closed the door. It was just the two of them in the ultra violet light.

"One last look around. This is a high stakes business, Finch."

"I get that."

"Every move. Your life depends on every move."

"I hear you."

"Good. Let's go."

They exited. Wayman killed the lights.

CHAPTER 22

Mae checked her makeup. Pulled up and dropped her bust, shook her hips a couple times to see how the weight rode. The day before she'd wandered into a department store's bathroom section and stepped on a display model bathroom scale. Up fourteen pounds since leaving Gleason, North Carolina. It didn't seem possible—a pound a day.

Wherever you put it, you're rockin' it.

"It's too cold for shorts," Ruth said.

"I have my jacket. And listen to you. I remember what you said about screwing every boy you could."

"That was years ago. And the reason I'm babysitting while you're off trying to become the future first lady of Arizona is that you've already tangled with every man you could."

"He's not even interested in running for governor. And you read the article before I even knew who he was."

"They all say that. Plus he as much as admitted he's courting the big money. He's a politician. Watch out. That's all I'm saying."

"You make it sound like I'm dating a serial killer."

"Like I said. He's a politician. That's much worse—"

"I'm leaving."

"Don't stay out all night. I want to get to bed at a reasonable hour."

Mae closed the door behind her. Shook down the steps and admired her jiggling reflection on the window at the turn in the stairwell.

The bar was a quick walk from the Monte Vista. Mae looked left and right at the hotel exit, a habit she'd taken at Baer's urging. *Always look for anything suspicious. Someday, if the shit ever falls apart, you might only get a moment to decide.*

Decide what? Leave my kids forever and run?

Still, she'd found herself unconsciously following his advice.

Nothing looked unusual. The air was already below freezing and the coldness on her legs hurried her across the street. She turned a corner, walked a little farther past the tourist shops, and stepped into the bar.

There were more people than the night before and thankfully the added patrons seemed to increase the average years of the crowd. A DJ played hip hop, and before she'd gotten used to the pulsing beat through the plank floor, Nat Cinder arrived at her side. He placed his hand at her ear. Leaned. She smelled Bay Rum.

"This shit's driving me nuts. You want to watch a movie or get some lobster mac instead?"

"Where?"

"Well, I have a cabin not a couple miles up the road."

"Uh."

"You're safe with the future governor. Fact, with politics nowadays, I ought to be afraid of you."

"You said —"

"I know. It's all bullshit. Either way, let's get out of here, okay?"

Mae thought of the .45 auto in her purse. "Sure. Let's do the movie. Or the lobster mac. Yeah, let's do the lobster mac."

They exited. A few steps away, Cinder nodded at a white Jeep Grand Cherokee. The four-ways flashed. He opened the door for her, took her hand to help her in.

"Oh shit, this seat's ice."

"Just a minute. It's heated."

He closed the door and circled to the driver's side. With the engine running, he turned on an interior light and showed her the controls for the seat. Turned off the light and drove.

"So what I've been able to learn about Nat Cinder, he's a right-wing zealot who hates Mexicans in particular, but anybody who isn't white in general, and who especially hates the gay and lesbian community—so much he fabricated evidence to destroy the state's first lesbian governor."

"Internet, right?"

Cinder put on his right signal. Turned. He checked his mirrors all the time, and never seemed to take his attention away from the main task ... keeping the vehicle on the road.

"Sometimes you get down in the pig shit, you find the pearl."

"I don't think the Good Book meant it that way."

"Yeah, but truth is truth regardless where you hear it. I just want to know if I'm going to have lobster mac with someone who thinks that way. Because I don't—and I don't know the protocol for dating someone famous, who has opinions all over the place."

"That's interesting. To date, I've given exactly one interview, and it was in the newspaper this morning."

"That's not an answer."

"Well—the events you reference—it went down like this. I was married. My wife died in an accident. I blamed myself because I was drunk when it happened. But I found out the former governor was involved. At the same time, my father-in-law was the state house minority leader. He planted nasty photographs of the governor in my path. Sex stuff. Before I could even think on how to get rid of them, the governor tried to have me murdered. I mean, within hours. So your answer is this. The only thing that matters is whether we can look ourselves in the mirror. I'll honor anyone who is honorable. Race, sex, religion, I don't give a royal yeehah. But people who want to pretend right and wrong are relative, I'm not their friend."

"Are you running Libertarian Party?"

"I'm not running for anything tonight. Let's shut this down, all right?" He turned. The Jeep bounced. "Sorry about that."

The headlights cut to a pair of parallel ruts wending through low-growing evergreens.

"Uh ..."

"Spooky in this part. But see those two lights up ahead? That's where we're going."

The vehicle bounced so much she couldn't bring the lights into focus.

After what seemed several jarring minutes, the double-track smoothed into a gravel driveway that opened into a clearing. Ahead, a log cabin with a light on each end of the porch.

"A single room cabin?"

"Not quite."

Cinder cut the wheel and stopped the vehicle with Mae's door in front of the steps.

"Hold on. Let me get the door for you."

"Wait. Before you do that. You're running for governor? Is it true?"

His eyes tightened. "I don't know."

He stepped out and around the vehicle. Opened her door. "But to tell the truth, I'd hoped we might spend a little more time on the other subjects."

Her hand in his, she exited the vehicle. He released her hand but kept an arm out as if she might stumble during the three steps to the porch. While he unlocked the front door, she said, "I'm going to be blunt. Here's what I'm thinking. I'm old. Twenty-eight. You're at least twenty-nine."

He snorted.

"If you're about to run for the highest executive office in the state, you don't want me at your side. You don't want me in your past. I'm not trouble or anything—well I am. And if people look at me very hard, they'll surely see it."

"Why don't we just enjoy some lobster mac?"

Nat pushed open the door. Turned on a light switch and waved her inside while he held the screen door open.

Mae leaned inside. Thought of the pistol in her purse.

Now's a good time to pull it. Before he drags you inside ...

The cabin was tiny—just a single room with ratty sofa, a tiny rabbit-eared television, probably black and white, on top of a book stand. A kitchenette on the other side, with a small round table and a single wood chair. She looked to her right and saw a single bed, even narrower than a real bed. A cot? The cabin had bare walls. No doors leading to a bathroom or anything else. After a few moments she knew why it seemed familiar. She'd seen a documentary. It looked like the Unabomber, Ted Kaczynski's hut.

"Okay, I'll go in first," Nat said. He stepped past her.

"You know, I think I'm just going to be up front with you. This is creepy as hell. I have a gun. I hope you're not a weirdo."

Cinder's smile ratcheted higher. "Perfect. I'm glad to hear it."

"What?"

"All of it. It's supposed to be creepy. Well, not creepy, but off-putting. And you carry? That's good too. And that last, I'm about the sanest man you've ever run across. It's the rest of the world that's off its rocker. Check this out."

He left her at the door and stood before the tiny round kitchen table, set in the middle of a rug. He bent at the knees, found something under the edge of the rug, and lifted.

A section of floor three feet wide and five long was hinged at the opposite side. He said, "Carpet's glued. Table's bolted." With the section vertical, the horizontal table rested neat against the sink cabinet.

Nat stepped into the hole, felt under the floor, and the subterranean chamber lit.

That's all she could see.

He motioned to her.

"Uh, that's even creepier."

"No, I assure you, it's cooler. Way cooler. But you aren't going to see it from over there."

"I told you. I have a gun."

"Go ahead, pull it. I don't give a shit. You'll put it away when you want."

Mae exhaled. Serial killers were always charming. Smiling.

Sexy.

You've already decided he can do anything he wants to you, short of murder. What's the worst it can be? A sex dungeon?

"What, is that where you keep the lobster mac?"

"It's where I keep my house."

"What?"

"We're in the attic right now, which was designed to look like a lonely cabin in the middle of nowhere. Come see the rest."

He disappeared down the steps.

Mae pulled the .45 from her purse. Switched the safe from the off position, and entered the cabin. She closed the door. Tested it to make sure it didn't somehow lock itself.

She descended the steps with the pistol in both hands, her arms ready to swing whatever direction needed. Each step took her into a different world.

Standing on the floor, she put the gun back into her purse.

"Okay, you win. This is way cool."

CHAPTER 23

The bandsaw had a large table extension. Asger placed the girl on the flat stainless steel and pushed her into the one-inch band; the teeth were better suited to oak or maple than meat, and the saw crashed through her flesh like a boulder crashes through water, splashing meat and blood out the back like so much wet sawdust.

Zip, pull the table back, push her over, zip. Arms gone. Pull her back, spin the body on the table, Zip. Zip. Legs gone.

When she was headless, armless, legless, Asger powered off the machine.

"Grab a knife," Wayman said.

Finch had grown up on the periphery of a massive butcher operation, not a meat cutter, but son of the owner. He'd been outside, looking in, but he'd seen how the men handled their knives, and as a child had imagined himself slicing, filleting, turning corpses into cuts.

Finch took a knife from the wall and grabbed the girl's leg—the one that hadn't been split open.

"There you go," Wayman said. "Remove the meat from the bone. Nothing pretty. We're not making steaks."

Finch put out of his mind that moments ago this was a dead Latina. A day ago, a live one—and a month before that, a live one he'd sedated while ferrying across Arizona and Utah.

Every move: your life depends on it.

Finch cut flesh like he'd found a lost calling. He rolled the leg to its front, plunged the blade at the back of her knee, and sawed upward, each motion halted with steel stabbing bone. The meat gave away tenderly before the blade and at the top of the thigh, he lay down the knife and pushed apart the sides. He slid the point of the blade around the bone, over and over, each time separating the girl's leg muscles from her frame. When he'd rolled the leg hard to the right, he re-centered and began slicing the other side. In minutes, her thigh and femur were apart.

He rolled the blade around the knee and all her thigh lay on the table.

Asger still worked on his leg.

Finch did the same to the lower leg, except working around the tibia and fibula, instead of just one bone.

Finished with the leg, he grabbed an arm.

Wayman had completed his arm, and said, "Finch, finish Asger's leg. They don't have meat in Sweden or wherever he's from."

Asger pushed the leg to Finch and swung the girl's torso. He probed with the knife blade below her sternum, then pushed until the tip sank a half inch. Leaning the blade backward, he pushed it forward.

"You have to be careful not to get the blade too deep," Wayman said. "You remember gutting deer, right? Cut the intestines, you might as well wash your hands in a bowl of shit."

With the blade slicing open her pubic region, Asger shoved and split her open. He now cut flaps on the left side of her stomach, below the rib, above the hip, then rolled her to the left. Her entrails fell to the table.

Finch remembered the single time he'd field dressed a deer. This was the same. Exactly.

He finished with the leg Asger started. About to rest his knife on the table, he wondered ... *could I kill them both, right now?*

Finch put down his knife.

The FBI wanted the whole operation. They wanted to know who sold the kids, and who paid to have sex with them. Well, they'd certainly want to know who paid to kill them. They'd take months and months trying to infiltrate the organization. They'd allow five more girls—every month—to be slain while getting their shit together.

He could end it all right now. Not another girl ... not even the one upstairs being murdered while he helped destroy the evidence of the last.

"I see your wheels turning," Wayman said. "You're wondering, what's the sense in cutting up a body? Why not just take it somewhere? Bury it. Burn it. Get it out of the building, fast. Am I right?"

"The thought crossed my mind. I mean, shouldn't the goal be to get a body out of here as fast as possible, so there's no evidence here, at all, except for the tiniest possible moment?"

"No. You're ass backwards. It's all about minimizing risk."

Asger, finished now with removing the organs of the upper chamber, hefted the torso to the bandsaw. He powered it on.

"Think it through," Wayman said. "The goal isn't to get rid of the body. The goal is to be as close to zero risk as possible. You don't do that by rushing through a routine to get rid of evidence. You do that by taking each step in terms of how much risk is involved, and where the risk comes from."

"I'm not following."

"So this girl, she was ready to move at noon today. That's when the knife went through her heart. Should I have thrown her over my back, carried her out on the sidewalk, and said, okay, no evidence inside the Butcher Shop?"

"No."

"Of course not. The goal isn't to get her out of here. It's to get her out of here with as close to zero risk as possible. That means, we don't move her in a state that allows her to be identified. Not as whatever the fuck her name was. Identified even as a person."

"I don't get it."

"If we threw her in a body bag into the truck, a chance stop by a cop, the whole gig's up. So we turn her into sausage to feed the homeless. And we mix her guts with hog and cattle hooves. Bones. It all gets ground up, dried, turned into meal."

Finished at the bandsaw, Asger stepped to an adjacent room and rolled a giant wheeled trash bin, like for recycling.

"Ah, refrigerated guts," Wayman said.

Asger pushed the container to the butcher table, opened the lid, slid the bones and guts into the bucket.

"In a few hours that'll be covered with hog and cow bone."

Asger placed the meat they'd removed from the girl into a giant tray. He then began an apparently practiced routine. He opened the bandsaw guards, removed the blade, hosed the saw, sprayed with an Oxy compound, and hosed again. Then he placed a new blade on the saw.

The grit of bone and meat washed from the saw went down the drain.

"What's next?" Finch said. "I'm ready for the blowjob in the hot tub."

"Nope." Wayman said. "Now we make sausage."

CHAPTER 24

They stood at the grinder, grease and blood slimed on their hands. The job was done: the product lay in a plastic tub.

"When we make the sausage, we always do it ourselves. It's the same problem I keep mentioning. Who do you trust?"

Wayman unbuckled his belt and pulled it from his pants.

"Don't your employees think it's weird the boss comes in and makes sausage late at night?" Finch said.

"Actually, no. They think it's part of my roots. I wear denim and flannel. I own a nightclub but look like Grizzly Adams. I haven't sold out. Coming in at night to work as my daddy and granddaddy worked ... it fits the theme."

Wayman untucked his shirt, began unbuttoning it from the bottom. "Now remember what I said about moving bodies. You drive around with a corpse in the trunk, get pulled over, you're thinking, now I have to kill a cop. This way, with the girl in the cooler, the cop sees I'm supplying sausage to a homeless shelter. I get a tax deduction. That's why we don't move bodies."

Wayman removed his shirt. Unbuttoned his pants and slid down the zipper.

"Last step, everything gets clean. There's still risk in the procedure. Not so much of someone accidentally seeing what's going on and recognizing it. The only risk we have is someday, one of our clients flips on us, or someone gets curious about what's on the top floors of the building, and starts watching us too closely. Eventually, almost any enterprise can be found out. At that point it comes down to gathering evidence. Well, if there's nobody saying someone's missing, no body, and no DNA, and no murder weapon, it's hard to prove a murder. The only way we go down is if someone on the inside goes rogue."

Finch looked at the trash bag containing bloodied bed linens, furniture covers, the murder weapon.

"Yep. You got it. We strip, put our clothes in the bag, clean the table, grinder, then hose ourselves too. Walk the bag to the incinerator in the basement, and then go to the dance floor. You've earned your five-thousand-dollar blowjob."

The wire!

"Yeah, cool. I can handle it. Can I get a cheeseburger or something first? I'm about to pass out. Low blood sugar. All the excitement."

"That's the thing." Wayman pointed at Finch's shirt. "You got blood all over you. We can't risk you leaving DNA everywhere you go. That's why we have procedures in place."

"I'm not walking out of here naked."

Wayman shook his head. "Your pecker too short?"

Wayman dropped his pants. Dragged his wife beater over his head. Pulled off his socks. Underwear. Opened the bag and placed the clothes inside.

Finch turned. Asger was naked as well.

Without looking at them, Finch remembered the knives on the wall. The garden hose. People hang themselves with garden hoses all the time. It's a weapon.

Wayman studied him.

Every move. Your life depends on every move.

The recording device was supposed to look like a band aid, and it did, so long as no one looked too close.

But Wayman had been talking about trust. The right people. And the whole evening was obviously a test.

I'm totally dead.

Which knife? The one with the longest blade. If he pushed aside Asger he could grab it from the wall. Misdirection would help.

Misdirection.

Finch exhaled.

A new idea arrived. He smiled.

He thought of tits. Perfect, not giant, not small, just medium perfectly drooped boobs. Bouncing, rubbing up against his face, dragging over his chest, hanging free, jiggling, glistening in oil and sweat. With milk dripping over them like a waterfall over a cave. He imagined breasts in his mouth, pressed against his cheeks—both cheeks, his face squeezed between. He thought of

Michele—the best lay of his life—bending over and swinging. He thought of her mouth, that first moment, the flicker of her tongue on him ....

And Finch unbuckled his pants. He dropped them.

Wayman looked at the bulge pressing Finch's underwear.

"Well, that explains a lot."

Asger snorted.

Wayman choked. "We're straight, little brother."

Finch turned away.

"You been queer this whole time? Is that it? The drugs, the lifestyle? All 'cause you go with men?" Wayman laughed. "Oh fuck, that explains it."

His back to both Wayman and Asger, Finch lifted his shirt. He dragged his fingernail over the bandage-like edge of the recording device. Catching the corner, he pulled. The strong adhesive tore out hair. It had to have left a red mark. Would they notice?

"Shit, I guess we better get you to the Range Rover dealer."

Finch lifted his shirt and t-shirt over his head and with the recording device inside, rolled them and placed them in the trash bag. The evidence would be incinerated.

Wayman said, "Put your underwear, shoes, socks, everything in the trash bag."

Finch kept his front angled away from Wayman and Asger.

"Follow."

Wayman pushed the giant stainless-steel sausage grinder to the tiled area with a massive drain and plastic walls. He lifted a hose, turned a spigot and sprayed the grinder while Asger disassembled the parts. Again, Asger produced a jug of oxy cleaner.

"Why don't you use bleach?"

"It doesn't get rid of the blood. Oxy pulverizes that shit."

A clump of meat fell from the basin to the tiled floor in a cascade of sudsy water. Wayman sprayed the hose directly on it and drove it drainward.

Asger nodded to Wayman.

"All right," Wayman said. "Your hands get cleaned with Oxy. The rest of your body, soap and water."

Asger stood next to the wall and Finch warily stepped next to him. Wayman hosed them, top to bottom.

"What's that on your chest?"

"Ringworm."

Asger shifted away from him. Shook his head.

"I'm taking something for it. Supposed to be gone in a week."

"Turn around."

Asger and Finch faced the wall. Wayman sprayed them again, top to bottom.

"Asger, you wanna hit me?"

Wayman gave Asger the hose and submitted to the spray.

When they were clean and rinsed, Wayman stepped to a steel work area with cabinets above and below. Opened the one at his knees, and withdrew a paper bag. "You're my size. Here."

He passed the bag to Finch. Inside, a towel. Finch lifted it, and saw clothes underneath.

CHAPTER 25

M ae sat naked on the bed with a glass of white wine in one hand and an empty cereal bowl next to the other. Hershey's syrup smudged her left areola.

"I'm satisfied about every way I can be," she said.

He'd made lobster mac with a box of spirals, a bag of shredded Mexican blend, heavy cream, and a couple of lobster tails from the freezer.

"You want the last strawberries?" he said.

"I couldn't."

"I'll toss 'em in the trash."

"Gimme."

He passed her the bowl.

Long before they crawled into bed, he'd given her a tour of the buried house's three stories. Kitchen, dining area, den, on the lowest level. The den was actually more of what she imagined the Situation Room at the White House might look like. Television monitors everywhere. Computers, side by side, cables, keyboards. Even with nothing on there were little lights flashing all over the place. She'd said, *You could run Arizona from here*, and his eyes had narrowed slightly, and he'd grinned.

Arizona? ...

The second floor was bedrooms. The third, above surface, was the cabin with the sideways table. He'd said a niche construction company out of Idaho made it for him. After the tour, she'd noticed it just so happened the biggest television was in the bedroom, and the most comfortable way to watch it, in bed.

She ate the last strawberry. Gulped her last wine.

"You want to open another bottle, or will that do for the evening?"

"That'll do. I hate to scrog and run, but I have kids to get back to. Their grandmother's watching them, and I don't want to leave them in her hands too long."

"Yeah," Cinder said. "Ruth Creighton."

Mae froze.

"Don't worry. But yeah, I figured out who you and your clan are."

My gun!

It was in her purse on the floor, tipped over.

She locked eyes with him.

"Did it live up to your expectations? What, you thought you'd feel like Clyde if you screwed Bonnie? Something like that?"

He laughed. "Easy, now. I already looked into the whole thing. I don't know if you've been following your own case, but there's been a couple of sympathetic reporters writing a series on Baer and all the corruption he exposed by poisoning half North Carolina. Most folks—and this is key—most folks think if you mess with a man's dog, you got shit coming."

"So, you figured it out just from talking to me? You haven't seen me with Baer."

"No, but I met him this morning. Same accent. Same pissy attitude."

"I don't have a pissy attitude."

"Endearingly blunt nature, then. Anyhow, I tend to stay on top of the news, since I'll need to convince a lot of people in a couple years I'm smarter than I am. Every cable show had your photo up for a week. Baer looks different with a buzz cut and clean shave, but a face like that, it don't matter what you put around it. And you should have dyed your hair or something. You look same as that prom photo they had up."

"I hate that photo."

"Does your rack justice."

"Well, priorities."

Cinder sat on the edge of the bed. "I suppose if you want I'll take you back."

"I better." She remembered being blunt with him before entering the cabin. She'd said she wasn't trouble, but looked like it. She'd said he wouldn't want her to be near him if he ran for governor, and he just now admitted he was running.

"I have a question."

Cinder twisted to her.

"You've as much said you're running. I told you a couple hours ago, I'm trouble. There's no way this is going anywhere, is there?"

He held her look a long time, his mouth flat. "You've got the wrong idea about politics."

"What's that supposed to mean?"

"It isn't where the clean people go."

CHAPTER 26

Wayman led Asger and Finch to the basement and watched as Asger placed the garbage bag inside the incinerator. He'd felt a little more at ease about his brother since learning he was gay. Somehow, it made his life choices coherent and explained the tension he always seemed to carry with him.

But Wayman needed more.

"You don't leave anything to chance," he said. "You watch every detail. You either do what is critical yourself, or you observe it. Always. Asger has been with me six years. Not a single failure, ever. But I observe everything that is critical. It's not about trusting people. It's about distrusting fate. Remember that."

They walked toward the elevator. "You're done for the night, Asger. I'm going to have a drink with my brother. See you tomorrow."

Asger nodded. He stayed on the elevator when Wayman and Finch got off on the third floor.

"You met Amy, on the fourth floor—the bitchy girl, likes to take charge? Asger's poking her."

Finch appeared thoughtful. "How does the whole thing work? I don't see anyone going up there."

"You don't need to know that, yet. You may never. The bottom line is our clients pay through the nose, and almost all our business is repeat. We only take new clients after we stick a microscope up their asses, and we only bring them up stairs if we already have something on them."

"What do you mean, on them?"

"Evidence that'll put them away a long time if they turn on us."

They entered Wayman's office. Below them, the nightclub flashed and bodies throbbed. Women in tight dresses, men in polos. Grinding, touching. Wayman thought of Claudia, how he missed her body.

How he would test her loyalty.

"Shit."

Wayman picked up his phone, hit a speed dial number.

"You see that beefy dago there against the wall? Prick's not doing his job."

The man pressed a bluetooth device at his ear.

"Tony, what the hell? Pay attention. Sofa, ten o'clock."

Tony looked up at the mirrored glass and nodded. He pushed through the writhing bodies and arrived at the sofa. He pulled a girl off a man.

"You can't have shit like that," Wayman said. "I own half the cops in this city and most of the judges, but little shit like that just invites trouble."

"I didn't see. What was she doing?"

"Head."

"Ah. By the way, are you going to say anything to Dad?"

"About you being what you are?"

Finch blinked.

"I doubt it. Dad's from a different time. Check this out."

Wayman wiggled his computer mouse. Wayman sat in the high-backed executive leather chair and motioned for Finch to come around behind the desk. He nodded at the screen.

"Fucking Microsoft. Wait a minute. Miracle. Okay, it's on. See this? Video of every room on the thirteenth floor, and the fifth. Pedos on the fifth. The black squares are cameras in rooms that are dark right now. But the rest ... You can see for yourself."

The monitor display was broken into sixteen squares, seven without images. The rest contained full color, crisp, moving scenes.

Wayman moved the pointer to the sidebar and clicked on Floor 13, room 4. All of the images were replaced, now, with four camera angles, each showing a different view of the same room.

"This is where you heard the girl scream," Wayman said.

Finch looked at the images. A girl on a bed, not tied to the bedposts like the other. She was curled on her side as if asleep. Another angle showed her eyes were closed. Another camera showed the man who'd bought the privilege of murdering her. He sat on the toilet, elbows on knees, head drooped.

"You own these people," Finch said. "Not just the cash they pay you. You own them the rest of their lives."

Wayman nodded, searched his brother's face. Was it admiration in his voice? Fear? He pulled open the bottom desk file drawer and withdrew a bottle of Maker's Mark and two glasses.

"Grab the ice tray out of the freezer. It's inside the cabinet, under the Keurig."

Finch opened the wood cabinet, then the refrigerator inside, and withdrew an ice tray from the freezer portion. He twisted it and the cubes popped free. He dropped two in each glass and his brother poured.

"I own them, and that's important. But it doesn't make the business run. The return on investment comes from one thing." Wayman drank whiskey. "They pay a hundred grand not because we remove the risk. And not because we provide the girl. They pay it because we provide those things in a package that says what they do is *okay*."

"You can't—that—are you serious?"

"Yeah, yeah. They're not monsters. They're normal. See, killing's the most natural thing a man can do. It didn't take one page in the bible before men started killing men. But they've been taught it's evil. Something that wells up natural out of the soul of man, and they've got all these neuroses built up around it. We silence the discord. We take it away. All value is perceived in the head, and revolves around wants. In men, there's only two: fucking and killing. That's why we're sitting on top of the biggest business in the history of man."

Finch replaced the ice tray. Received his glass from Wayman.

"Remember what I said earlier about every decision. Now I have a question and need a *damn* compelling answer." He lifted his glass. "Would you say that's half full?"

Finch swallowed his Maker's Mark in one long pull.

"I'll keep the flowery bullshit to a minimum. I had no idea the show was this big. I want in. I'll never have the brains to run a shop like you do, and I don't want to. But I want more than I got. I want the Land Rover and enough cash to be who I am. I'm sick of faking it. I want fuck-you money. I want a lot of it. That's it."

"Good. Come back over here." Wayman again moved the mouse. Clicked on Room 13, and dragged the cursor back the time line until a stunned and frantic Finch entered the room, followed by Wayman and Asger.

"You'll see in this video, no one's holding a gun to your head. No one's pushing you around. Not inside the room, on camera. As far as the video proves, you're an accessory after the fact."

Finch sat on Wayman's desk.

Wayman said, "Accessories get the same firing squad as conspirators and murderers."

Finch exhaled. "Like I said. I'm in. Every single girl you turned into sausage came to Salt Lake City on a truck I drove twenty hours from Sierra Vista. You didn't need a video to know I'm part of this. What I want to know is, when am I going to get my cheeseburger?"

CHAPTER 27

F inch stood at the sink splashing water into his face. His father slept in the next room. Wayman had driven him to a motel and left him at his father's door, and Luke had appeared surprised to see him. He didn't usually make the run from Williams with the boys. He didn't know how they did things. He'd gotten a room with a single bed.

Of course he had.

Finch went to the motel front desk and paid for a room.

It's better this way. Don't want to sleep on the ratty couch, and don't want to hear you snore, Dad.

Finch lowered his head to the faucet and dropped cupped hands of water over the back of his head. He worked it through his dreadlocked hair so it would keep his head cool and give him a chance to wake up and think.

He'd incinerated the wire.

He should call his FBI contact right now and tell her what had happened. She'd want to know as soon as shit went sideways. She was a hardass. He had to make sure she understood he didn't want to be complicit. He was acting out of fear for his life.

But the video would show him playing along. Quipping jokes, wiping blood off the walls with aplomb.

He should have gone to the FBI in the very beginning, when he was twenty and first started putting things together. It's what he should have done. When you see evil shit, you do something, not sit and wonder about personal consequences.

But he'd never been taught that. He had to learn it on his own. Had to develop his own personal sense of right and wrong based on the hurts other people gave him, and his guiding sense that he didn't want to do that to other people. He'd barely been aware of himself at twenty years old. All he wanted was beer and women. But eventually he'd figured out it sucks to be on the receiving end of self-absorbed inconsiderate assholes, and he became hyper aware of when he was causing harm. Not just real pain, like from a fist fight. But emotional harm. Even frustration. Finch couldn't pull out in front of another car. If his entry into the lane would cause the other driver to have to tap his brakes, Finch would wait. It just wasn't cool to be an asshole to someone until they were an asshole to you.

After a couple years of listening to his father talk about the differences between the races—not that one was better than another—that's how it started out—and then the tripe about how there's so much more opportunity in the great United States because of free markets and capitalism, and how delivering truckloads of kids into the country to explore the miracle of capitalism was a noble endeavor ... after a few years of piecing things together, the boy who just wanted to get drunk and laid realized he was smuggling kids so his father and brother could sell their sex. He'd started out believing what he'd been taught: my family is good, and loyalty to family is one of the highest ideals.

But after years of service, he'd found his loyalty hadn't been toward good people doing good things. He'd been loyal to an evil enterprise.

The realization took a long time to come top of mind. He was more and more troubled as the years went by. He lived more and more recklessly. Drank and used drugs. Steeled himself for the monthly round trip to Sierra Vista and Salt Lake City, and tried to make himself almost useless any time other business came up that they might want him to help with.

He'd contacted the FBI, came clean to Agent Lou Rivers, the woman who looked and acted like a man, and she'd told him if what he said was true, he could go to prison for a long time, and the only way out was to give the FBI what it needed to take down the entire operation. Everyone, top to bottom. Names, dates, video, audio, financial records. She wanted him to deliver enough evidence they could show probable cause for search warrants in Williams, Arizona and Salt Lake City, plus where ever else the girls were shipped afterward.

She always wanted more, and never acknowledged how much he'd already given her, and how much he risked every time they met.

He'd begun wearing a recording device for the trip from Williams to Sierra Vista, all the way through to Salt Lake City and back. But the recordings only had him and Cephus jawing about bullshit. Cephus pretended to not know much about the rest of the operation, and Finch worried that prying too hard would signal something was wrong. Finch had never been interested before.

Why now?

After months of tiny progress, Agent Lou Rivers began to pressure Finch to become more involved in the dirtier parts of the business. She'd told him to volunteer, and say something about how he needed more money, and he was willing to do what it took.

But every time he thought about going there, his stomach tightened. He saw images of kids and old men, and he wanted to run from it.

Finch backed away from the sink with his hair dripping onto his shirt. His face was cool. He still hadn't eaten—there were no fast food joints open on the ride from The Butcher Shop to the motel. His stomach was tight but the cool water brought an adrenaline charge. He was hungry, but strong. The situation was fluid. He'd bought time with Wayman by pretending to be gay, and that seemed to change Wayman's behavior entirely. As if all his apparent lack of interest in the family business could be explained by feeling sexually out of place.

Hell, maybe Wayman was gay.

Either way, Finch realized, Luke and Wayman had either planned to test him tonight and then kill him or, judging from his father's surprise, just kill him. He'd played things right so far, and had bought another day. An hour or two.

If they were going to kill him, wouldn't they have done it where they have the perfect operation in place already, to disappear his body? Wasn't that the implied threat in the entire night's activities?

Finch pushed aside the curtain with his finger and looked at the cars outside. The nearest street lamp had a half-lit purple appearance, as if unconvinced it was night.

The clock read 3:00 a.m.

I need food.

Finch unzipped his satchel and dumped a pair of worn jeans, a shirt, underwear, socks, and jacket on the bed. He only ever brought enough for one night.

Turning, he noticed the coffee pot. Good idea. He filled a paper cup with water and dumped it into the maker. Loaded a single serve pouch. There was room. He stacked another pouch on top. He could use the jolt. He opened the accoutrement packages and dumped the cream and sugar from both in the bottom of the paper cup. Hit the on button.

Finch extracted his wallet and stripped off Wayman's clothes, throwing

139

them to the floor. Jumped in the shower, scrubbed his body with the rough white washcloth, and rubbed himself red with the scratchy towel. Stirred his coffee and sipped while naked in front of the wall mirror. Is this what a vigilante looks like? Pooch stomach, slack shoulders, limp dick looking like a stack of nickels?

Finch squared his shoulders and drank more coffee.

He donned his clothes from the top of the bed and slipped into Wayman's shoes.

He threw on his jacket and at the door looked back on the room. Wayman's clothes were on the floor and the plastic hotel key on the dresser top.

The newspaper he'd carried from the truck, and still hadn't read, lay beside the television.

Finch grabbed the paper, tucked it inside his jacket like another layer of insulation, and let the door close, or not close, behind him.

CHAPTER 28

The night was cold. Snow glistened in the air. After a block, Finch placed his numb hands in his pockets. His wet hair froze. He should have toweled it more.

As he walked, his mind wandered. What did it mean that he'd embraced the girl's butchering well enough to convince his brother to let him live?

Did Wayman know him better than he knew himself?

Was he a good guy, or did the right reward make the difference? Could he embrace his father's business? Because while the moral aspect of the decision seemed relevant, he needed to live long enough to make it. The danger aspect was more palpable.

Finch turned his head without slowing his pace. A car's headlights a block back ... the car didn't seem to be moving forward.

He turned right at an intersection. Around the corner, he ducked into a shop entrance and squatted; if his head was visible through the glass, maybe it would look like a handbag.

The car eased around the corner and stopped next to the curb, headlights cutting a swath that left Finch in no danger of being seen. He lowered himself farther and peered around the corner, near the concrete step.

A cigarette glowed on the driver's side.

This dude was following him. The driver leaned closer to his windshield. The car inched forward. Stopped.

You're wondering how I could disappear in ten seconds, and you're not buying it at all.

You know I'm not from around here, so I don't have a friend's place to duck into. And in five seconds you're going to realize I'm probably hiding nearby.

Very nearby.

Finch trembled. Adrenaline shot into the mix of coffee and sugar already in his blood.

The car engine turned off. The door opened, and a tall man stepped out. The street lamps here were bright. He wasn't the one Wayman called the dago on the dance floor, but similar. Long black hair, a thick upper body, like he was used to pumping iron and cracking heads. He stepped in front of the vehicle. In his left hand, he carried a pistol with a long barrel.

From where the man now stood, Finch would be easy to see.

He eased into a sprinter's stance, ready to leap. But the man walked as if assuming Finch had turned the corner and made a run for it.

With his adversary at an angle past him, Finch slipped out of the entry and, on feet as light as possible, ran for shelter behind the man's car. Coming to a stop, he skittered a pebble across the pavement.

The man twisted, lifted his gun arm and hurried back to the car. Still stooped, Finch circled the car. His senses distorted. Fear created a new dimension. He saw the pavement like it was inches from his face, but nothing around it; he heard his footfalls as if amplified through a rock band's sound stage. His heart shook and his body felt nothing, not his fingertips on the concrete, not the cold on his face.

Finch saw the man's feet. He looked up.

The gun barrel, inches away, was a perfect circle, the man's face a cold menace behind it.

No way would he miss.

Finch swung his hand at the gun and connected with air. His vision warped back to reality. The man stood two feet away—where he'd been all along. The safety release snicked.

Finch leapt. He reached with his arms and shifted sideways. Expecting a flash and blackness, he instead felt the barrel of the gun in his hands, felt the man's body against his shoulder as he drove into him and twisted the gun away.

The man bucked him backward. Growled. Connected a fist to his shoulder and then slammed it down on his neck.

Finch brought his crossed arms up hard. His voice tore his throat in a scream that had no end. The man stumbled backward and Finch advanced, slipped a foot behind him, tripping them both onto the ground. Still grasping the handgun, Finch's fury surged. Here was a man who represented all the evil of his father's empire. A man who was prepared to kill him to ensure his silence, all on the order of his father ... or his brother ... his *family* ...

Holding the pistol away from him, he slammed the heel of his other hand against the man's nose, bouncing his head off concrete. The man's gun grip loosened and Finch smashed his right hand to the man's face again, and again, and pried the handgun free.

He turned it in his hand, shoved the barrel into the man's stomach and pulled the trigger. It popped into the man's guts.

It was a .22.

Finch pulled the pistol back and snapped the entire magazine into the man's chest.

He looked up the street. Back the other way. Still kneeling, he dug out the man's wallet and put it in his jacket pocket. Put the .22 automatic in the other.

Finch stood, pulled his collar higher about his neck, and resumed walking toward the bus station.

Dizzy, he closed his eyes as he walked. Somehow everything in his world had changed in a day. Nothing made sense. This guy came for him, and was fair game.

Wayman would understand that.

They should have given him more time to come around.

CHAPTER 29

Wake with the sun, colder'n a witch's bippy. Got Stinky Joe nuggled in, couldn't zip the bag all the way. Didn't wanna tote a blanket for a dog won't carry his own food. Not when I's traveling paramilitary light. So we freeze our asses on bare ground.

Try and shake myself warm and that don't work, but I can't get up and around, 'cause the house ain't two hundred yard, and the whole front's exposed. Got the zillion acres of golden grass toward the highway side, south the house. Got the wooded hills behind. I's edge of wood, can't see but the side the house.

Check the Timex. Six thirty. Got to be in the low twenties, from the joints. Throw back the tarp and get the feet out the bag. Slip 'em into leather ice blocks called boots. Lace 'em with shaky hands, then since I can't get up and walk around, bring legs up, knee to chest—or that direction—till the stomach tires but the shivering stops. Put on my coat and throw the bag back over me.

Times of discomfort a man gotta think on what he likes. And in real discomfort, what he hate.

I hate them shitheads in that house.

Sun shine bright on the Graves place, log cabin like the magazine covers. Big ass logs, mebbe foot round. Two story. Got the green roof made a tin. Black windows. Mile long deck. Swimming pool in back. Whole thing lit up at night with spotlights pointed at the walls and little lights 'long the drive.

Day or night they's no approach without if someone's a-lookin', they's a-seein'.

I think on my location. I'll spot anybody come or go but nothing in the house. But if I switch to the back, the house'll block the drive. Figger I'll wait here and bust inside when they leave. Or sooner if I'm a mind. Meanwhile, I stow my shit and crawl to a mess a brush. Rig the tarp over a bush so the camoflage'll mebbe blend. I can stand behind without drawing the eye, and watch from below.

Joe don't seem interested in nothing but sleep, and I can understand. We didn't get our spot picked till half the night was gone.

CHAPTER 30

FBI agent in charge Gordon Emerson squatted next to the body of a murder victim, discovered on the street at four in the morning, beside a car stopped in the street in front of a men's clothing store. The dead man's open shirt displayed ten blood spots, giving the appearance he'd been repeatedly stabbed with a skewer and bled out from the holes. One was in the stomach, the rest, above the heart.

"What the hell are you doing here?" Gordon said. "Aren't you working something under cover?"

The woman glanced up the street. "It's six a.m. My bad guys are in bed."

"So what are you doing here?"

"I was going to ask you the same. Why isn't the Salt Lake City PD handling this?"

"We're rolling it into another investigation. How'd you even know about it?"

"Heard about it from Junior. Wanted to see if I recognize the vic or not."

"Well?"

"Yeah. He worked in the Butcher Shop nightclub. So how'd it go down?"

Gordon studied Maggie. Decided to try to draw her out.

"Well, the perpetrator fought him. There's damage to the back of his head. The nose is bent, and he was bleeding from it before death. Then whoever did that shot him ten times. Looks like a twenty-two."

"What investigation?"

"What do you mean?"

"You're rolling it into what?"

"Need to know. But bigger than you might imagine."

"Yeah, okay. So listen, you got a line on the perp yet?"

"Around the corner, maybe thirty yards back, we got video from an ATM and from a camera facing up the street. There's a kid on it, and right after, this car. The kid's wearing a hoodie but the face is visible enough."

"You got video already?"

"The bank's been robbed six times in the last three years. We have a good relationship. The head of security has a standing authorization from the bank owners to give us the video without subpoena."

"I want to take a look."

"No need. We know the kid."

"Who is it?"

"Wait a minute. I've given you too much already. What are you working? What's the tie-in here? Or I'll tell you to leave."

"You know the nightclub where this guy worked?"

"Yeah."

"They've got a prostitution outfit, run on the upper floors. Pedo shit."

Emerson looked away. Nodded. "Okay. The nightclub owner—Wayman Graves. The perp's his kid brother. I just haven't decided whether the vic was supposed to take out the kid, or the other way around. The car is registered to the vic, and the killer was on foot. Usually the guy with the advantage—in this case the car—is the killer. But not here."

"Maybe the kid got lucky. Turned the tables?"

"Maybe."

"How'd you identify the kid?"

"Like I said. This investigation is way bigger than you know. It goes all the way to D.C., and from there, only higher."

"And me. Point of the spear."

"Get the hell out of here."

Maggie left and Gordon Emerson watched her, marveling how her shape somehow communicated through her winter clothes.

He wondered why she wasn't strutting on a runway, or half naked on the cover of Sports Illustrated.

He wondered what Wayman would do to her when he found out.

CHAPTER 31

Noon. Bunch a bullshit. No one doing nothing. Freeze my balls white up here. Who in the house? Who ain't? Man said they'd take the kids to Salt Lake after he bury his boy. Mebbe he clear out yesterday. House empty.

If they's a wife down there and she don't want a pop knot on her head, she shoulda cleared out.

Them clouds up north over the hill keep rolling in. Got lightning with no boom. Suspect in short order I's 'bout to get wet, and telling the honest truth, don't make sense me—saving the fucking world—oughtta be cold and wet, while them kid traffickers is dry in the log mansion.

Do a couple knee bends and damn near topple over. Get myself aright with a sapling and bend at the waist, limber like to poke standin' up.

Them clouds cover the sky now. Sun blacked out, look like nightfall. No traffic on the road, so I figger to come in from the garage side, they won't be no windows. Get next the house unseen.

I restring the tarp and Joe build a nest with my sleeping bag under it. No time to trench it, and no place around but slope, so too much rain just mean the bag get wet. All goes good, they be no need for a three day reconnoiter. I march on Flagstaff tonight.

"You stay put, Joe. Y'hear?"

You mind that blackhair girl. She didn't treat you right, and you's too stupid to see it cause you pressed your arm up on her titties.

"That's a lie—and I won't be lectured on morals by a animal licks his nuts."

You'd lick yours if you could reach them. You mind covering me with that flap there?

"Well, shit. Is all. Here. That good?"

I march off.

"And I would fuckin' not."

I climb the hill straight up, thinking the wood and dark'll give me cover. They'd have to look out the back windows at a wicked angle to see this direction, and mebbe the glass would distort. Plus I got the cammies on, so long as I go slow I hope to cause no alarm.

First rain water on my bare neck. Drop hit fat, heavy and cold, then join the shiver rolling down my back. Shoulda never let Mae chop off my hair. Nothing good ever come from short hair men.

Rain fall here and there, not quite committed to the storm.

Huff and puff and once I get a good way up the hill, turn west and cut behind the house. Hundred yards I got a gap in the cover and take a spot under a pine. Draw binocular to eye and scope the house, top, bottom, left and right. Got the big windows upstairs—house look like a church. Deck got the gas grill, open to the kitchen with the big patio doors. Driveway feed to the garage on the far end and who know what on the close. No motion in the house. Basement windows—no lights.

I watch the whole morning, and no Mrs. Graves drove off. Mebbe she in bed, crying her baby boy shot in the face.

Head west another hundred yard, then downhill, slow, mind wandering. What Stinky Joe said on that young girl—me being soft on account her sex ... She ain't pretty. But accourse he right.

But being aware the sex don't gotta make a man horned up. Suppose to work the other way. Man got a code, he see them young girls sex as the jewel in the castle. It's there. Accourse he know it there! He's a man, shit's sake. *He know it there!* But he'd ruther put his back to the wall, draw the sword and die to keep it pristine. Not climb the wall and have at it like some animal.

But in an age of vandalism and marauding deviants, ready to steal what they see, don't matter if its pennies or puss, the bad man'll take what he got no business taking. Accourse I noticed her titties on my arm. Accourse. But I ain't no pervert.

And I wouldn't lick my nuts, neither.

Bottom the hill, I got to find the route to the house. They's no cover, no trees, shrubs, nothing. So I watch and see the road and driveway's empty, then walk upright like I own the joint. Get up the back wall of the garage, then follow 'long to the deck. Creep slow. Duck below the kitchen window. Push on glass doors and they's locked. Gotta think on that. Not sure now's the time to bust glass.

Back the way I come, to the garage. Around the corner, up front the house.

Garage door open, just like that. Just sit open. Wait a minute for sound. None. Draw Smith from the hip and ease through. Four bays. Got the Cadillac Escalade in cow milk white. Got the red corvette. The RAM truck in black. And an open bay where I suppose they hide the meat truck with the kids.

Duck inside agin the wall where they's cover behind vehicles, case someone come. Look at tools on the walls, shelf with drill and Sawzall, got the grinder and a big ass vice like to hold a giant man's head. Three hundred Craftsman wrenches on the peg-board wall.

In back is a wire cage, like for security. Got it padlocked. Behind is hard to see on account the shit on the racks, but appears they's a stairway.

Since these boys troubled theyselves to hide it, make a fella wonder what down there.

Hold the padlock, give it a tug. Solid. Look about the tool benchtop but they's no keys laying 'round. But they's a coffee can with screws and bolts and nuts, and tin snips on the wall.

Mebbe, but that tin prolly too thick.

They's a garbage by the door. Inside, empty Coke can.

Cut the top and bottom off the can, then up the middle the tube, lay the metal out flat. Then snip a rectangle, two-inch-long, one inch tall, and a half moon tongue at the bottom. Cut another like the first. Take a metal file Luke Graves left handy on the benchtop, and run the cut tin over it so no barbs hang up.

Next with the pliers I fold over the one-inch side so it's half that. Add a little strength.

Lessee. Luke Graves got drill bits in plastic holder. Take it to the padlock and eyeball the diameter. Look like three-eighths. Back at the table, I put the bit in the jaws and clamp down on the spiral blade. It'll bust the shit out his sharp, but all this work go the way I want, only drilling Luke Graves'll do is behind bars, ass up with another man working the tool.

Or I kill him.

One.

Press the tin agin the shaft and bend it. With the general shape where I want, loose the vice and stick the half-moon in so it clamps too. Now it's in place, I work it with pliers, press, release, press, till the shape is right close to perfect 'round the drill bit.

Get the second tin the same and leave the bit in the vice for a memento. Flirt with his wife and Luke Graves'll be pissed. But a man keeps three hundred wrenches in lines on the pegboard, you fuck with his tools, he likely lose his mind.

Last I spot a grease gun with a knob at the tip; I daub it on the tin half-moons, inside and out.

Slip each tin over the padlock shaft and push the half-moon tongue down in the hole. Gotta jigger it 'cause the tension, but the grease help it slide in. Rotate the tin and the half-moon displace the bearings inside. Pull, and the padlock open.

I drag open the wire cage door, careful the scrape sound. Don't know where in the house the missus is, but I suspect this hidey hole might have some kids in it.

They got all manner cardboard boxes on the shelves; one look to have white uniforms like you see in the butcher shop. At the end the cage you turn the corner and double back and like I thought it's a downstairs, and at the bottom another damn padlock.

Go back and fetch my shims. Same brand lock. Got it open in no time. Silent. Draw Smith off the hip and twist the door knob. Ease it a crack. Dim light inside. Push open a little more.

Silent.

Swing it all the way and raise Smith to say hello, but the room is empty. Just a row of mattresses agin the wall. Blankets in a pile. A sink. Toilet. Like a big prison cell.

I leave the door open and the light on.

CHAPTER 32

Open the unlocked door from garage to house. Step into a thin room with wash and dry machine stacked. Pretty table for folding clothes. Smell like perfume chemicals. I ease the door shut behind me and see framed words on the wall next the garage.

> *Our Father,*
> *Who art in Heaven,*
> *Hallowed be Thy name;*
> *Thy Kingdom come,*
> *Thy will be done*
> *On earth as it is in Heaven.*
> *Give us this day our daily bread;*
> *And forgive us our trespasses*
> *As we forgive those*
> *Who trespass against us;*
> *And lead us not into temptation,*
> *But deliver us from evil.*
> *Amen.*

I THINK on them words and how I don't forgive and it dooms me.

I think on them words and the house they in.

In the laundry room.

"Who are you?"

Woman voice got the confidence comes with a firearm. I turn, easy. Gun belt bonk the wash machine. She fifty something. Pretty, like in high school she was queen. Married right and had the money to keep the face tight. But today's dark clouds and storm fill the shadows dark, the lines bold. The red underneath from a mess of tears is maroon, and the cheeks is flushed and salty from a recent cry.

"I come about the kids."

"What?"

"You live here?"

"Get out."

"Nope."

"I'll shoot you."

Little red glow in the eye, mebbe not enough to stake my life on it. Trickle of juice on forearms.

"You ever shoot a man before?"

"Yes."

Hot red. Liar.

I walk in the kitchen, slow. Hands up. "I need a glass water. Maybe some cheddar cheese if you got any. Cabbage. Been out the wood two week and some Mexican girl stole all my camp. These illegals come through and ain't nothing but thieves and liars and cheats. Test a Christian man's patience, but I let her off with it. Didn't even try to hunt the heathen Papist down. Stole my food and everything. That was two day ago. Miss, you mind not pointing that thing at me?"

She's a good jump away but no need to jump. Her eyes turn uncertain.

"I saw your Lord's prayer there on the wall. Prayer answered, I come across good, kind, Christian folk. Miss, ain't no need to keep that gun on me. Where you keep the water glass?"

She nod to a cabinet over the sink. Outside window, clouds is rolled in so black and rain picked up, deck is soaked. Up on the hill Stinky Joe liable wet by now, even under the tarp.

Open the cabinet and grab a glass. See Mrs. Graves's reflection in the window. She look to the side and the gun shift off me. I swing the glass at her head with the base heading first like a glass bullet. Bounces her skull, shatters on the wall. She step back like I pegged her temple with a ball peen. I got Smith up and friendly, wants to say hello.

"Put the gun down, Mrs. Graves. You ain't shot a man, and I shot twenty in the last week. Well, I only shot mebbe five. The rest was other means. But they dead just same."

She don't move.

"Drop the pistol to the floor. Don't bend down. Don't do shit but what I say. Drop it."

She don't move. Wonder if that glass bust her brain.

I step at her and she stay still. Take the pistol out her hand.

She face me. Eyes go narrow. See the blood veins in the white. The shine of fresh salt. She say, "You're the one who shot Cephus."

"Howdy."

She smacks me good, open hand.

I cinch the hair at back her head and steer her to the other room. "Need some information. Soon's I get it, be on my way."

Twist her 'round, ass in front a rocking chair. Drop her in it.

"What information?"

"That meat truck. Where it go?"

"Why?"

"Where's the meat truck go?"

Sparks on my arms.

"We deliver meat with it. It's refrigerated. We have butcher shops all over Arizona. We—"

Smith tell her shut up and think.

"Yer boys picked up a load Mexican kids two day ago. Shot one a couple mile down the road. Then another got free when I shot your boy in the face. Where's the meat truck takin' the rest the blackhairs?"

"Fuck you."

"You got a lot of money in that pretty face. I could beat it with metal for ten minute and not kill you."

"Salt Lake City."

"Where?"

"There's a restaurant. A nightclub. My husband owns it with my son. I don't have anything to do with any of it. They're all planning for the revolution. They're nuts. I've been trapped here for twenty years. I can't get out. I can't do anything about it. They just do whatever they want to make money, and it's all okay because soon the race wars will leave us on top. We've got an arsenal in the basement. We've got booby traps all over the mountain, and a hideaway dug in with enough provisions for five years. Oh Christ I didn't have anything to do with it."

Whole time she talkin', I got the juice flowing, and her eyes glow like the last two coals.

"Yeah, well, I don't know your book too good, but they's a part about feeding the poor, ain't they? Or you just read the part about stonin' babies at the river?"

"What?"

"Say the name. What's the joint in Salt Lake City?"

"The Butcher Shop. It's restaurant on one side and nightclub on the other. That's where everything happens. They bring them through. It's just transportation. They'll be there a couple days and then ship them to other places, where they can find jobs. Some of them are being connected with their families."

"Yeah? How that work?"

"Some of the men come up here for work, and when they get enough money, send back for their kids."

"You think that's what your man do? You think?"

She nod, then adds vigor. Glow red. More she nods more juice I get. She fulla shit and know it. Queen of the log cabin castle.

"Let's be clear on one thing. Nevermind the rest yer bullshit. That place you say. Meat Shop?"

"The Butcher Shop."

No red.

"Good."

I could end her torment and bust in her skull. Make the world better by one. But she just look the other way, never pull the trigger.

"You's goin' to the garage basement, where you keep the blackhairs. Grab whatever food you need for a week."

"What?"

Outside the rain come down something fierce. Any don't run off'll be solid ice tonight. And maybe snow start coming in on top. By now, the bag's wet and I'll be walkin' in ice and be iced over too. Got the stove, and two day food. Pick up supplies while I's here?

"I'm not going in that prison cell. I didn't do anything and you can shoot me now if you think you can make me."

Uh-huh. Got the Lord's prayer on the wall, but just now while she talked her face was ugly like scrunched up asshole.

"How long your man been saving these kids from Latin America?"

"I don't know. At least five years. Ten."

"Every month?"

"Sometimes more."

Kids in the hundreds. She live off their suffering, but don't make 'em suffer. She eat filet off their suffering, but don't make 'em suffer. Drive the milk white caddy and put on her princess white gloves.

I bring Smith to her head. Blast lights the room orange, and it's Halloween a split second, black, orange, blood all over the white carpet and furniture.

I look at what I done and blink it clear. Remember the last twenty second. I'da let her live, but she just went on like before.

Evil won't change. So no mercy.

That's Baer Creighton's law.

Any man or woman bring evil on a kid, real evil, I shoot him. Someday someone'll bring me low, and I'll be at the other end the barrel. I know it. But till then, I don't tolerate the evil. I don't turn away the evil. I shoot it in the head.

That ain't by God, and I know it.

It's by Baer.

WOMAN DIDN'T KID. Downstairs is a fortress. Tile floors. Six gun safes next a cement block wall. Wouldn't mind a peek inside. Pull each wheel and they's locked. Got an entire wall of shelves made of two by fours and ply. Coolers, plastic cases. Read the labels. Dehydrated veggies. Dehydrated meat. Whole bottom shelf, twenty feet long, is plastic water bottles.

Another shelf got a good section a books. *Advanced Mantrapping Techniques.* Another on building bombs from household chemicals. Escape and evasion. What you can eat in the woods. Must be fifty books. Accourse, got the Holy Bible.

Find an OD green wool blanket and swipe it for Joe. Waterproof sack. They's a bin with clothes. Grab a wool set of long undies; strip down and step in em quick. 'Bout does it.

Upstairs, find the liquor cabinet. Open up. Johnnie Walker Blue Label. Can't be too bad. I swipe it. Got a bottle of Crown Royal XR. Don't know 'bout that. Them Canadians. Ah, hell. Beggars ain't choosers.

Pack 'em in Joe's wool blanket. Check on Mrs. Graves. Still dead. Outside the rain come down sideways. Soon's I step out the door I be soaked. Head back the garage, sack on my shoulder. I wait a break in the storm but none comes.

Set out in the cold rain with another body behind me.

CLIMBING THE HILL, I think on what she said 'bout them having a cave or fortress up here somewheres hid. And traps. Don't seem civil, traps in the wood. 'Cept I did it to Cory Smiley and it worked real nice. A fella might say one less asshole in the world don't matter, but it sure did to Corey Smiley.

Whooeee. Tired. Got the lungs a pushing. Recall a line.

> *Once a fella*
> *Met a fella*
> *In a patch a beans.*
> *Said a fella*
> *To a fella*
> *Can't a fella*
> *Tell a fella*
> *What a fella means?*[1]

SEEMS HIGHER I CLIMB, colder the wind. Don't think it's the elevation, just the cold front settling in. And soon as I think it, the rain stop, and five minute later the snow start. Gotta get a move on, else I won't see the tarp and Stinky Joe under it.

Tromp along the low side a line of trees—white birch. Grab a mess of curly bark and stick it in my pocket. Even wet it'll light a fire quick. And seeing clouds fulla snow make me wonder if I screwed a goose 'cause I only brought supply for a three day reconnoiter.

Moving on. Got my hand on a sapling and to avoid a fallen tree, swing a little uphill. Plant the foot, and the whole ground give out beneath. I fall forward—save my hand on the sapling slow me.

Leg go straight down. Fire shoot up my calf like a bomb blow it off.

"*!* — — — — — — *!*"

Suck the wind out my lungs and yank the voice out my throat. Blink hard tears and rage squirt out my pores. They trapped the wood!

I don't move.

Blood rush up in my head and ears and save that, the world is silent as snowfall.

I look down the pit and see what they done: a square hole where you step if you miss the log, corralled in by the row of saplings. Pit covered by twigs covered in leaves. Each stake is an inch thick and I suspect the one shoved up my calf is too. I look on the pit and try to collect the brain. Want to jump back but mebbe they's another trap behind? And what'll happen to the hole in my leg when I pull out the stake? That wound gonna bleed.

I recall what they put on them punji stakes in the foreign wars. Human shit, get infected and kill a man in days, so say Joe Burke, who was there.

I concentrate all my wherewithal on breathing slow and steady. I got the hooch I stole. Mebbe disinfect the wound, if I can get it up inside. And while I ponder, any shit they rubbed on the stake is thawing.

Heart jumps out the body.

Yank my leg but—way I's standing—thigh ain't got the pull. Get upright, brace on the sapling, and stand with my left leg to drag the right free. That spike come out my leg and I look at it, smooth and shiny in blood. No way to know what they put on it. Maybe the black plague.

Pricks. Any man that'd sell a kid—you got no way to guess what he'd rub on a punji stake.

Extra glad I shot that woman. Might be I only get to kill two of the Graves.

Blood rolls out the hole, down the sock and over the boot. I think on it quick. If they's poison up in there, mebbe flowing blood help get it out.

Let it bleed.

Afore I set off for Stinky Joe I wonder if mebbe I need that stake. I get on all fours then my belly in the light snow. It's coming down hard and them thick flakes add up quick. Reach in the pit and give that peg a yank. It won't come. I push and pull; after a minute my arm warm and tired and the stake pull out. Get a close look and I can't see gobs of nothing on it, but it don't take much bacteria to set a man under.

Now I try and walk. Right leg got zero ambition. I drag it forward but can't control the foot. And can't push off to make the walk go forward. So I got a half walk. Pull the leg with the thigh, stop; next leg forward with the thigh, push through, pull forward, stop. Never felt so nekkid in the wood—but if somebody come upon me now, man or mountain lion—Baer Creighton's doomed. I got my bullets but after that, nothing but a knife blade.

More steps I take the tighter that calf get, like it cinch on itself. All I can do to keep my voice in my throat and not cuss the whole miserable creation.

Off my right, down the hill, think I see the tarp, covered in snow. Still dark like dusk, though it can't be but mid-afternoon. Now I cut downhill and wonder, why'd I climb up there anyway? After I shot the Mrs. Graves? Just dumb as dick.

And I know it gonna cost me.

With the right leg bum I head downslope sideways. Can't control the foot enough to not fall on my ass if I walk straight. But sideways seems I got about the same control as otherwise. Boot keep the foot and ankle straight, thigh and knee do the rest. Snow already cover the leaves and the path I cut got a red splotchy line with it.

Glorious. Found the tarp.

"Stinky Joe, I got us a 'mergency."

I pull back the tarp and underneath is the camouflage sleeping bag twisted up, solid ice on the top side but where Joe's coiled, he dry and warm.

Joe stretch. Grin. Sigh.

I damn near got it.

What?

The rabbit.

"Well I stepped on a punji stake, and I's liable to die here in a minute."

It'll take longer than that. You remember what Joe Burke said, right?

"Just lookin' a little sympathy is all."

I's plenty warm from the walk but the heat in my leg don't feel like when you cut a finger whittling an elderberry whistle.

Open the bag and sit on a dry part. Pull the right pant leg up and the wool underskivvie.

It's like I try to drill a hole coming in at the steep angle. The stake drag and scrape two inch, then where the calf is thick, they's a hole right in. Press the meat and pain like I never feel all my life. Work the muscle spite the agony and the blood clumps push out the hole at the bottom.

Feel the calf and from the tightness, seems that punji almost bust out the top.

Stake in hand, I rest it along the calf, line up the blood marks with the skin, see how deep it go.

Shit. Pert near the whole way.

Pull the leg all up the knee an they's blue under the joint.

Look out the valley. Got the interstate. Could hitch a ride mebbe. But in Flagstaff they'd say, who this man got the punji in his leg? And I say, you take payment in gold maple leaf? They say, you's that crazy stone-cold killer wanted back east.

I got to solve this one myself.

Got two-day food. With the likker I stole, mebbe last a week. Got the water from the snow. But the elements ... They say these storm can dump feet in hours. Bury a man.

Meanwhile down the hill, two hundred yard off, sits a house with all the food I want and heat to boot. Got the dead woman there—that's nice. Suppose I could get her on the back deck. And when Mister Luke Graves come home, I just shoot him too. 'Long with that dreadlock piece a shit. Once the leg heal, drive on up to Salt Lake to the Butcher Shop and go in guns blazing. Man got to die someday. Why not Salt Lake City?

I don't like the look on your face.

"Oh, you'll like some of it. We's headed to that house down there."

"You're injured." Girl voice.

What?

Turn.

It's the blackhair stole my shit. Snow in her hair and melted on the face. Got my pack on her back, stands bowed to hold the weight.

---

1. Author's Note: I did not write this poem. My wife related it to me many years ago after learning it from a man in a nursing home. I wish I could credit him by name. Given the choice of not including the line or of giving its author anonymous credit, I chose the latter.

CHAPTER 33

"You speak English. Why ain't you said anything back when I saved yer silly ass?"

"If you knew, you wouldn't speak free."

"Sure would. You hungry? You warm? Got no gloves on yer hands."

She say, "What happened to your leg?"

"You be careful on this hill. Them pricks live in that house booby trapped the wood. Dug a pit with stakes."

I wave the punji.

"Stepped in the pit and drove this thing up the calf. You wouldn't be an itinerant med student like ole Che Guevara would ya?"

She smile. "No. They teach English at my school."

"Well, you's a hardy lass. That pack gotta be forty pound."

She get on her knees next me. Take my leg, with ginger fingers, push agin the calf.

"How come you run off?"

"You're a man."

"But I saved yer silly ass."

She look at me.

"I shot the man was gonna kill you. Took ya in when you's freezin."

She look away.

Now it seems more important she gimme some kinda answer.

"So how come you run off with all my shit when I's good to you?"

"You're a man."

She push an prod like she want to cause some pain. More blood clumps drop out the bottom.

"It's already infected. See the red, up here?"

I push off her hands. Square her by the shoulder.

"I ain't like them fellers. I ain't. And you gotta do what you gotta. To protect yerself. I know it. But I ain't one a them bastards. I hate 'em with all I got, and I got this hole in my leg 'cause I hate 'em so much I's huntin' 'em down. That's they house right there. And the man runs the whole operation dug the hole and set this spike. His wife inside the house got a hole in her head I put there. You'd like it. And I know where they drove that truck with the rest you kids, and I's goin' there next. So don't you put me in that same place as men fuck kids. Don't you dare."

Eyes is wet from the leg pain. Mebbe the snow. Got myself riled. So much hate for these evil sonsabitches—and she say I's one em? I save her from the Cephus so I can poker myself?

"Get outta here. I don't need ya. Go on. Shoo."

I give her a shove. Joe perk up. Girl roll sideways to the snow. Struggle with the backpack to get her weight situated and her feet back underneath.

"Go. Damn ingrate!"

The girl pushes up with bare hands in the snow and gets her feet. Step back a few. Look around at the sky, the snow, the hills, the house. The trail of blood, most covered in fresh white. Now her face is wet with melted snowflakes, and her mouth pulls back and her eyes taut.

"You—the storm—you can die."

"Mebbe so. But I won't tolerate bein' near ya."

She look at me a long time, but I don't look away. I done my part to save her once, and if she hell bent on death in the cold, wants to talk shit to me, then fuck her.

She turn. Go back up the hill where she come from, each step slow like she got a mountain chained her ass.

Watch her trudge till she's a flash a color in the trees. Each step she take, the world is more silenter. The air colder. Then I can't see the backpack no more.

I got the dog.

"Hey you brute. I still got you."

Didn't see that coming.

"What's left to do? I ain't a kid fucker."

Fetch that bottle of Canadian whiskey, sketchy Crown Royal XR shit. Pull the top and gurgle a good swaller.

Make a man believe.

If I live through this punji shit and make it to Salt Lake City—and survive the killing I intend there—I's moving to Canada. Someone up there's gonna school me on whiskey.

Gurgle more. Taste like they pulled all that's good and righteous out a jug a likker an put it in a single bottle. Then mebbe polished it in Rita Hayworth's hair. Something. Down the gullet so smooth and easy, a feller wanna drink the whole thing. Two three pulls, I's about there. Gulp like it spring water.

Shit go to work quick. Ain't been appropriately lubricated in weeks; now I got the leg wound I got the time. An nothin' cure the pain like a good knock out drunk. Finish the bottle. Lordy the taste is like honeyed milk and cinnamon.

Stinky Joe stands. Hold my eye.

> *Once a feller*
> *Met a feller*
> *In a dusty barn.*
> *Said a feller*
> *To a feller*
> *Can't a feller*
> *Tell a feller*
> *That girl didn't mean no harm.*
> *You's a dumbass.*
> *She liable to freeze out there,*
> *And you run her off.*
> *Mebbe she come to get help—not give it.*
> *And you got yer high and mighty up.*
> *Oughtta be ashamed.*
> *Dumbass fuckin' redneck brute.*
> *You only wish you was a dog.*

"NOT YOU TOO. SHIT."

Joe stretch ass high, get the pucker hole up in the wind and decide agin it. Run off, lift a leg to a tree. Come back.

That girl looked pretty wore out. Like she coulda used yer help.

"I got rights too. I won't be accused."

You better go after her.

"How? Lookit this snow."

You got here in it.

"Ahhh. Bullshit."

Pull down the wool skivvy. Pantleg over. Try to get on my knees an pack the bag.

You don't need that. Jest get the house.

I look at Joe. Got the drunk on, don't exactly know who to trust. My talking dog or my doodlefucked brain.

Joe cock his head.

Once a feller
Said a feller
Getcher dumbass to the house.

"ALL RIGHT ALL RIGHT."

I get on my feet and find they don't got the balance they used to.

Start up the hill, after the girl.

Hey! The house is thataway!

I look up the mountain. Then left to the house. "What I climbing the hill fer? House thataway."

You'd just step on more spikes up there.

"And 'sides. They rigged the wood with traps. I'd prolly step on more spikes."

Joe sniff the ground, head for the house. Stop and look back.

I start down the hill, right leg out, and zip slip boom that's it.

Black.

GOT the pounding in the brain like log traps swinging agin the noggin from both sides and hitting at the once.

Come aware with Stinky Joe licking the nose. Somehow, though I recall planting my face in two inches snow, I's inside the bag snug. Feel down my side to Smith, and he's cold ready to shoot, was ready all the time. Joe whine and I open the eyes. Dark out. Joe quit licking and the face is cold. Moon high and bright—got the camouflage tarp over me. Bottom side agin the ground numb cold. Got the pain up the leg like a fire, up in my thigh. Recall the whole sordid mess I's in.

"Ah. Fuck."

Use your words, Baer.

"How you set up the tarp?"

That was the girl.

"She still here?"

Nope. Dunno where she went.

"How long ago?"

In dog time?

"Shit. My other bottle around?"

Up the hill a couple feet. You didn't fall far.

"Can you grab me that other bottle?"

Hunh?

"Can you grab me that other bottle?"

Okay. I'll stand watch.

Close the eyes and let the brain settle in for the full mortal experience. Half afraid to see the leg. Throbs like nothing ever in the history man. Without looking I feel the swelling, like the cellulitis mebbe. Get the dirt infection and it move so fast, all you get is hours.

All the people I killed quick, all the mercy I showed, and I got to go like this. Dog won't even fetch a drink.

Try and lift my head, but the throb is only worse. Close my eyes and let the pain float through and above; that don't work, so mebbe I just own it. All right, I's here.

Come git me.

I got a knife. I'll cut the leg off at the knee. Something. Can't let that poison keep going. Though the throb is murder, I squint hard and get to the elbows. Roll the side. Unzip the bag and toss it open. Pull out the leg and press about the calf and knee. Twice the normal size. Thigh growing.

Was it the woman, Lord? Was that it? I shouldn't a shot the woman?

I throw the cover back over me, try and stay warm. Change my mind.

"Come git me."

Open the bag all the way. Unzip the coat so it's flannel agin the freezing air.

"Fuck y'all. I's from North Carolina."

Close my eyes.

Wait.

CHAPTER 34

F inch Graves pulled a magazine from the rack and opened it. The cover photo showed a log cabin on the side of a mountain, similar to his father's, but grand on a scale that boggled his brain. The inside spread showed the details. Cobalt sky. Blazing orange and red trees. A deck made of the exotic, super-dense tropical hardwood Ipe, that spanned an acre and was covered in teak lounges. In front, a dark lake reflected the cabin mansion's majesty toward heaven, where it seemed only a personality as vast as God's might fully appreciate it.

$3,232,999.

It was the kind of house Finch could own, someday, if he went all in with his father and brother.

In fact, Wayman's profits could buy it in less than a year, if his numbers held. No expansion needed, and not counting the wealth he'd already created in past years.

"We're closing the office, now," the red headed woman said. She'd allowed him to stand by the front window the last hour.

Finch stood in the real estate office where he'd several times met Agent Lou Rivers.

"No problem," Finch said. "I'll wait for her outside. Thanks."

He replaced the sales magazine on the rack and exited.

He'd sat at a bus station in Salt Lake City until dawn. Ate a scary ham salad sandwich from a vending machine and napped on the bench. He bought a ticket, boarded the first bus to Flagstaff, and quickly dozed. When he woke two hours from Flagstaff, he pondered the only two escapes from his predicament that seemed possible.

He could continue his present Lone Ranger course. He could try to explain to the FBI, without the recorded evidence, how his father and brother not only trafficked in brown kids, but sold them to murderers and ground them into sausage when it was done. He could hope to live long enough to testify in court.

Or ... he continued a line of introspection begun after killing the man who'd been sent to whack him.

In truth, he felt unconflicted. Their sole interaction was when the man attacked him. Examined from every angle, Finch had not broken a moral code. It wasn't like killing a kid.

And he felt pretty good about it. Not just that he'd defended himself against a mortal threat and totally kicked ass.

He'd killed a man.

The power of putting a gun to another man's chest and pulling the trigger —it was incomparable. He could possibly understand how serial killers became addicted.

The last two hours on the bus ride to Flagstaff were productive.

Follow the thought process all the way ...

He'd felt no remorse, and what if his father had been right all along? What if the people from south of the border were different? What if—by their own choices—they were intrinsically less ... something ... than him, or his family?

Less human?

He saw himself in a white bathrobe on the deck of the log mansion, gazing at the two-story glass, experiencing the sky reflected in it. Or perhaps he sat in one of the lounges with fine women next to him, on either side, sunning the very bodies they would wrap around him that afternoon, before he napped.

Could that be him?

Did Finch Graves have it in him to kill—not just to defend his life—but to defend a lifestyle?

People died all the time anyway, regardless of Finch's decisions. The total of human pain and misery was infinite.

Why shouldn't he be on the side of it that gave him a mansion?

And the part he hadn't really considered, that animated the rest of his thinking ...

Do I want to die?

Already?

Because the path he was on, that was the inevitable conclusion. If he took the fight to his brother and father, he'd wind up dead. The question was just how long he got away with living.

And seen from that light, was it really his fight to save the whole world?

Was it his obligation to save every deadbeat Latina who didn't have the sense to avoid the *coyotes*?

If Latin America valued its kids, wouldn't it keep them from coming north? It wasn't like Luke and Wayman Graves were the first men to discover pedophiles.

The sun had set a half hour ago. The wall clock said six. Where the hell was she?

It'd be just his luck that if he decided to bolt, that's when she'd show. He looked behind him, at the glass of the real estate office. The dial in the window read forty degrees. The temperature would drop fast, without the sun.

Lou Rivers's car swung into the lot.

He had to figure out what to say to her.

He couldn't go back to the family. The FBI was on him.

But he didn't have what the FBI wanted.

For the moment, he'd have to play both sides.

AGENT LOU RIVERS had parked with her trunk to the building. Finch approached the driver side and stood beside the door.

The window dropped. She said, "Get in. Come on."

Finch walked in front of the car. Opened the passenger door and sat inside.

"You look different," he said. "New shaving cream?"

"What do you have for me?"

"Nothing but a story."

"Where's the wire? The recording?"

"That's part of the story."

"Shit. This better be good."

"I can give you politicians. Clergy. Cops. Billionaires."

"But no recording?"

"Like I said. It's part of the story. It was incinerated. But I know where the real evidence is. Video of not just the men and the kids. It's way bigger."

"Yeah?"

"They're selling the kids to killers. Like, billionaire serial killers."

"You're jerking me off."

"Uh." Finch blinked. "No, there's like a hundred thousand billionaires. A million or some shit. A crazy number. And you'd have to be half psychotic to want that much money anyways. So there's zillions of them that want to rape and kill kids. My brother's business corners that market."

Lou Rivers looked forward. The weight of the accusation had clearly rattled her. Finch continued, "He made me help clean up after one of them cut a girl to death. He made me sanitize the room with him. He'd have killed me if I tried to get away. So I helped, and even made it look like I was happy to. You know? But that isn't the worst."

"What's the worst, Finch?"

Finch stared out the front windshield. "He makes the bodies of the dead girls into sausage and donates it to homeless shelters."

Rivers thumped the steering wheel. She looked across the street to the old railroad depot. "But you don't have any direct evidence of this, yet? Just what you witnessed?"

"No. They made me strip, and I tore the wire off with my shirt."

She looked at him.

"I had to strip so I could clean off the blood. They're fanatical about getting rid of the evidence."

"Okay. Stop talking. I need to get all of this recorded. I need your testimony to be legit. Straight up legit. If you've seen this stuff, it'll be enough for the warrant we need."

"Now?"

"Yes, now. We need to go to the station. You're willing to make a statement?"

"I mean, of course, with protection or something. They have body guards. They're making millions. They'll kill me."

"We can protect you. I promise. Hey, I need you in the back seat. And throw on these cuffs. Just can't take you in without cuffs on. No one will see."

"Yeah ... That's how it's done?"

"You're part of a criminal organization. Until we have an agreement on paper, to the Bureau, this is all smoke. I mean, I believe you ..."

"No problem." He picked up the cuffs and opened the car door. "Back unlocked?"

She hit the button on the door panel. The mechanism thunked. "Hop in."

Lou pulled out of the realtor's parking and turned right on Milton Road, then slowed approaching the onramp to Interstate 40.

"Isn't the office up ahead?"

Lou Rivers didn't answer.

"Hey?"

"I want you to show me the scene from the other night. Where you said your brother killed the Mexican boy. Something about this whole thing isn't adding up."

"I already told you all about that."

"I know. I want to see it. We'll have to get some people on it."

"You haven't been out there yet? I told you where to find him. The red jacket."

"Look, it's been a busy day."

She merged onto the highway and Finch looked out the window. Something didn't add up about him?

Him?

Finch thought about Lou Rivers. Her age. Masculinity. The way she seemed to hold something back, in her eyes. Never really there with him. How she always delayed doing anything about the shit he told her.

How she wanted me handcuffed in the back seat.

"Just taking a wild guess," Finch said. "How long have you been working with my father?"

Agent Lou Rivers connected eyes through the rearview, then returned her look to the road. "Known him a long time. We went to high school together."

"Uh-huh."

"So you're not driving to the site of the body."

"No."

"You've been feeding everything I've been telling you to my Dad."

Lou Rivers said nothing.

"You know he's going to kill me."

"That's his business."

Finch saw himself handcuffed to the rail in the back of the Isuzu refrigerated truck. He thought of the basement where they kept the girls and boys, the piss-smelling mattresses and rough wool blankets. He thought of the interminable ride from Sierra Vista to Salt Lake City, all of it on a wood floor, bouncing along with a wrist handcuffed to the rail. And he thought of the ultimate destination. Getting drugged, raped, murdered, and fed to the homeless.

"What's he have on you? Video, like the stuff I saw at my brother's place?"

"I'm not into kids."

"No, I figured it was something else. Who knows. You guys are just as corrupt as anyone else. So hey, you know where you're going? The exit to take?"

"I know where I'm going."

"Good. That's just terrific."

Finch inhaled deep but kept the breath in his lungs. Let it out slow. He filled them again and felt the intoxicating oxygen replenish him. His heart raced and the more he tried to calm himself, the more adrenaline surged.

Lou Rivers put on her turn signal and braked. As the vehicle slowed toward the stop sign, Finch slipped sideways.

She drove the Impala to a rolling stop. The engine idled. The car eased forward. There was never traffic at the intersection. In his entire life, he'd seen maybe one other vehicle there at the same time.

He could trust it.

Finch threw his handcuffed wrists over the seat ahead, catching Lou Rivers by surprise. He yanked back hard. The chain between his handcuffs crossed her throat and pinned her head to the rest.

The car drifted into the intersection. Lou Rivers bucked, hit the gas; the car surged. She twisted right and gagged. He pulled harder, now against the side of her neck. Her knees collided with the steering wheel and the car wobbled. Her feet off the gas, it slowed. They'd crossed the intersection and now rolled up the edge of the onramp, as if to resume travel on 40 west.

Finch didn't remember which side of the neck carried the blood to the brain. He couldn't suffocate her with her head turned sideways, and it was possible she wouldn't even pass out. If she could work both of her hands, she might be able to free her pistol and point it back at him through the seat.

Finch pushed his hands forward, releasing the pressure. He swung his left hand over the head rest and with both wrists side by side, jerked backward. She brought her hands to her neck.

Finch pulled harder.

She spasmed.

Finch drew her closer.

She gurgled. Her hands fell away. Finch heaved until he felt something in her neck dislodge. Maybe her throat collapsed. Or a vertebra shifted. He jerked again, felt the handcuffs cut into his wrists, and held the pressure until long after Lou Rivers was limp.

Finch eased the pressure, keeping his hands about her neck and the cuff chain in place, should she revive. The car had stopped on the wide curb of the on-ramp. A tractor trailer passed on in the interstate. Finch looked over his shoulder, through the rear window. No traffic behind him. He pulled his hands over Lou's head and, like a swimmer, dove between the seats, landing with his head in her lap. She smelled of released bowels.

Finch put the car in park. Checked her pulse to be sure. Her eyes were glassy and fractured with a thousand blood vessels.

He patted her pockets, found a key in the left.

It had to be the left.

Finch adjusted Lou Rivers sideways, her back to the center of the car. She fell over to the console. He reached with both hands and dug with the left into her pocket for the key.

In a few minutes, he had the cuffs off his wrists.

Finch exited the car and stood in the free air, knowing his remaining life would be counted in minutes if he didn't get his shit together.

There was no way to escape the FBI forever. Not when he'd killed one of them.

There was no way to evade his father and brother. They'd hunt him down. He couldn't trust the law; given his father's reach, he couldn't trust anyone.

He pulled the keys from the ignition. Opened the trunk, dragged Lou Rivers from the driver's seat and dropped her in. The woman couldn't have weighed a hundred pounds. At the front seat, he looked at the mess she'd made releasing her bladder. Inside the door pocket was a roll of paper towels. He wiped the seat, threw the towels in the trunk with the body, then let out another ten feet of paper and folded it into a cushion. Finch fired the engine, sat starting at the windshield.

Now what?

Finch thought of the log cabin mansion under the cobalt sky and the glassy stare of the Latina he'd cut to pieces.

CHAPTER 35

"Wake up."

Girl voice.

I shake with cold. Hands on me. Pull my face. Shake shoulder. Open eyes. Still dark. Pain in the leg crowds everything I know. Can't make thoughts cohere. Dreamed of pain then woke to it.

"Take this."

She push a plastic doohickey in my mouth.

"Spffff!"

"Take it." She push it in. Hold up the box. Can't read fer shit.

"Fentanyl. It will help your pain."

I can't rest. The head pounds and the whole right leg's on fire.

"Keep that in your mouth. It will help. This is going to hurt but you must trust me."

She work out a bag. Take an item, do something, back the bag. With scissors she cut pant leg and under skivvie.

"Do you feel this?"

"Nothin' special."

"Good."

She shove a bristle brush up the hole.

Fire all inside and overwhelm the rest my misery. Brain go off and float somewhere the lights is bright and pulsing. Skin on my teeth peels back. Bones crumble to mush. Gotta think I's somewhere else.

She do it again, calf-fucked with a wire brush. Pushing that torment deep in the muscle.

"This part will hurt a little too."

She shake a can, like spray paint.

"Whoa." My voice brittle like a little girl. "Just shoot me. No more torture."

Hear the whoosh from a can.

Fire in the leg go nuclear. Burn like flesh melts off the bone. I twist and holler an cuss, and she move out the way so's I don't whack her. Moonlight show the label.

Lysol.

She shove a hose up the hole an fill it with Lysol. I get a thought and can't hold it. Then another and I partly remember the first. Some a me's filled in wonder she come back. Lysol a good idea. Kill anything it touch. Good start. But rest a me can't hold it together for the agony.

"The pain killer I gave you will help. I want to wait but the infection is very bad. Lysol will slow it. But some might be too far inside. The leg is swollen. We must go to the hospital. There is a Cadillac in the garage. Can you drive?"

"Sure."

"You must teach me."

My eyes is drippy with water. Throat sore and raspy. Brain like hammered mud.

"Okay."

She unhook the tarp, pull it back and it's white all over everywhere and moon sharp as a knife up there above. Specks of light—clearest night I ever see. I blink and my eyes don't feel right. The leg kinda go distant. Still throb, but like the leg a mile off. Close my eyes and open again. Now this girl's the prettiest in the world—even with the orange clown hair.

Wow, is all a feller can say.

"You got some pretty ass hair. Why don't you press it agin some kindlin' and start a fire?"

Way back somewhere I got paper birch bark. Was that in Arizona? Or as a boy?

She stare, mouth tight. Then smile. "The fentanyl."

"I like to still some of that." Then, "You come back after I say some mean stuff."

"You get on this." She drag a plastic boat sled next me. Got a yellow nylon rope with knots up front. "Can you roll over?"

I twist and land on Smith in the bed of the boat. "You gonna tie up Stinky Joe and holler *mush*?"

She wrinkle her face.

"Who is Stinky Joe?"

"That dog was here. Where Joe?"

"He has not been here. We need your legs on the sled." She gets in front of me and something's different. She lift my leg and put 'em on the sled. Then the other. She wearin' gloves.

"You see Mrs. Graves?"

"I saw."

"Wicked woman, that."

Blackhair lift the rope and pull.

"Hey, my sleepin bag. And pack." Reach and touch Smith. Okay. Forgot I already checked. "What you say this lollipop is?"

She lean hard and get the rope over the shoulder. Plant the feet sideways, squat, cinch up, stand. Sled move off the flat an alla sudden the silent night filled with the crunch a snow. She pull and trot, and the boat cut the hill with speed. Rope go limp.

"Out the way! Whooooeeee!"

Glide downhill. Grab the boat sled rails and pull the left; lean right. Pass the girl; drift toward the house. Lose speed cause I ain't headed straight down hill, but save the trek at the bottom. Look like six-inch snow if one. Come to the flat and I's at the edge they lawn. Sled stop. I push with the arms and pain clouds the brain. Druther walk. Brain about as loopy as a ten day drunk all at once. Try an figger how to stand. Right leg won't bend worth a shit. Roll over an push up. Stress the head like to pop, and through the giddy loopy I sense if I don't get the antibiotics soon I'll pull up the green corn and stomp little chickens.

Standing, I plant the right leg and move the left. Drag the right along. Got mebbe twenty thirty yards to the driveway.

Girl catches up.

"Hey. What yer name?"

"Tat."

"What? Tat?"

"Tathiana."

"Hello, Tat."

"Hello. Keep going. The car is on the other side."

"Tat. I got—hey, lissen." Grab her shoulder. "Tat. I sorry. I apologize."

She look at my face and nary a muscle twitch. Nothing 'bout the eyes. Nothing 'bout the mouth. Cold as sauerkraut.

Mind move on. Fentanyl drug. Can't make sense that orange hair. But it make the girl pretty. Mebbe her coming back make her pretty. Sometime a man just want a hole to curl up and cry in.

Fuckanyl drug.

"What drug you gimme? Sheeit."

Wonder if she could drag me. Stinky Joe could. Where Stinky Joe? I stop. Turn. "Joe! Hey-Ah. Joe!"

"We don't have time."

"You find keys in the house for the Cadillac?"

Head shake.

I walk. "Mebbe run ahead? Look in the house. Find her purse?"

She go ahead. I look from there to my feet, a mile and back. Got the vertigo. No balance in the feet. Look ahead and a star flare off the left, down the road. Two star, ground level.

Mebbe I get to kill one more Graves.

CHAPTER 36

Wayman Graves powered off his computer. He glanced at his watch. Claudia was probably downstairs already. She'd said she'd meet him, rather than allow him to send a car.

He'd wondered about that. Other girls thrilled at the idea of dating a man wealthy enough, and confident enough, to send a limo to pick up his date. But Claudia had demurred, saying she'd be coming from—she'd jumbled the words together and he hadn't understood—so she may as well just drop by the club.

Maybe she wanted to hide where she lived.

Maybe.

Wayman had been troubled each time he thought of her since the moment he'd told her he intended to marry her.

Even a small passage of time increased the ease of walking back the statement. *I was joking. You were looking so good I spoke without thinking ... We don't even know each other.*

If he didn't mention it again, she'd never bring it up. Women were smart about that. Women know not to believe a man feels something until he says it a hundred times—and then they doubt it forever. The ephemeral could never be absolute.

But he didn't want to walk it back.

Wayman didn't love her. He didn't know what love was or how to do it. He was attracted to her in a way that perplexed his understanding, as if a physical string tethered his eyes to her face.

In thinking of her, he didn't see a future with them cuddled up before the fireplace whispering their deepest secrets. He wasn't stupid. That future wasn't available to him, ever. One, he was a man, and two, no woman would be cool with the shit buried in his soul. Not after he'd learned he could take whatever he wanted from the girls upstairs, zero risk.

But Wayman could see Claudia with their children, raising them right, respectful, square-shouldered and strong. He saw her as a potential partner in creating a home, bearing sons to pass the business to.

Would she ever work beside him?

Wayman's mother had assisted his father early in their marriage when the meat business grew, and Luke often said she was critical to their success when the second phase kicked in. His mother spoke Spanish, and taught Wayman and Cephus. Luke had always refused to lower himself, so Caroline Graves negotiated the first truckloads of girls, then oversaw the fledgling operation in Salt Lake City until Wayman promoted Amy out of the ranks to do it instead.

Would Claudia take to the business the way his mother did? Claudia wouldn't *have to* participate, but she needed to believe in the cause, or building a household would be impossible. It wasn't like the old days, when a man could correct a woman. Not with iPhones everywhere. And he wanted harmony in the household, not strife. A woman strong enough to submit, but without cowering or groveling.

Wayman shook his head. He hated brooding moods.

He stood at the mirrored window, surveyed the dance floor, and saw Claudia alone by a pillar, looking up at the glass, but not where he stood. The effect was strange, as if she looked past him, the two of them not connecting.

Wayman left the room, locking the door behind him. He joined Claudia on the dance floor, took her hand, let his hips move with the beat, spun her, led her to the door. The motion cheered him.

On the sidewalk he led her away from the line and said, "Would you like to go to another place, or have dinner at my place?"

"Here. I'm on a keto diet, so I can eat meat all night."

"Ah."

She punched him.

"Let's go."

They walked another twenty feet to the entrance for the restaurant side of the Butcher Shop. He opened the door, allowing her to lead him inside.

The Maître D' wore a black tuxedo; his shoes looked like polished onyx.

"Will you have a private booth, this evening, Mister Graves?"

"That will be fine. But don't kick anyone out."

The man nodded and led them.

"He wouldn't really tell someone to move would he?"

Wayman smiled.

They sat in a booth that offered both size and seclusion. The walls extended to the ceiling—as did all the booths—and the front, open now, would be closed by a curtain when the waiter brought their dishes.

"Oh good," Claudia said. "The menus are in English. I hate places that use other languages. Like English isn't good enough."

Wayman nodded, studied her. "Yeah. Like I want to press one to speak my own language. You want to come here, talk like the people who live here."

"Well, that's the way it is. Nothing's going to change it." She held up the menu. "So what's good?"

"Anything. You might like the elk. Wait, the pronghorn is a sweet meat—add to that, the chef makes it in a white wine sauce with truffles, rosemary and black pepper. Or you could have good old beef and A1 sauce."

"They both sound delicious. I feel like I haven't eaten in weeks."

"You know what? We have a chef's special. I just remembered. It's a sausage combining our most exotic meats. We only make it every now and again. I promise, it'll be the sweetest, most tender meat you've ever had."

"Sausage?"

"Yeah. It's not like a bratwurst or something. This is the real deal. Tell you what, I'll have the sausage and give you a taste."

"I didn't think it was legal to sell wild game at a restaurant."

"It isn't. We can only sell farm raised animals that were slaughtered and inspected by the meat folks. It sucks for freedom, you know. Can't do anything without big brother's permission. I resent the hell out of that. But in the end, it works better anyway. When you buy meat killed by a hunter, there's no telling what he did to the animal. Gut shot, let it run a mile, pumping adrenaline. It's better to give an animal a quick death. You can taste panic."

"That's so interesting."

"Yeah, but it's another case of the government forcing everyone to do something, when the market would police it better. If I served meat that tasted like it was fried in cat whiz, I'd be out of business. Government doesn't need to participate."

"Well, that's the nanny state."

"Only problem is nanny states turn into dictatorships. Countries never evolve to more freedom."

"You know more about it than I do. I can see your passion."

"You can have security, or you can have freedom. You can't have both. Ben Franklin said that. Or somebody."

The busboy entered, followed by their waiter. The busboy set the table and poured water into their glasses.

Claudia ordered the pronghorn and Wayman, the sausage.

Again alone, Claudia said, "Was that busboy Mexican?"

"No, I don't hire Mexicans. That guy's Croatian. Gets a lot of sun I guess. Why?"

"No real reason."

"Tell me."

She inhaled. Let it out. "It isn't polite."

He leaned. "Tell me."

"I hate them."

"Why?"

She looked at the curtain, still open, and the other people dining. Then met his eyes.

"I was in high school. Nineteen ninety-five. Coming home from school. I was born in Texas and lived outside El Paso, and I thought the Mexicans were like everybody else. They fit in. They'd been there so long, they had the same beliefs. Later my dad's company transferred him—us—to San Francisco. One day I was walking home from play practice after school ..."

Wayman placed his arm across the table, hand open. Claudia stared off, eyes glassy.

"You don't have to tell me."

"No. I don't, but this is why I hate Hispanic people. Because three of them cornered me. Two held me down while the other raped me. And then they switched. And every time I fought they punched me in the stomach so hard I couldn't resist. They kept talking to each other, across me. Think of that. Think of being held down, and they're talking to each other in that gibberish language."

"What happened to them?"

"Nothing. They were gang members. Their parents came from El Salvador in the eighties. There was a civil war there and a lot of them came here instead of fighting for their own damn country. San Francisco declared itself a sanctuary city in 1985. Well, the kids they brought up became the gangbangers that raped me. And it wasn't just me. There were others I heard about. But because they were protected, no one went after them. And there's all these assholes out there who like to say sanctuary cities have less violent crime. I don't get it."

"You see, that's the kind of story that just pisses me off. These people."

"And here's the thing. I'm supposed to be the racist. Three thugs see a little white girl and rape her. I'm the racist? I understand judging each person by his actions. Personal responsibility, fair justice for all. But when you have a class of people who all behave the same way, you have to judge them by the class, because they have a power as a class that they don't have as an individual. As a class, they can overwhelm you. That's my brain speaking. My heart? I'll cross the street to avoid them. I'll leave a party if I see one there. They make my skin crawl. In *fear*."

Claudia placed her hand in Wayman's. "So you don't think I'm crazy? An ugly hearted hater?"

He shook his head. "It's a shitty deal. The only response is to allow it to make us stronger. Otherwise ..."

"Yeah." She smiled. "But I don't dwell on it. I can't. There's only so much room in your mind. You either dwell on the stuff that hurts you, or on the stuff that makes you happy. It's a choice. So I try to not think about those days."

"I'm glad you told me. I was thinking about showing you something. A surprise."

"Really?"

"Wait till you see what I've got upstairs. You're going to love it. Oh, our food's arriving. You have to try this sausage. Trust me. You'll love it."

CHAPTER 37

F inch sat in the dark with the engine running and the headlights off but the parking lights on. Windows down. He wanted the clarity that came with cold air.

At night, truckers pulled over on whatever exit found them tired; in the west, vehicles parked at exits were common.

An FBI agent growing stiff in the trunk, less so …

After all the action of the last couple of days, his brother's death, his participation in the grotesqueness of the family business, and his two killings, Finch found he desired nothing more than a few hits off a fat joint, a couple shots of house whiskey, and bed.

Eyes closed, he pressed his head to the headrest and realized an hour before—a half hour?—Lou Rivers's head had been where his was now, her eyes shattering as he choked her. Right where he lay his head, closed his eyes, and rested.

What a cosmic joke.

A vehicle rumbled over the potholes on the intersection behind him. Only a handful of people lived back that way, his father one of them.

Finch opened his eyes. Checked the mirror, then turned in the seat.

Through the dark, he recognized the vehicle by its reflected shape in the moonlight. It was the Isuzu refrigerated truck.

He looked at the clock. Five minutes. He'd been sitting, thinking, only five minutes.

The tunnel vision and acute hearing that had overwhelmed his senses when he killed—*in self-defense*—the hit man in Salt Lake City had not occurred when he killed Lou Rivers.

He'd been in a different zone, but without warped senses.

With Lou Rivers, he'd plotted. He knew her destination, knew the route. Identified a method of attack, weighed the best time, given the risks the violence would create. He could have throttled her with the handcuff chain while the car raced down the interstate at seventy-five miles per hour, but that would have resulted in a wreck, likely killing them both. Instead, he'd waited until she came to a stop at an untraveled intersection.

He'd had more time to think things through. In the back seat of the Impala, he was a different man: Someone who already had experienced killing.

A voice in the back of his mind yipped, *you've got a body in the trunk! You killed an FBI agent!*

But the rest of him was calm like throwing out junk mail. He lived in the same world as a day ago, populated with the same evil, but in his own estimation, he'd grown, he commanded his fate and who he would choose to be. The values he would choose to enforce.

He didn't have to run. Didn't have to be a victim of family pressure. He had balls.

Fact.

On the bus ride from Salt Lake City, right after he'd boarded, he was too jittery from caffeine, sugar, and adrenaline to sleep. Finch had removed the newspaper he'd taken from the night before, and had stowed under his jacket, and opened it. His father had been looking at the paper on the drive to Salt Lake City. On a rest stop, Finch had noticed the interview section his father had been reading.

A fellow named Nat Cinder—easy enough name to remember—had a year ago managed to have half of the Arizona government removed on various charges ranging from conspiracy to murder. Now it seemed the grassroots wanted him to run for governor.

Finch could give a shit about politics. But he'd noticed a couple words on the folded paper.

Nat Cinder was on a mission to end human trafficking in Arizona.

And from what Finch understood of how he brought down the governor, there was a chance Nat Cinder was the one guy in Arizona who might have both the stones to take on Wayman Graves, and the decency to not already be in his grasp.

Finch resolved to find Nat Cinder.

But first, work.

He pressed the trunk release and stepped out of the vehicle. At the back, he lifted the lid, unfastened Lou Rivers's belt, and dragged it clean of her body. Her holstered pistol fell aside. Finch grabbed it. The holster had a compartment for a spare magazine. He withdrew it, held it to the trunk light. Thirteen rounds. Next, he withdrew the pistol, a Glock 21, .45 automatic.

A lot of gun for a hundred-pound woman.

He released the magazine, saw it full, slipped it back in. Pulled back the slide and observed brass.

Ready to go.

Finch sat in the driver's seat, checked his rearview, put the car in reverse. He slowed at the intersection and, seeing no lights, backed onto the road.

CHAPTER 38

C laudia let Wayman take her hand as they exited the restaurant through the kitchen. She paid her compliments to the chef—the pronghorn was not what she expected, but she didn't tell the chef. The sausage she sampled from Wayman's dish was much better.

They entered a hall and, after a couple turns, stood waiting at an elevator.

"So what's the surprise?"

"I'm going to show you something that will maybe make you feel better."

"I feel fine. About what?"

"What happened to you. What you told me."

"Oh—see, like I said. I don't think about it."

The elevator door opened. Wayman blocked if from closing with his foot.

"You do think about it. All the time. It's built into who you are. That's why you feel what you feel toward certain people."

"Again, you're right."

"You're going to appreciate this."

They entered the elevator. The door closed, and she was alone with him. He'd never indicated the capacity for violence toward her, but below his surface boiled the kind of passion that, confined by the rigidity of his belief system, could easily churn itself into viciousness. She sensed it was a constant struggle with him, keeping the froth of emotion closed off around those who would judge him. An act of survival he longed to cast off. He spoke of freedom because he was not free.

The elevator chime rang. The silver doors parted.

"Are these real?"

"They are real paintings. But they're not worth millions. Tens of thousands."

"Beautiful. Is this what you wanted to show me?"

"Nope." He glanced at his watch. "We've only got a couple of minutes." Wayman led down the hall. Stood before a door, and it opened without his knocking.

"Claudia, this is Amy. She's my floor manager."

Amy nodded one time. Stepped back. Wayman led inside the room. A desktop similar to a kitchen counter top spanned one wall, with file drawers underneath, and what must have been twenty video monitors above, stacked four high, across the entire wall. Several screens were black. Some of the screens showed people having sex.

Older men. Younger girls.

Claudia was still, sensing much depended on how she framed her expression, and the words she chose.

"What on earth?"

She forced herself to step closer.

A cell phone buzzed. Wayman sighed. He pulled the phone from his pocket.

"My dad."

He swiped. Answered.

"I'm tied up. What's up? ... What's he look like? ... You should back away. Regroup ..." Wayman caught Claudia's eye. He turned away and exited the room.

Claudia noticed Amy raking her up and down.

"What is this?" Claudia said.

"Whores. You never see whores?"

They were children. Claudia fought the tightness in her stomach, closing in around the meal she just ate, wanting to expel it.

"I just noticed they're all, I don't know. Like you. Are they from Mexico?"

"All over. Panama, and up."

Wayman entered the room. "I'm sorry. That was my father."

"Is everything all right? Sounded like—"

"Yeah, he's all right. He's negotiating a contract. There's always something." Wayman nodded at the video wall. "What do you think?"

"It's like, what? Live porn? Is this for the Internet?"

"That's a good idea. I hadn't thought of that. No, this is live, just for the sake of live. Notice anything about the girls?"

"Yeah. They're all like her."

"I wanted you to meet one of them."

Claudia heard his foot scrape on the floor. Saw him turn as if in slow motion. She opened her mouth and closed it, dry.

"I need some water or something. That wine sauce." She pressed her hands to her pants to dry them.

"I'm sorry. You're not enjoying this?" He moved to a small refrigerator. Gave her a bottle of water.

She drank.

"No, I'm just surprised. A little overwhelmed. That you would trust me with this. I mean. This can't be legal?"

"Nowhere close. This is a good old-fashioned brothel, and those girls are fresh from L'America. We bring them up every month, give them instruction in capitalism and when they've satisfied our customers, we introduce them to new employers, in other cities."

He's testing me.

"I think it's disgusting."

He shifted.

"What on earth would make a white man desire *that*?"

Wayman exhaled hard. Laughed. "It's called Strange. Most men want a little strange, time to time."

"And you? Is that what this is about? You defining the rules of the relationship? You want to have this conversation here, with her?"

"No, no," Wayman said. He grinned. "No. I just wanted to show you some of the business. Because I told you a couple days ago. I'm going to marry you."

"Not if you want strange."

"I don't want strange."

"Okay."

"You want to meet one of the girls?"

"Not particularly. I told you." Claudia curled her lip at Amy. "I don't like these people."

"It's important. For us to be able to trust one another," Wayman said.

"Fine."

Claudia steeled herself.

Wayman turned. Amy led them out of the room and down the hall to a door. She opened it with a key and stepped aside.

A young girl was on the bed, under the sheets. Claudia stepped into the room. Wayman followed.

"This one has been here for two months. She's used to the routine. She's been a good earner."

Claudia stood at the side of the bed. The girl sat up. The sheet fell away. The girl reached to Claudia's waist.

Claudia stepped back. With a set jaw and squinty eyes, she opened her hand and smacked the girl across the face. "Don't you ever touch me."

She marched past Wayman. "And don't *you* ever bring me around these people again. *Don't do it.*"

Claudia strode to the elevator and waited for him to arrive with the code. "I'm furious with you."

"You'll get over it."

"I hate these people. Why did you do this?"

"I had to know. Because the business has another floor."

"I don't want the tour."

"Let's go down to my place. Have a drink."

"I don't want a drink. I'm going home. I need to do my yoga. My hypnotherapy technique. Why did you stir all this shit up in me?"

They rode the elevator to the bottom floor. He exited with her, walked beside her through the nightclub's storage rooms, through the back of the bar. Glaring, she allowed him to peck her cheek with a goodnight kiss, and left him there.

Outside the Butcher Shop, she walked quickly to her Chevy Nova, unlocked it and sat inside. Claudia stared out the window a long while, then opened the door, and threw up on the blacktop.

CHAPTER 39

Headlights up the drive like a flying saucer buzzing the field. Got the main lamps, and my fentanyl head make 'em spin.

"Girl. Tat! The man kill your boyfriend—he comin' up the road!"

I's in front the house. Nowhere to hide and couldn't get there if they was. Standing on the fire leg, pain come and go. Most time it's way off, but I move sudden it jumps in like a flash. Give a man a scare.

Truck come up and stop without going in the bay. He back twenty feet at least. Maybe a quarter mile. Perception come and go. I remember I got the drunk on 'fore the orange hair gimme the pills. Poor liver about to give up on account the hate.

Door open and the Isuzu refrigerator truck lights stay on.

"That a diesel?"

"What?"

"I say, that a diesel?"

"Who are you?"

"I'm the feller executed your boy Cephus. He was gonna shoot the Tatti girl. Tat. What the hell kinda bringin' up you give that boy?"

Can't see the man too well with the headlights behind him. Though the snow is bright and light come from the open garage bay.

"Oh, and I shot yer wife."

He step closer. Hands in the pockets. That's where his gun is. I bet.

"She in the house," I say. "Couldn't let her go, not with how I's fittin' to kill all the rest y'all."

Realize I don't yet got Smith in hand. And he prolly got a gun in the coat already pointed at my belly.

"Oh, hey. Don't worry though. I didn't violate her. Just shot her in the head. And by the way. Some sick shit, you got the punji stakes up there. Thought you might like to know you got me."

He pull his hand out his coat and it's like I thought. Had the gun on me. Can't see the size but it some kind automatic.

"See? Look my leg." I twist it.

"So what's your story? You come out of nowhere and just start murdering my family, and we've never met? Who are you?"

"I's nobody. To you at least. That Stinky Joe—I's his whole world. But nobody special to you. I was campin' is all. An your boy shot the Mexican. He come back with the girl. You know I thought she was a boy till I pressed them li'l hooties on accident. Anyways, I was ready fer yer boy. God favors me that way."

"And that's it? Our paths have never crossed?"

"Nope. Well, I coulda pissed on ya when you was at my camp. The tent. That Mexican girl stole all my shit. But she a good girl and y'all shoulda just let her go."

"Who else knows about all this?"

"Oh, hell. You know that fella ain't running for governor? He don't know. And that girl your boy was 'bout to shoot. She don't know either."

Luke Graves stop walking. Now he close, I see his face. Uncertain eyes. Don't know if we's alone. Prolly wishing he could have what I's having.

"Well I guess it's time to play cowboy." I reach for Smith and miss. Catch Luke Graves by surprise and he don't shoot. Make another swing at Smith & Wesson; get hand on grip and 'fore tube leave leather Luke Graves shoot.

Gun a little twenty-two or something.

Smith & Wesson drop the snow.

I got the bullet in my arm—like getting stuck with a lawn dart. It hurt, but the arm still there. So that's good. In all. But that's mebbe the fentanyl dope.

"Hold on," Luke Graves say. "Don't move. I want to understand a couple things, 'fore I kill you."

I keep the eyes on Luke Graves, but out the peripherals a black shape move quick and silent on the snow. They's a sparkle in the light. Tat coming up from his blind side, back around the truck. If she make a sound the diesel engine cover it.

"Sure. What you wanna know? Yer old lady didn't see it comin'. If that mean something to ya. One second she's the queen of the log cabin, royal highness above all the blackhairs. Next her head got a hole like a football bat screwed a cantaloupe."

"Baseball bat."

"Yep."

Tat's up on him. Only a couple feet behind. She musta got Mrs. Graves's pistol—the one she pulled on me—from the house. Or mebbe took it and had it all along, since she come back to help me. She ain't but four feet and change and Luke Graves's mebbe six. She point the gun at his head, then like afraid she'll miss, lower the tube.

"I'm still not sure I understand why you'd inject yourself in someone else's business?"

Tat ain't shootin. All she gotta do is squeeze but she don't. Meantime my hand's slippy and cold in blood. Got the right leg pert near dead. Got the right arm shot. That oxy drug got the steadying effect, but shit if this ain't enough to stretch a man's patience.

"Mister Luke Graves. You buy them kids from south. The blackhairs, and sell them up north. You sell their sex. Yea, or no?"

Luke Graves a wary sombitch. He shift the gun to me, center mass.

"Go ahead."

"What?"

Fire blast out Tat's silver tube. Luke stumble forward; his arm off pitch. I go to the left knee while the right won't bend. Fall to the side. Luke swing the gun after me and Tat fire again, this one in Luke's neck. He go limp. Drop.

Tat's face is messed like the crick washed away the bank and showed all the tangled roots. Pulled back here, snarling there. Tears. She keep the gun up though Graves gargles blood to death in the snow.

Helluva gunfight and me not even getting Smith out the holster.

"You can put that pistol down now."

Tat keep it up like she's thinking on whether to keep shooting.

I bet that's the first man she kill outta fifty she wanted. Need a minute get her brain back.

"You don't mind, I's gonna get back to what we was occupied at 'fore we was interrupted."

I crawl the house, climb the wall for balance, let the left leg catch up the right. Standing, I set for the garage.

I can open my hand and close it but the bullet in the top of my arm make it weak. Couldn't pull the plug out a jug to save my life.

"You get them Cadillac keys?"

She lower the automatic.

"Mebbe put the safety on that?"

She bring it to me. I point to the switch. "Push that."

She do.

"Point over there and pull the trigger again."

No fire. She nod.

"You got the keys?"

Tat pulls 'em from her pocket.

She help me in the Cadillac, and I watch while she stick in the key and get her started. Mebbe learned something on the streets in L' America. But not snow driving.

Tat put the pistol barrel down the cup holder.

I show her reverse, look out the window inside the garage and wonder how we get through the wall. Vehicle burps backward, and I go forward. Knock the noggin on the glove box. She hit the brake and slam me back in the seat. Now I recall that pesky bullet in my arm. Fucker hurts, then I don't feel it at all. Tat's head's on fire with the orange, all aflame and bright.

"Trouble," she say. Pushes the shifter into first, then reverse, then park. She grab the gun, open the door, and vanish while I look at the radio just went out. Suspect my brain don't work well as mebbe I need it to.

Got bright lights in the eyes, through the side mirror. Now who drive up on us?

And where the hell Tat go?

Then I understand. The headlights lit her hair all bright like on fire.

A car door slam. Still got the light in the mirror. Move my head and the light go. That's how that work.

Hell with it. Head back on the rest. Ain't my fight, today. Not with my leg destroyed and a hole in my arm.

But Tat come back for me and, shit, I's conscious. Can't lift the right arm too easy, so I reach over and unlatch the door with my other. Throw legs over the seat and try to land on the left, with no punji wound. Right leg sets about the torment, stirred up, spiteful.

"Shush, ya prick."

Out front, twenty thirty yards off is a car with bright lamps on the high beams. Impolite like the city. I steady myself on the Escalade.

Car door. Black figure.

I reach for Smith and he ain't there so I hook my thumb on the holster.

A man come forward through the headlights and floating snowflakes. His right hand is longer than his left by mebbe six inches. Or he got a gun.

He say, "Who are you?"

"Baer ass Creighton. Who you?"

"Finch Graves. Why are you here?"

I know the voice from sitting in the tree. And I sure as hell pick up on the last name. This is Blond Dreadlocks.

"Suspect you and yer daddy wasn't on the same page, exactly. Mebbe. You had a tone with him. Mebbe I was hearing things. It was right after the girl run off with all my shit."

"No, I'm not part of that anymore. Where's my father?"

"Other side the Sinuzu, here."

"Isuzu."

"That one."

"You fucked up or something?"

"Oh, I's a touch more'n fucked up. Fucked down, fucked in, fucked out. Every way a feller can—without gettin' laid." Smile, that was good. I slip down on the Escalade hoping my ass'll find purchase on the bumper, but it don't and I drop. But the back my head find the bumper fine. About knock me out.

"That blood?" say Finch Graves.

"That blood."

"You say my father's just the other side of the truck?"

"Deader'n shit."

"Good."

"Whoa, now?"

"I come to kill him."

A shadow cross behind Finch. No mystery this time; Tat figger it worked the first, mebbe she try it again. In two second she's beside Finch, got the gun on his chest.

He put up his arms.

Tat's hand shake and she make a mean face, wince like, and the gun thrust like she's fake shooting. Then I ken it: she forgot the safe switch.

"You forgot that safe switch, Tat."

"Stop, don't do that," Finch say. He turn to her. "Don't you recognize me? I'm the one who gave the key to your boyfriend. I thought he would help all of you with the handcuffs, so you could escape. Not just him. And I planned on letting you loose at a gas station, so Cephus couldn't could do anything to you."

Tat still got her mean face on. Gun shake in her hand.

"He's telling the truth," I say. "He don't got no red or juice comin' off him. He ain't lyin'. It's this gift I got, see? I can tell —."

Finch step aside out the line of Tat's gun. Go behind the truck to look his father. Tat still trying to squeeze the trigger. Got sparkles on her face but her hair is black again. She put the gun down. Look at me. Eyes swim in water and cheeks is shiny. She see me lookin' and wipe her face with her arm.

Finch come up by the garage from other side the truck. Got the grave look on his face.

"Who killed him?"

"I did," Tat say.

"Thank you. My mother?"

"I did her," I say. "Not I *did* her. I shot her, what I meant to say."

"Good. She was part of it from the beginning."

Finch Graves still got the pistol in his hand. He look around the house, the falling snow. Stick the gun down his pants in back. "You were about to get some help in the Escalade?"

"Yeah. I got stuck on a punji stick. And shot."

"Well, I'd take you in the Impala, but I got a dead FBI agent in the trunk."

"No shit? I'd like to see that."

"I was trying to tell her about my dad, the whole operation. She was snitching on me the whole time. Years."

"See," I say, "my experience, you shouldn't even try to work with them federal police. Nor the local, come to think of it."

"Well, let me park the Impala so we can get the Escalade out. I'll take you. Where were you going to go for help?"

"Flag, over night. Then I don't know what."

"I got an idea."

"I got one too."

He get in the Impala and move it other side. Tat help me in the seat again and climb in the back.

Finch pops in the driver seat and throw his body 'round like he know where each device is at. Four-wheel drive. Reverse. Out we go. Turn around and head into the flying snow.

Finch wanna go fast but I tell him we's better off late than dead. Like Ma used to say. And we ain't going the hospital, so what's the rush?

We mount the interstate and I see nobody bother to plow. Just the semi-trucks with they tires. Finch keep it going easy, and though it twenty-five-mile mebbe thirty, we arrive no worse the wear.

Hardly recall the lay of town. And the dope gimme incentive to sleep. But I spot the right turn and point the Monte Vista where Ruth and Mae stay. We'll visit Mae. Ruth'd just wanta bounce off my nethers and I don't think I could fetch a boner if she brought Racquel from the cave man poster.

Finch run the Cadillac up on the sidewalk and gotta back up and pull forward to get back on the road and parallel.

"You go upstairs first. Up on the second floor. The room is twenty-two. You tell the girl Baer needs her help on account I's shot. Tell her to get the kids out the room. Put 'em with Ruth. Then come back for me. You got all that?"

Finch leave the keys in and the heater running. Go inside.

"Can we trust him?" Tat say.

"I dunno. I jest know he didn't lie 'bout what he said back there. You saw. Did he give the key to your boyfriend?"

I twist around and see her out the peripheral. She nod, got the tears going again.

And I wonder, where the hell is Stinky Joe?

CHAPTER 40

They got the sofa clear but it don't make sense a man dripping blood to sit on it, so Mae pull trash out the tin and she got a few spare bag underneath. She cover part the cushion and I switch from wood chair to soft sofa.

Rap on the door. Mae open it: Ruth come in.

"I left the kids with you," says Mae.

"I put Morgan in charge of Bree and Joseph. She's a better mother than I ever was. Oh, *shit! Baer!* What'd you do now?"

"Come on in," I say. "Join the fracas."

Finch sit in the other wood chair by the kitchenette table, looking off at the wall. Tat come out the bathroom like she washed her face, and though the hair ain't orange, it don't do her no harm. Tat clean up nice. Put a prom dress on her, you got a regular girl. But Tat wasn't born to crush the hearts of wall flowers. Mankiller got a different future.

"Let me look at this." Ruth wrestle me for my coat and wins. Then my shirt. I's pert near nekkid 'cept—certain places—I got hair like an ape. She look at the gunshot hole in my arm and her manner ain't like I seen before, not on the road trip west nor before, when we was thinking on saving the buried girl, and didn't. Something got a hold Ruth, something distort her so she's all action and take charge, but it's like a thin coat of stain don't convince the wood beneath. Ruth say, "You're going to come through this just fine." But she don't believe her words, and that make me question something so far I ain't.

Mae see my face. Crowds Ruth. Take my hand. "Mom, would you go in my room and find the first aid kit we bought the other day?"

Mae hold my right arm up, press here and there.

"The bullet passed through. And it looks like it didn't hit the bone or anything," Mae say. "We'll wrap this one so it doesn't keep bleeding. It's the leg that's going to be a little more trouble. I'm sure a doctor can handle it."

Mae works while Ruth cast a sober on me. Been a good couple hour since I guzzled that Canadian booze. And I's a little more accustomed the dope Tat give me. Ain't bragging.

"Was thinkin'," I say. "I know a feller might have the wherewithal, locate a surgeon, maybe outside the system. Don't much care for his smartass way, but you know what they say. Beggars don't choose shit."

"I know someone," Finch say. "I mean, I know *of* someone. I was going to get in touch with him about what I want to do in Salt Lake City, about the rest of the girls up there. He'd know a doctor, maybe."

"What girls?" Mae say.

"Oh, his daddy runs a traffic operation," I say. "Tat was one his kids up from Mexico. Tat shot him. I shot his wife and son. Both in the head. And once I mend, we's all three gonna go up and shoot his other brother, so the girls can escape back home to Mexico."

Finch look at Tat. Tat look away.

"Oh," Mae say.

Ruth come out Mae's bedroom with a red nylon first aid kit. Unzip it as she walk.

Mae say, "I met a man, Baer. A few nights ago. He's pretty connected. People who can get things done without being official about it. I could call him."

"Good. Somebody call somebody, and if none of your people step up, my feller's name is Nat Cinder. He'll be across the street for breakfast in the morning.

"I know Nat!" Mae say. "I mean, we went out a couple times. That's who I was thinking of."

"You know Nat Cinder?" says Finch. "*The* Nat Cinder?"

"Whoa, hold on," says me. "You date him?"

"We had a drink. He said he met you. How'd that happen?"

"Hitch hikin'. Bought me breakfast. Fucked me on a gold coin."

Mae roll her eyes. "Should've asked me. Just a sec." She pull out a cellular telephone. Press a couple places. "Hi, yeah ... I was thinking of you too. Hey listen, I can't really talk. You know Baer—my dad—we talked about? Yeah? Well, he needs a doctor, but we can't exactly go to the hospital ... He stepped on a punji stick. You will? Oh that's so sweet. Okay. Bye."

KNOCK ON THE DOOR. My head already pointed that way, so it's no trouble seeing Mae open it. Nat Cinder enter with a pudgy Jerry Garcia-long hair frizz guy truck in after him. He carry a black bag like the ole timey doctor took payment in chicken and rhubarb.

"Baer."

"Nat."

We nod like shaking hands. Nat look at Mae and she look at me.

"You pokin' her?"

"Dad!"

"Baer!"

"What you say?"

"Just pickin'. Hell. I hope y' are. Check out this punji hole in my leg, doc. That little blackhair agin the wall shoved a plastic tube inside and fill it with Lysol. How 'bout that?"

Doc Jerry puts out his chin, frowns. Tilts head left and right like he's weighing earrings. "Might have saved your life."

Nat say, "For the record, Mae and I've had a couple beers and conversations. And I'm old fashioned enough, I'd have a word with you if my intentions got serious enough to warrant you sticking your nose in them."

"Well I figger a man that gets me over the barrel on a gold coin deserve a little ribbin', and with these punji-type injuries, I'm sure doc here'll say, I's good as done fer. So in a sense, wouldn't be right, I didn't give you shit when I had the chance."

Cinder come over and swings a hand, holds it till I slap mine in it. Grab hard. He say, "You got a good girl. You shouldn't say shit like that."

Jest what I need. Philosophy from a rapscallion think like me. "Aright, dammit. I know. I know. Mae, shit. Fuck. All right?"

"Apology accepted. I'll poke any damn body I want anyway."

Nat snort and Mae smile and Doc Jerry look back and forth and grin like he party the humor, and no one looking but me, Doc unloads his weight on his knees, set the black bag on the floor and open it.

"Here."

He put a thermometer in my mouth. Take my calf in his hands.

Shift the thermometer to the corner my mouth. "See how the Lysol been drippin' out all night?"

He lift the pantleg. "I need to cut this away."

"Hep yerself."

He pull a Leatherman tool from his hip. "Stop talking. I need a good read on that thermometer."

"Oh, sure. Yessir. Doc—you mind me askin? What kinda—"

"Veterinarian."

"Ah. Good."

He open the blade and work it agin the cloth, all the way 'round.

"Yeah, that was good thinking on her part. Of course, Lysol is a pesticide, in terms of its effectiveness. But only mildly toxic to mammals. I suspect you'll feel sick when—I take it you're on some kind of pain medication right now?"

Tat say, "Fentanyl."

"That explains why you're not on the floor crying in pain. Are you breathing okay?"

"Hell. Suppose."

Doc pull the thermometer out my mouth. Look at it. "You have a mild fever. That's normal. I'm going to leave this thermometer with you. Call me if the temperature goes to 101." He look at Mae. Ruth. "Got it?"

They got it.

Doc Jerry pull away the pantleg and press calf meat. "That hurt?"

"Not particular."

"Ah, wow. Almost all the way through. Did you realize that the stake almost came out the top?"

"Sure did. Held it up agin the hole, after."

He nod. "Well, there's a considerable amount of heat around the wound, but that's likely from the size. The redness doesn't radiate far, and the seepage is mostly clear. I doubt much of it at this point is Lysol. Were it a darker color, more greenish or brown, combined with a decaying smell, we'd have a serious problem. But as things stand, I think a heavy round of cephalexin — I brought you a couple days' worth—ought to hold you over until my lab tech can work up a culture and see what we have that kills whatever bacteria are causing your infection."

I nod 'cause I don't know what else make better sense.

"So," Ruth say, "He's not going to die or anything? That's what you're saying?"

"No, I don't think so. It'll take a few days of close supervision, but we ought to be able to eliminate the infection. I'll take a sample, and be off. I'll come back tomorrow and see how the cephalexin is doing. You should notice an improvement every day. If you feel lethargic, uh, that means tired, you might—"

"I know lethargic. Is all."

"Oh, well. If you feel it, that's a cause of concern. I'll want to know about it."

"Fair 'nough. What I owe ya?"

He shake his head. "Nothing. No payment, in any way. Last thing I need is word to get out, make people think I practice medicine on people. No sir, this is just friendly advice. Given, I might add, on account of my friendship with the next governor of the great state of Arizona."

I shake his hand.

Cinder shake his hand.

Doc Jerry look at his watch. Gimme a business card, got a horse on it. Mae come take it.

"I'll check in on you in about sixteen hours. It's the earliest I can make it."

Doc leave and Nat step out with him. Keep the door open while he mumble. Come back inside, alone.

"So," Nat Cinder say. "You're Finch Graves."

Finch look up from the floor.

Cinder step closer. "What the hell are you doing here?"

"I—Tat and I—brought Baer here."

"I know something about your family operation. I suspect the girl here, what's your name, miss?"

"Tathiana."

"I guess Tathiana knows something about you as well. So tell me what I don't know."

Finch talk like a double-pussed cow cutting bladder on a rock.

"I started informing to the FBI on my father and brothers almost two years ago. They kept wanting more information. I've been providing recordings of conversations. When I finally discovered what they're really about—the killing —I told my FBI contact, and she tried to take me to my father's. She'd been working for him the whole time. I guess they let me live because they knew they'd find out as soon as I put everything together, about what they were doing. Anyhow, when I was just in Salt Lake City, they tried to kill me, and I had to escape. It's because I saw all the video evidence. All the pedophiles and murderers."

"Wait," Cinder say. "Murderers?"

"They're selling the privilege of killing their prostitutes for a hundred grand a piece. So if I'd have let her take me to my father's place, I'd have wound up dead. She's in the trunk of her Impala, back at Dad's house."

Cinder nodded. "Dead?"

"Uh-huh."

Cinder shake his head. "Mae, Miss Ruth? I hope you can appreciate this, but I need to have the room with Baer, Finch, and Tathiana. You understand? We're going to talk about things. Or we can leave if you prefer."

"No, I'll go check on the kids. Ruth. Let's go check on the kids."

They leave. Cinder look around the room, listen a few second.

"I've been through a round of this before. You said video of pedophiles and murders. When a criminal knows his shit, he gets evidence on the enforcer. It's the only way a crook stays free, in the long run. They can't evade the law, so they have to own it. The only way to do that is to own the enforcer. That leaves us with two options. First scenario, we forget about everything. Go our separate ways, and hope God forgives our part. The second, take down the evil, ourselves. There's no one else'll do it. Not with video being held on them."

"Less take them assholes down," says I.

Nat look at me. "You ain't doing shit but healing."

"We'll take them down," Finch say. "I was on my way to kill my father when I found Tathiana and Baer had already done it. Next is Wayman. I know how to get in, where he keeps what we need. I say we take him down."

"Tathiana?" Nat say.

She nod.

"Atta girl," I say. "Toughest I ever see. You want that one."

"All right," Nat Cinder say. "Let's figure this shit out."

CHAPTER 41

I t felt good to get it all off his chest. Maybe that's why Catholic people confessed. He'd carried the guilt for years, participating in unspeakable evil, knowing what he was doing, not doing enough to end it.

Not doing *anything* to end it.

Because while he informed on his family to the law, nothing happened.

He'd been trying to buy absolution at the cheapest price. By confessing his sins to the FBI, he'd sought to remove not just responsibility for his actions, but for being the solution. As Cinder had told him, you can't turn over a problem to an agency that is part of it.

Deferring your morality to someone else has the same consequence as having no morality at all, and no one gets a free ride. No one gets to hang out beyond the fray.

You uphold the standard or you destroy it. Zero sum.

Providing the details to Nat Cinder, Tathiana, and the ever-charming Baer Creighton, felt better than mere confession. Finch didn't give the weepy, woe-is-me routine, and no one offered pardon. Instead he took a place in the group that would hammer out justice and save the remaining girls.

Almost as a formality, they'd talked about turning over the details of the operation to the Salt Lake City police, instead of further trusting the FBI. But with Wayman bragging about owning the law, they doubted he would have overlooked the local cops.

The locals would be trustworthy enough to go in and rescue the girls, but then what? One corrupt badge with everything to lose disappears the video evidence that puts away dozens, maybe hundreds of pedophiles and killers.

No, Cinder had said. They needed to control the evidence. Saving the girls was nice, no offense Tat, but our first mission is to secure the evidence. After that, we save the girls. Then we distribute the evidence all at once to a hundred news organizations, and provide each with a list of the others. That way, instead of delaying while they call their money masters, they rush to publish. Raw capitalism would force the press to do its job.

They'd formulated their plan based off everything Finch told them about the layout of the building and the location of Wayman's office. Cinder had volunteered to bring the needed resources to complete the mission. They'd meet at eight, have breakfast, and hit the road to Salt Lake City.

The last part of the plan, according to Cinder, was deniability. There were two unfortunate things about living in a corrupt society. First, justice was rarely served. Second, the people who went about securing it on their own were considered the bigger threat, not because they used violence as a tool, but because they upended the police cartel's power.

Long story short, Cinder said, "We do this, according to them, we're the bad guys. And since I don't want to die just yet, we can't leave any finger prints on any of this."

With that, Baer— still drugged and drunk, but with glee that showed his true calling—related his part in the execution of Cephus and Finch's mother, Caroline. He'd left no evidence he could think of that would tie him to either act of justice.

Tathiana had killed Luke, and with fierce eyes, she'd displayed the weapon to Cinder. Baer explained the firearm had belonged to Caroline.

"Okay, that works," Cinder said. "Cops look for the path of least resistance. This'll be murder suicide." Cinder took the gun from Tat. "I'll give you one tomorrow you'll like better and can keep forever."

Cinder turned to Finch. "You said you choked the agent with the handcuffs on your wrist. That means your DNA is all over them. Where are they?"

Finch pulled the handcuffs from his pocket.

"Ideally, we'd clean the DNA from the cuffs and leave the chain alone. That way they have the murder weapon and can blame it on Luke. But any of your DNA at all, they'll match it to you, whether they have a sample of yours, or not. They'll know you're family, and that'll compel you to give a sample. So those cuffs have to disappear. I'd soak them in battery acid and bury them in the woods. You want me to do it, or you?"

Finch tossed him the cuffs.

"Any loose ends?"

"My car," Finch said. "It's at my father's place. I took it there the morning we found Cephus, and with everything that happened, never went back to get it. I drove Tat and Baer here in Mom's Escalade."

"Okay. The Escalade probably has Baer's DNA all over it. We don't have time to give it a good cleaning. Take it back to your father's place, dump a can of gas inside, leave the windows open, and light it. Remember, we're leaving the FBI agent there in her trunk, so there'll be plenty of confusion for them. A burned-out vehicle ... their skinny little minds'll be working overtime to figure out why Luke Graves shot his wife, killed the agent, then half a day later, set his wife's vehicle on fire, and killed himself. So long as no other evidence is in the mix to make them look outside that scenario, it's as good as solved."

"You want me to do that?"

"Yes, I want you to do that."

"Okay."

"Last thing," Cinder said. "Baer, you're out. You know that, right?"

Baer looked wistful. Sighed. Shook his head, frowned. Then smiled. "They's plenty other evil people. Shit. Fer later."

They adjourned, everyone to meet in the same room the next morning.

Finch drove the Escalade to his father's. The garage door was still open, his Mustang parked where he left it. As he'd been instructed, Finch found a can of fuel in the garage, emptied it all over the upholstery, most where Baer had sat, and lit it.

He drove home at one, opened the sunroof, cranked the heat, and put one hand into the opening above, like toes in cold water.

He was on the right path. He knew it. He may never be right with God on the whole affair, but he damn sure wasn't lining up with the devil.

Finch pulled into the lot at his apartment, exited the car, and closed the door. The sound echoed off building bricks. When the silence returned, Finch leaned against the Mustang, listening.

He felt peace.

He climbed the stairs and unlocked the door.

CHAPTER 42

W ayman's cell phone buzzed. He put up his finger. Asger and the new guy Louie quieted.

"Hey, Nick, hang on minute. I'm finishing a conversation."

Wayman pressed the face of the phone to his leg and looked at Asger. "You vouch for him?"

"I know him."

"Yeah, well, you knew Tommy too, and he ended up shot by his own gun. Ten times. And now I have to handle it."

"Louie's a good guy. We worked together before. Tommy—he wasn't my guy. Your friend Dane introduced him and I said I'd take a look, but he wasn't my guy."

Wayman closed his eyes. "Show him his post."

Asger and Louie exited the office. The nightclub thudded. Was quieted again with the closing of the doors.

"Nick?"

"Wayman, Nick Carpenter."

Wayman glanced at his watch. 1:00 a.m. "Hello, Nick. What's wrong?"

Carpenter had retired from the Phoenix police department years back and fulfilled a lifelong dream by moving out of the furnace to the cool high plain of Williams, Arizona. He bought a place a lot nicer than a retired cop ought to be able to afford and, from time to time, worked with Wayman's father handling local issues where a retired cop's connections could smooth things over. That graduated into occasional wet jobs, simple busting kneecaps kind of work.

Except, in the meat business, it usually involved fingers and band saws. From there, the sky was the limit. Carpenter liked the tax-free income because it didn't trigger more of his Social Security being taxed. Amen, brother. Nick Carpenter fit the Graves mindset just fine and, in the space of a decade, became a reliable freelance help for anything Luke Graves needed.

In addition, he was trustworthy because he had everything to lose if his part-time job ever became news.

Nick Carpenter said, "I'm standing at your daddy's place. I got the shittiest news you'll get in this life. Someone hit him, Wayman. This place is a war zone. Got the burned-out SUV on the turnaround. Your father's face down in front of the garage, shot, and son, I went inside to look for help, and they got your mother too. One shot in the head. And worse. She's cut up something ugly."

"You say they?"

"We got a little snow. There's three sets of footprints."

"Okay. I'm coming down. Don't call it in. Right?"

"Uh, you might want to think on that. I can turn around and leave, and make like I was never here. I haven't touched anything but a doorknob. But whoever did this gets a bigger lead each hour I don't get someone in here. You want them to find out who did it, don't you?"

"Yes, but what I don't want is a bunch of cops going through my dad's house, you understand? I don't know what he left in the open."

"Your daddy didn't operate that way. He covered his tracks."

"Don't talk like that on the phone."

"All right. Are you flying down? Want me to get you at the airport?"

"How much snow did you get?"

"Inch, two."

"You sure?"

"I'm standing in it. Doesn't come to my toe."

"Okay. I'm going to use the grass strip. I'll be there in four hours or so. Meet me there."

Wayman ended the call.

He lifted his office phone, hit #2.

"Asger. I'm flying to Williams. It's going to be a few days. Emergency. Need anything, go to the burners."

Wayman hated communicating business-critical information over any sort of technology. His father had preferred coded communication, but Wayman figured even codes can be broken. Better if they didn't know there was a conversation at all. He and Asger each kept a burner phone charged and ready.

Wayman searched a number on his cell phone.

"Peter, sorry to call at this hour. Wayman Graves. Yeah. I just got some bad news. Family emergency. I need to come in on your strip in about four hours. West? Okay. I got Nick Carpenter going to pick me up .... Okay, thank you, I will."

WAYMAN LEARNED to fly because while he was in high school, Tom Cruise convinced him being a Navy fighter pilot was the coolest thing a young man could aspire to.

His father had redirected his thinking. If he was going to die for a country that viewed him as a serf without rights and worth nothing but the confiscatory taxes he would pay, he should do it as a Marine, where at least he'd line up every morning with the best, and if he survived, emerge with skills that might be useful in the dystopian world he would inherit.

By the time high school ended, the family had taken its first steps toward surviving the coming race war apocalypse, and Luke had shared some ideas on how the family might both help instigate the conflict and profit from it, so when the inevitable came, they'd have the resources to defend themselves.

In pursuit of that plan, Wayman joined a different group of uniformed men for a three-year tour behind bars.

He came out still wanting to fly airplanes, but more along the lines of running guns or drugs. Whatever his father needed. A year after his release from prison, he took lessons. The FAA granted his license.

He didn't fly as much as he thought he would, but the exhilaration was the same every time the engine pushed him into the seat and his stomach floated on takeoff. His first plane, he paid cash for a Cessna 172. Today he owned a Piper Malibu Mirage, a 1.5-million-dollar delight financed through the bank. His father had shaken his head at the extravagance of it, but grinned like a fool when Wayman said he'd financed it, and then threw his own words back at him. *Why pay with real money today when the whole shithouse'll go up in flames before you'd ever pay off the note?*

Lot of wisdom in that man.

His father was dead.

Wayman rolled the thought over. Adjusted the headset cushions around his ears.

Off the port side, Flagstaff twinkled below. He was minutes from seeing what happened to his family and figuring out what he would do about it.

Someone had cut up his mother? What did that mean? He should have pressed Nick for details.

What about the Graves assets?

Part of the justification for the airplane was that when the shit hit the fan for the last time, he'd haul ass home and join his father, mother and Cephus in the shelter. His father had built it as a family home, foreseeing the day they'd declare a kingdom over the surrounding lands.

But in the back of his mind, Wayman always wondered. Shit was bad out there. This new jackass president was trying to turn the country socialist in the space of a year. Still, average folks didn't pay attention, and much as he agreed with his father about the deplorable situation with American politics, he also thought they were a pretty clever bunch, on whole. The people they kept disenfranchising were relatively small in number. The people who'd have to rise up were kept sedated on reality television, opiates, and welfare. Wayman never said it to his father, but he doubted the country would fall as fast as Luke seemed to hope. And meanwhile, there was a lot of good living to have. A lot of money to make.

With Cephus dead and Finch just a matter of time, Luke's house would become Wayman's house. He'd inherit the underground shelter. The meat business. His life was about to change in ways he knew he couldn't yet grasp.

He'd need to appoint Asger to run the Salt Lake City operation. No one would have Wayman's eye for the business, so Wayman would have to learn how to delegate from a distance.

Maybe insulation was good.

If he moved back to Williams and ran the meat company, he'd be sitting pretty.

Like Luke had been.

Wayman shook his head. He'd always known his position was more precarious than his father's. Even sensed it was by design. But with his father dead and the son needing to learn in a hurry, he saw the cold efficiency of it. In placing Wayman in Salt Lake City and limiting their communication, Luke had set his son up to take the fall for the whole operation. Wayman had said to Nick Carpenter he wanted to check the house and make sure nothing could blow back on him, but he now saw that was a useless worry. His father wouldn't have anything about their Salt Lake City business at the house, or anywhere at all.

The man had been cold.

It was inspiring.

The last he'd spoken with his father, Wayman was with Claudia, in the video room with Amy. Luke had called and said there was a man standing in front of the garage. A grizzled man, bald head, leg solid blood. Wearing a camouflage outfit and a leather-holstered pistol at his side. Luke had said it was probably the man who killed Cephus.

Hours later he learned his father was dead.

Wayman kept coming back to the same disbelief. Luke was bigger than any threat. Smarter—and more committed to being careful—than any adversary.

His father couldn't be dead.

It couldn't be true. But it was and Wayman knew it. A lightning bolt had hit Luke. Some rare accident no man, no matter how diligent, could avoid. It showed the precariousness of life, and the importance of making it worthwhile. Of extracting every joy, every satisfaction, from the surrounding environment.

Wayman saw the landing strip. Drank the last of his coffee.

His father was dead.

Others would be soon.

PETER CORSON STOOD with Nick Carpenter at the end of the grass strip. They all called it the grass strip, but it was an inside joke. The private runway had begun as grass, but with dollars earned from hauling marijuana northward, had quickly been covered in asphalt.

"You want to put it inside? Good chance we got more snow coming," Corson said.

"Yeah."

They used a tow bar and backed the plane into the hangar. Wayman grabbed the small duffel he'd packed.

"Nick told me about your family, Wayman. I'm real sorry. If any of my resources can be of help, holler at me. Country's gone to shit."

Wayman slapped Corson's shoulder. No one knew the man's worth, but Luke always figured it was a couple zeros past the Graves's combined wealth.

"I appreciate the offer. I might need help locating a man. I'll let you know."

"Well, I know you got the business up north, and now all this on your plate. Plus your daddy's concern too. Come and go on the grass strip whenever you need."

Wayman followed Carpenter to his Buick. Threw his duffel in the back seat. As Carpenter drove down the lane, Wayman looked at his watch. "I want to make a stop. Go to Flag."

Carpenter nodded.

Wayman opened his bag. Withdrew a .380 revolver.

Carpenter was silent.

After a few minutes, Wayman said, "Left up here."

As dawn broke, they arrived. Wayman directed each turn and finally, they parked.

"I'll be fifteen or twenty. Maybe go get us a couple coffees. Something to eat. Anything but McDonalds."

Wayman got out of the car and headed across the street, through an alley. He pulled the sweatshirt hood from below his jacket over his head. Emerged on the other side of the block and ducked into an apartment building. He kept his eyes on the building walls. Two years before, when their FBI contact Lou Rivers first made them aware Finch was snitching, Wayman had scouted a route to his brother's apartment with no video surveillance. Luke had said to hold off. Give it time. They'd know his every move. Maybe he'd wise up. See the light.

If Wayman would have listened to his father the night before in Salt Lake City, this errand with Finch would have already been taken care of. Minutes after dropping Finch off at the motel, he'd gotten a phone call from his father. *"No way. He's had two years. I put it to him straight and he as good as told me to fuck myself. It's over."* So Wayman sent Tony to handle it.

Now, it was up to Wayman to do. It was better this way.

He climbed the steps with careful quiet footfalls, drawing his weapon from his jacket as he entered the hallway. He pulled his hood lower on his face. Looked downward in case anyone joined him in the hall.

He stood at Finch's door—the man who'd tried to turn in his father and brothers to the FBI.

Knock?

Wayman lashed out with his boot. The door crashed inward. He followed. Looked left. Right. Straight through to the bedroom. He kicked in that door as well, and Finch stood on his bed in his boxers, cagey like a linebacker ready to leap whatever direction the game said jump.

"We knew two years ago."

Wayman fired, saw death blossom on Finch's chest.

Finch fell to the bed.

Wayman approached, fired one more into his brother's forehead, and left.

CHAPTER 43

Nick Carpenter turned onto the Graves's lane. Wayman braced himself. He'd imagined his mother as Carpenter described, the darkening of her face as death laid irreversible claim and decay ascended. The meat missing from her thigh, like someone had wanted to make a statement about the butcher business.

It wasn't right, in a sense he couldn't quite place, that a woman could die at all.

His eyes burned with the need for sleep. Wayman drank from the large coffee Carpenter had grabbed while Wayman visited Finch.

"I'll hang back and give you a minute to check things out if you like."

"Good."

"What the hell? You see that?"

A dog was beside what Wayman assumed was his father's corpse.

"What is that? Coyote?"

"Nah. Hell. That's a dog."

"And that's my dad, there?"

"That's him."

Wayman lifted his revolver from the floor where it had been since he rejoined Carpenter. He powered down the window.

"Don't shoot toward the house," Nick said. "You don't want your bullet holes in the house when the investigation starts."

Wayman's phone buzzed. It was the one in his left pocket. His regular phone, not the burner.

He answered. "Yeah."

"Wayman?"

"Yeah."

"This is Emerson. Something you need to know now."

It was one of his FBI contacts in Salt Lake City. "You sure you want to say it on the phone?"

"It's okay. We don't have your cell tapped. Just the office."

"Great to hear. What's up?"

"Just learned a little bit ago one of our agents has found her way into your organization."

"Yeah? Who?"

"Her name's Maggie. I don't know what name she gave you. But she's unmistakable. Tall, probably the prettiest woman you've seen in your life. You know who that could be?"

Wayman felt a punch to the gut. "Yeah. I know. She's FBI? No shit?"

"Hey, I called as soon as I found out."

Wayman ended the call.

Carpenter stopped the car.

The dog was pissing on his father.

Wayman pulled the door handle and climbed out, partly slipping on the snow. He hadn't slept since the night before. He'd worked all night, then learned his family was murdered. Piloted his craft to Flagstaff, murdered his brother. He needed more caffeine. A line of coke. Something. He rubbed the pistol to his forehead, grinding the grit-rubber grip into his skin. He stooped and scooped snow powder in his hand, pressed it to his eyes while thinking about Claudia's lies about her childhood, how she was raped, how she hated who he hated.

How she'd played him.

The dog looked up and put its hind leg down.

Wayman pointed the pistol. Squeezed one off. The blast numbed his ears. The bullet flaked a log behind the dog. The recoil affirmed and provoked his rage. The dog bolted, and Wayman followed around the garage.

He fired again.

The dog yelped and fell. Then bounded away.

Wayman trotted. Finding the spot where the dog's prints became a body roll, he saw bright red blood. It incited his lust. Woman betray him? She could have been the mother of his children.

Focus.

He stomped after the dog. The blood drops increased in frequency and size. It'd been a good hit. He'd find the dog cowering somewhere and maybe, just maybe, filling the animal with holes would alleviate his fury.

Wayman's lungs burned. He hurried after the tracks, circling behind the house and beginning up the hill.

The blood sign lessened. The dog's tracks expanded—he ran uphill and only every five yards or so left a red spot.

Wayman slowed, grabbed a birch tree for support. His lungs were on fire from the cold air and exertion. He looked uphill for the dog and, not seeing it, twisted downhill. He swung out his left leg and dropped it...

Something was wrong.

His foot travelled beyond ground level another six inches, but Wayman's body weight had already shifted forward. He buckled at the knee to prevent the footplate from making contact, but failed.

He'd walked into one of Luke's or Cephus's mantraps. A memory flashed— his father and brother farting around the shop one Christmas, making landmines.

The plate below Wayman's foot connected with another positioned several inches below it. They were separated by springs on each side, and in the middle of each, on top and bottom, copper connected with copper. An electric circuit completed, connecting an electric charge from a battery to an electric fuse, which in turn was housed in a canister of homemade black powder.

Wayman followed through on his attempt to lift his leg, resulting in him rolling to his left and jerking his leg away from the trap.

He heard a fizz, a sound like a burp of steam, and nothing. He lay on his side a moment, aware an explosive was only a few feet away. He saw the bright morning sky and was stunned by the turn of events. He was alive. He had his leg. He was alive.

Wayman laughed, full throat, to the sky.

ACROSS THE LEAVES galloped a pit bull, twice shot in the last three days, once a lover of men, but now a hater, face drawn in snarling rage and brain spastic in fury. The dog flew the last ten feet downhill and landed with its teeth on Wayman's neck. In a single clasp and jerk, Wayman's throat collapsed. With the second, the dog pulled it free.

It stepped away a few feet and watched Wayman kick and spew blood onto the snow. Then licked the wound on its hind leg, where Wayman's bullet had creased it.

CHAPTER 44

Nat Cinder knocked on Mae's door, a sense of unease riding high in his abdomen. He'd slept five hours, woke early, prepped gear, rented a van, swiped a pair of license plates, then bought a bag of burritos and a gallon of coffee for the drive.

He didn't relish the task at hand. Finch seemed vested in manifesting good out of the evil he'd helped create, but worthy motives didn't always translate to noble outcomes. It might have been the dreadlocks, Cinder didn't know. Maybe there was just something jarring about working with a person who'd been on the wrong side for so long, and suddenly wanted on the right.

Finch seemed like a man who valued his life so little, he'd trade it for even a fleeting sense of absolution.

The door opened.

"Mae."

She stepped back from him, a wary wrinkle to her brow. She was barefoot and wore flannel pajamas.

At the table, in the same chair she sat in the night before, Tathiana ate fried eggs and bacon. She'd cleaned up into a completely different person. She wore clothes that didn't fit her—Mae's most likely—but her hair was brushed and her face clean. She looked up from her plate, and Cinder felt the heaviness of her judgment.

Just as, he imagined, she now felt his.

Baer Creighton snored on the sofa.

"Man needs a bath. And check that leg. Make sure none of that smell is coming from the wound. It's trouble if it is."

"I checked first thing this morning," Mae said. "He just needs a bath."

"You want to open a window or something. Tathiana's trying to eat."

"Ha ha."

"Where's Finch?"

"Not here."

Cinder had looked at the van's clock before leaving it. Finch was late.

"Tathiana, you ready to go?"

She placed her fork on the plate. Stood.

"Why don't you use the bathroom. We have a long drive."

Her eyes narrowed.

"Okay, would you go to the bathroom so I can talk to Mae without you hearing it?"

Tat stepped around the table and entered the bathroom. Closed the door.

Cinder took Mae's hands. "When this is all done, if those videos exist like Finch says, there's no telling the amount of heat we're about to bring down on a lot of people. People with a lot of power. That means no matter how anonymous I set things up, eventually it comes back to me. So if you're in it for a shot at the governor's mansion—"

Mae giggled.

"—you might oughtta put that out your head."

"You'd trade the governor's job for saving those girls in Salt Lake City?"

"No, I'm doing both. But I just wanted to give you advance warning. There's gonna be shit follows this. I don't think either of us has ever seen what damage a hundred billionaires can do."

Mae pulled him down by the shoulders and kissed him.

"You built that buried house for a reason."

"Atta girl."

Cinder looked at the bathroom door. Tat's eye watched from the gap. "You hear all that? Come on out."

Tat joined them.

"Okay," Cinder said. "If Finch shows, tell him we left on time and he can try to catch us if he wants. We're in a blue Chevy van with a plate that starts A3J. Got it?"

Mae nodded.

He kissed her again.

On the steps to the entry, Tathiana said, "How will we know where to go?"

"We'll figure it out."

"What if—"

Cinder stopped and Tat stumbled into him. He stood her back up.

"Tat. Here's the answer. We'll knock down enough walls. All your life, that's the only strategy you'll ever need. Detailed plans always fall to shit. So knock down walls."

TAT PUT the seat back and slept most of the way to Salt Lake City. The drive took nine hours with rest stops. Cinder drove into the city, then figured it made sense to lay low until night. He took Lincoln Highway east and passed Mountain Dell Reservoir, passed the golf course, and stopped at a turnaround beside Little Dell Reservoir. The temperature was falling, and dusk was upon them.

She'd learned during her short life that other people say and do what they want, and rarely considered her welfare. Had she not acted violently on her own behalf, she could have been raped or murdered multiple times, just in the last two years.

Her mousy size belied her seventeen years. She had lived with her younger sister Corazon, fourteen, since her parents were murdered by a cartel. Her father had been a police captain. Her mother, a nurse. She had lived well, but her parents had never led her to believe the world was anything other than corrupt and violent.

After two years on their own, traveling through cities and jungles, Tathiana understood. People were no better than the wild they pretended to abhor. Animals that would cause her harm were rare and easy to avoid. But human predators were everywhere, and their harm was of a different magnitude. They'd force you to do things. Steal your possessions. Steal your freedom. Some would kill you, given opportunity.

She and her sister had survived in Mexico by the generosity of the churches, old women, dumpsters, and by their wiles. They eschewed human contact, but especially avoided men, and more especially young men. However, they found that even men who were very old were susceptible to finding homeless girls irresistible.

While aware her safety often depended on invisibility, Tathiana at the same time developed a teenager's rage-fueled recklessness. After killing a priest with a pair of steel scissors in a town outside Puebla City, she began trusting herself more around population centers. She carried the scissors with her afterward, held to her hip with a looped cord she'd tied through holes cut into her waistband. She and Corazon ate often and avoided most trouble, until waking one night surrounded by men who tied her and her sister and threw them onto a truck. Then they ate rarely, were drugged and sleepy, and within two days were in Sierra Vista, Arizona, and the next day, were transferred to a different truck, and hauled farther north. Tathiana took the pills they forced her to take on the first day, learned from her mistake, and faked swallowing them afterward. When the boy Francisco received the key from the blond dread-locked man, and escaped without freeing anyone else, and was subsequently shot, Tathiana's rage gave way to rebellious desperation. If she was going to be a captive, she would not be a compliant one. Regardless of the consequences.

Only after the man emptied the truck of all the girls save her did she realize she'd left her younger sister alone amid the wolves.

She'd seen something different in the gruff man who saved her from being murdered that night. He behaved much like her father. Mostly silent, always wary, but with her father she'd grown to understand—especially in thinking about him after his death—that although he distrusted people because he was a police officer and saw their perpetual, artesian spring of stupidity and evil, he served them in the police because he loved them.

Tathiana sensed in the wildman who saved her something similar. Or maybe she wanted to see it. Her instinct for years had been to trust no man, and but for the freezing cold, she would not have violated that. But the temperature drove her to his fire, and the man proved unlike any she'd been near since her father. He'd not been familiar with her. He brooded and took offense easier than a highbrow woman, but his actions proclaimed him to be her protector, not owner or suitor.

So she came back for him when he bled.

This new man, the one called Nat, drew water from the same well as the other, though he seemed less protective. Maybe because he was partly respectful, but mostly, it seemed, he was uninterested.

It was a relief—and allowed her to make her own plans regarding the fates of the people who held her sister.

Now her biggest fear was arriving too late and learning her sister had already been murdered.

"I'M GOING TO SLEEP," Nat said. "Don't talk so damn much, all right?"

Tat broke her steel look and smiled.

"I shouldn't have brought you along. Just so you know. But you have a right. When people do shit to you, that confers rights of retribution. I'm going to write a book on it someday. Goodnight."

Nat leaned back the seat and closed his eyes.

"What is our plan?"

"The restaurant is open until ten. We go in at nine."

"That's it?"

"Like I said. We knock down walls."

CHAPTER 45

They slept in the front seats with the back of the van to the reservoir.

Nat Cinder woke to Tathiana's soft snores, instantly cognizant of his surroundings and the mission at hand. Almost as if he hadn't slept, but only relaxed four hours, while his mind probed the plan for weaknesses.

The night before, when they outlined the broad parameters of the rescue, Finch had drawn a map of the floors, the hallways and rooms he knew. The hallway through the inner building, behind the restaurant and nightclub, was secured by locked doors. On the nightclub side they were also guarded.

Although Wayman hadn't told Finch his process for escorting pedophiles and murderers to the upper floors, Finch had described to Nat what he had observed over the years. Cinder, with what he already knew of human trafficking, surmised Wayman's likely process.

Men would either first meet with Wayman in his office or, if they were long established, would be taken through the double doors leading to the storage room, which in turn led to the ground floor hallway and elevators. If it were merely a brothel, Nat figured that wouldn't be the case. The girl named Amy would be reliable enough to handle the business. Not so with running a pedo operation. It was a different order of risk for all involved. No client would trust a late-teen madam, and no owner would trust a client he hadn't looked in the eye.

That was magnified a hundredfold for customers wanting the killing floor. Cinder figured they'd be escorted up the steps, across the balcony, and to Wayman's office. You wouldn't run a business transferring so much risk onto your own shoulders without a display of power and thorough understanding with your client of the rules at play. Not if you wanted to stay in business more than a day.

Finch had worries about how to pick the locks to get through unseen. Nat told him to see the big picture, and the little details would sort themselves out.

Nat straightened his seat. Stepped out of the vehicle and dropped a golden braid on the driver side rear tire. The thought struck him it was what a dog would do, and he wondered if a dog would also risk its life, fortune and freedom on a rescue mission such as this.

Probably more often than a man would.

The other door opened and Nat finished before Tat could come around the back. In a moment he heard her urine on the pavement.

He liked her. She communicated something in her silence, in her focus. Maybe in translating her manner he added his own purposed fury to the mix, embellishing hers. Either way, she came across as the most no-bullshit teen he'd ever seen.

Her splatter ended, and she came around the front of the van. He saw her silhouetted against the flat, black reservoir, a bare starlight glow to her brown skin and black hair.

"I brought you a couple things. C'mere."

He moved to the rear and opened the van doors. Dragged a black nylon bag and unzipped it. She stood beside him.

"I guessed your size. Climb up in the van and put on these clothes."

Tat unrolled the outfit. Black camouflage pants. Black t-shirt. Black nylon insulated jacket. Cargo pockets everywhere. Keeping her eyes on Nat, she shed her coat. Tossed it inside the van. She dropped her pants and pulled off her top. Nat closed his eyes and turned around. Heard clothing sounds.

"Now I look like you," Tat said.

Judging by the fit of the clothes, he'd guessed right on the size.

Nat gave her a black nylon belt from the bag and she threaded it through her pants loops.

"Okay, you got the clothes. Here's what you've been waiting for."

Nat withdrew a Glock 19, a compact 9-millimeter in a black Alien concealed-carry holster. He demonstrated on his waist how to attach the holster so the Glock was instantly grabbable, but rode without discomfort on the inside of his pants waist.

Tat affixed the holster clip to her belt.

"That's the easiest gun in the world. Just point and shoot. Pull it out."

Tat grasped the gun and pulled. It was stuck.

"Hold on. The holster is fitted to the gun so it won't fall out. You have to give it a solid pull."

Tat jerked the gun clean.

"Okay, good. Now point over there at the water. Hang on good. Squeeze the trigger."

The gun blasted orange.

Tat snorted. It sounded like a surprised laugh. She fired five more rapid shots into the black nothing.

"Nice. You got a sense for the trigger pull. How's it fit the hand?"

"Very good. I like this."

"It's yours forever. Let me show you one more thing. Always keep it pointed at the ground, or away from people unless you want them dead." He stood beside her. "Hold it in your right hand, open. Okay, see this? Press it."

She depressed the magazine release. It dropped into Nat's hand.

"First off, remember when you take the magazine out, you still have a bullet in the chamber." He waved the magazine. "This holds fifteen. You need to reload it."

He opened a box of ammo and showed how to press one into the magazine. Then gave it to her. "You have to press pretty hard. See if you can get it."

She did. Then filled it.

"Okay. One last piece of advice. Don't use that gun unless you know you have to. Don't pull it unless you have to. Let me do the heavy work, all right?"

"No."

"What?"

"I'm here to kill people."

"Well—shit. I know that. I mean, only kill the people who need it. That's all."

"Okay."

Nat stood at the back of the van and added a second holster to his hip, this one on the left side.

"What is that?" Tat said.

"Just a gun."

Her eyes wouldn't leave it.

Nat Cinder nodded. "It's as wonderful as it looks."

NAT DROVE into the city and parked in the alley behind the Butcher Shop restaurant, next to a dumpster.

He'd considered wearing a mask, but decided against, because no one

231

staring at a badge and gun would remember a face, and he planned to carry the building's video evidence with him when he left.

Nat tried the door. Locked. He pounded on it with the base of his gloved fist. Repeated. The door opened. A man with tattoos up his neck opened the door. He was already turning away when Nat pulled the door the rest of the way open. The man must have thought someone from the kitchen had locked himself out running trash to the dumpster.

"Excuse me," Nat said. "Take me to your boss." He opened his jacket, displaying a fake badge hanging by a chain from his neck, and a nylon shoulder holster almost braying with implied threat.

The man looked from Nat's face to Tat's and hesitated.

"Friend," Nat said. "This is a tactical emergency. Take me to your boss, now."

The man froze.

Wayman's operation was tight. Probably prepared for something like this. Nat trusted God to favor the bold. He strode through the kitchen toward the dining area, looking for someone with obvious authority, and spotted a gray-haired man in a suit, leaning down as he spoke to the couple seated at a table.

Nat waved to him. The man straightened with a jolt. Regaining his composure, he excused himself from the table.

Nat stepped around the wall hiding the kitchen. Tat followed. The suited man joined them.

"Who are you? What is this?"

Nat showed his badge. Pointed to the double doors on the other side, near an area set up for butchering animals. "Unlock those."

"I cannot. And I didn't see your badge. Or get your name and who you represent."

Nat pulled his Glock. "I'm going through those doors. Either you open them, or I find a cleaver back there to hack off your head, so I can get your keys no fuss no muss. Right?"

The man's eyes shifted toward the kitchen.

Tat drew her Glock and lowered her stance. Keeping the pistol pointed low, she covered the area for threats.

Nat smiled inside.

"I don't have keys. No one goes back there from this side. We just can't do it."

Nat had already considered the possibility he would have to use force at the first barrier. Although more violence would likely ensue, Wayman and his bodyguards were unlikely to call law enforcement to deal with their security problems. So as long as Nat kept moving, and kept surprising his adversaries, he kept the advantage.

"Let's go."

Inside the kitchen, he searched and quickly found what he wanted: a giant freezer on wheels. He moved forward with purpose. Kitchen staff saw their weapons and put up their hands and backed away. "Keep doing what you're doing, Tat."

Nat rolled the ten-foot horizontal freezer away from its wall and with all his strength, pushed it to the double doors.

It bounced away with a thud.

Nat pulled back the freezer. Turned it so its back corner would make first contact with the center of the double doors. As he pushed, the suited man joined him. The freezer bounced again, but the doors emitted a cracking sound and the gap between them expanded.

"The lock secures into the concrete below. Once it's broken, we may be able to open the doors inward." The man waved at a waiter. "Joe, come here. Help."

Nat wondered if the suited man had suspected the other business going on in the same building, and now sensed his last chance to get on the right side of things.

Together, all three men rammed the freezer forward; the doors broke from their hinges. One hung like a severed limb connected by a flap of skin.

Cinder said, "If you know what's going on upstairs, you know why we're here. Keep the commotion down here to a minimum. And if you hear gunfire, feel free to evacuate."

The suited man stepped away.

Nat jumped onto the stainless-steel freezer, sliding across the top, and Tat followed.

They hurried down the hall. Following Nat's hand signal, Tat stopped at the elevator. Nat ran past. At the end of the hall he pulled his Sig Sauer P220 Elite .45 and from inside his jacket pocket, a Dead Air Armament Ghost 45 suppressor and a vial of water. He dumped the water into the suppressor, then threaded it on the pistol.

"Stay where you are."

He stood at a bare angle to the industrial steel doors, aimed at the lock above the handle, and fired. The bullet smacking into the metal was louder than his firing it. Blowback irritated his eyes. He always forgot shooting glasses. Squinting, he fired twice more. Pistol at his side, he kicked the door open.

Nat waved Tat forward. She joined him. "We advance one door at a time. I'm going to the next. You guard the rear. Understand?"

She nodded and assumed his space inside the door. She held her Glock groundward but ready.

Nat climbed the steps. At the second floor, he repeated the procedure. The sound echoed in the concrete block stairwell, but he was unconcerned. They were on the opposite side of the building from the dance club, and the priority was to secure the video evidence of the murderers and pedophiles from Wayman's office. They were close to their first target. Freeing the girls upstairs came next.

The second doors open, Nat peered into the hall. It led straight to a set of glass doors, and beyond, a balcony with dancing women. According to Finch, Wayman's office was at the end of the hall on the left, right before the glass doors. Another set of glass doors led to his office, and a final set allowed him direct access to the balcony.

Depending on his mood, any of the doors may or may not be open during club operating hours.

Nat presumed Wayman sat inside his office watching the club, working on his computer or whatever shithead evil assholes do at work. He also expected to see his bodyguard, the blond named Asger.

No one stood guard outside the office.

Maybe Asger was inside with Wayman discussing something. Or maybe taking a leak somewhere.

"I'm going upstairs," Tat said, behind him.

"No, you're guarding the rear."

"My sister is up there."

"We'll get them next. First, we need the evidence in that office. Do as you're told."

"I'm going up."

"No."

"I'm not leaving her."

"We do things in the right order. We need the evidence first because if we get it, this whole place is shut down forever, and the bad guys go to jail."

"I'm going for my sister. If your plan doesn't work, she is still captive."

Nat closed his eyes, exhaled long. Could he just smack the insubordinate shit?

Tat ran up the steps.

"Stop! Don't shoot in the door with your gun!"

Nat ran after her. Caught up once she'd stopped at the next level up, at the third floor.

"Wait, stop. Just a minute. A lot of girls are probably on the next floor, working. And if there are any on the top floor, that's where we need to start. So I'll open the door on the fourth floor. You go in and get any of the girls there. I'll run up the fifth floor and clear it. Then whichever of us gets to the third floor first, goes in. Got it?"

"Okay."

They climbed to the fourth floor. Nat shot it twice and tried the handle. It opened.

"Wait for me to get up there."

He climbed to the fifth floor, where Finch said they killed girls. Shot open the door, replaced his magazine with a fresh one.

"All right Tat, let's go."

He entered the hallway. The floor was darker than the others. Silent. He tried the handle on the first door he found, and it was locked.

He heard a gun blast from the floor below.

Tat.

Shit.

Nat shot the first door's lock. Pushed it open. Empty.

The next.

The next, and all the rest.

Another shot from below. Then another.

Tat was shooting open doors?

He finished clearing the floor. There was no one being murdered on the fifth tonight.

Just on the fourth, by Tat.

CHAPTER 46

Tathiana pushed open the door and strode into the hall, her Glock pointed straight ahead.

She moved down the hall mindful of what Finch had said. There was a Latina who used the name Amy, who served the slave keepers as their whoremaster. Because each room was locked, this woman was vital to finding her sister. She held a physical key.

No one was in the hallway. She expected that to change. Tat holstered her pistol.

A door at the far end opened and a girl came out. Long black hair. She carried herself with authority.

"Amy?"

The woman hesitated.

"Amy, help," Tat said. She looked to the door beside her, as if something behind it was wrong.

Amy approached slowly. "Who are you?"

Tat drew her Glock and closed the distance between them. Amy put her hands to her head. Tat pressed the barrel to her forehead.

"Where are the keys?"

"One key. My neck chain."

"Take it off."

Amy used one hand to find the key under her shirt and pulled the chain over her head.

Tat took it.

"This opens each door?"

"Yes."

"Don't move."

Keeping her Glock on Amy, Tat tested the key on the door beside her. It opened. Tat placed the barrel to Amy's forehead.

"Where is Corazon?"

Amy looked away.

"Where is Corazon!"

Amy pointed down the hallway.

Tat grabbed her neck and lifted. Amy stood. Tat jabbed the Glock into her back, jolting Amy forward. She poked her hard twice more until they stood at the door. Keeping the gun on Amy, Tat opened it and motioned Amy inside.

A girl—maybe her sister—was bent over the edge of the bed. A hairy man was on top of her. He looked sideways at them and stopped moving; his mouth fell. His eyes darted.

Tat prodded Amy again. "Over there. Beside him. You, get up. Stand by the wall."

He pulled himself from the girl and covered himself with his hands.

The girl on the bed lifted her head and looked at Tat.

"Corazon!"

Her sister looked back at her, barely aware.

Tat blinked away the water in her eyes. "Get up. Stand over here with me." Corazon stumbled. Caught herself. Turned.

She was still drugged, and Tat noticed something.

Blood, down the back of her leg.

Tat pointed at the man's hands, covering the instrument of his evil. She fired. The man leaped and screamed. Waved his hands. Lunged for the bed and brought his knees to his chest.

Tat shifted the Glock to Amy. Placed her ugly stare above the three sight post dots and squeezed the trigger.

Amy's head popped backward. She dropped.

The man whimpered. Tat stepped to the bed. Kicked Amy's head out of the way of her foot, and placed the Glock to the man's anus.

"No!"

She fired.

Tat faced her sister. "Use the bathroom. Get this man off you. I will be back for you."

She ran to the end of the hall and opened the first door. A man was on top of a girl. She stepped inside. "Get off her."

The man went to his knees, then straightened. He was white. Gray hair disheveled in oily tangles. His belly was huge. Legs and arms skinny. She raised the Glock and fired at his head. The man collapsed. The girl stared wide eyed.

In Spanish Tat said, "Put on your clothes and wait for me here. We are taking you to safety."

Tat left the room and opened the next.

Empty.

The next. A man sat on the bed. A girl knelt before him.

Tat pointed. Fired. The man fell back to the bed into his own red spatter.

"Put on your clothes. Stay here. We are all leaving today."

At the next room, a man held the girl in front of him, as a shield. Tat approached. He backed away until he met the wall. She walked forward until the gun was so close to the man's eye she could not possibly miss. The man released the girl. He said, "Please ..."

"Okay."

Tat fired and felt blood spatter on her face.

She left it.

"Put on your clothes ..."

She went to the following room. It was empty. Then she killed two more men. From the floor above, she heard Nat's gun blast. At last, she came to the final room. Inside were a man and a bent-over boy. The man hadn't heard the gunfire or had not cared. Tat shot him in the chest. She waved the gun indicating for the boy to stand.

She held the pistol on him.

What would he become? One of them?

A scream rose in her chest, adrenaline-fury seeking outlet, stoked further by her hesitation.

Tat wavered.

At last she said, "Put on your clothes. Follow me."

She gathered the girls and led them to the stairwell. Her sister barely seemed aware of her rescue. Of anything at all. Tat blinked away more tears, and when that didn't work, snarled. There was work to be done.

One floor down, she ran into Nat.

He raised his eyebrows at the girl standing behind her shoulder. "Your sister?"

"Yes."

"Good. This is where the rest are."

"Why hasn't anyone come for us?"

"Did you shoot Amy?"

"Yes."

"Then there's no one here to tell them. You're two floors above, and there's a nightclub right next to the office. They probably didn't hear anything."

Tat nodded.

"Can you get the other girls? I want to go after the evidence."

"Okay."

"If you get back to the stairwell before I do, take everyone out to the van and wait."

CHAPTER 47

Tat's insubordination turned out helpful. The girls would all be secured before Nat confronted Wayman and his crew.

Nat expected the situation to get dicey. The business had profits in the millions, and since the product was murder, it made sense the owner would be willing to quickly cross the line. Plus, he had bodyguards. Nat watched for the blond Asger, but also the crew of mafioso-looking bouncers that doubled as enforcers. Wayman might call in any of them for support. A smart man would not leave a multimillion dollar business exposed to a single foreseeable risk. Nat assumed Wayman was smart. He had to have thought through the possibility of a gang or mob hit, just to grab some of the nightly cash.

Nat almost wished Tat was there to back him up. At least she didn't hesitate.

Using his silenced Sig Sauer P220 Elite .45, Nat shot holes through the lock. He swapped magazines and entered the hallway.

Empty.

Ahead thirty yards were the glass doors. Beyond them danced half naked women, unaware of the gunfire and chaos behind the mirrored glass. To the left, still unseen, would be the office doors.

What if Wayman was not inside the office?

What if he was inside, and the door was locked?

Nat had something for that strapped to his hip.

He stood next to the left wall and approached with speed. He stopped before arriving at the office and looked inside from an angle. The light was on.

Motion reflected off the double glass doors leading to the balcony. Nat tried to figure the angles, to guess where the person stood inside the room.

He saw a blond head move quickly and realized his reflection must also be visible inside the office. Nat swung around the corner and fired into the glass. The bullet zinged but the glass held.

Behind the glass stood Asger, the blond lieutenant. His narrow eyes glinted with nightclub light and rhythm, and he drew a gun from his hip and pointed. Nat recognized the distinct shape. Asger carried a Glock.

But would it penetrate the glass?

They faced each other.

Asger nodded his head, as if he and Nat had come to terms. He raised his pistol arm, and took a bead on Nat's head.

Asger fired. The glass percussed. The bullet fragmented under the first layer of plexi and shattered into a starburst pattern, captured in place between layers.

Nat placed his silenced Sig on the floor and stepped fully into view of Asger. He pulled a cannon from his left hip, a Smith & Wesson 500, and placed the barrel's half inch hole against the glass.

Asger's eyes bulged. He put up his hands.

"No!"

He scrambled around a desk and fell to his knees before the glass and twisted the lock.

Nat pushed open the door. It bounced against Asger's head. He scrambled back, hands up.

"Where's Wayman?"

"He said he had to take care of an emergency at home. He left last night."

"Where's he keep the video?"

"What video?"

Nat swung the .500, pointed at Asger's head.

"It's on the computer. And the backups."

"What backups?"

Asger pointed to a desk drawer. "Wayman backed up every video on micro SD cards. They're in a black book."

"Unplug it all, and get me the book."

Asger moved to the computer. Unplugged cables. He looked up.

"No!"

Nat turned.

Tat stood at the door with her Glock aimed at Asger.

"Tat, don't!"

"You have the computer."

She fired. Asger's head snapped back and he fell. On the floor, his body jerked but his eyes went blank.

"Fucking dammit!"

"He saw your face. You can't be governor if he saw your face."

"Shit." Nat holstered his cannon, found the black book with the SD cards, and grabbed the computer. "Where are the girls?"

"Where is Wayman?"

"Already back at Flagstaff. I guess you can hunt him down there. So where are the girls?"

"Hallway, waiting."

"I told you to take them out."

"I didn't."

"And I didn't figure you would. Get the door for me. And watch front and back while I carry this."

It was unlikely they'd face any new threats. Wayman's bouncers and body-guards worked on the dance floor, and likely wouldn't learn of Nat's operation until someone came looking for the boss. That could be hours.

"Let's go," Nat said.

Tat led the way.

CHAPTER 48

They argued as soon as Nat fired the van's engine. He'd already put the plan in motion—already had queued a contact he knew from his work fighting human trafficking, to be ready to take over once the girls were rescued.

"I'm taking the girls to someone who will get them to the Mexican embassy."

"No."

"Pull your gun. I don't give a rat's ass. This is going down my way."

"No. I don't trust them. Men in business. Men in government. Men in church. It doesn't matter."

Nat allowed himself to cool down. Missed the turn and kept going straight. He'd circle back. It wasn't Tat's fault she'd been dealt her set of life circumstances. Any decent person owed her a little grace. But it was her fault how she chose to be a constant insubordinate prima donna snit, and that needed a resolute correction.

Eleven girls and one boy? crammed into the back of the van. He didn't have the capacity to care for them in Arizona, and even if he did, he couldn't keep them. Soon they'd have the same status as any other illegal.

A shelter didn't have the clout, but the Mexican government, through the embassy in Salt Lake City, would advocate for the girls' rights in a powerful way. Even if it became a political game between two nations, the girls would be better off than if he allowed them to disappear into the United States with no one to look after them.

Last, neither Nat nor Tat could allow themselves to be connected to the girls' rescue. There were too many corpses for that.

"I'll grant you've come through some shitty situations," Nat said. "And you don't trust anyone."

"You don't know—"

"Shut up. Don't interrupt me. You're young and all you've seen is the ugly. It's big and real. I don't deny it. But if you live your whole life thinking it's you against the world, and everyone else is rotten, then you're already the asshole to someone else, and *you're always going to be the asshole to someone else.* I risked my life for you and your girls. So stop being the asshole."

Nat glanced at her, partly to read her expression, partly to make sure she hadn't pulled her new Glock on him.

"Okay," she whispered. Her eyes glistened.

"Okay," he said.

"But not my sister. I will never lose my sister again. And I know where to stay for the winter in Flagstaff. And then we return to Mexico ourselves."

Nat waited. Thought. Nodded. "Okay. I'll help."

He turned the van and resumed driving to the parking garage he'd designated with his contact, a female attorney working at the Utah Domestic Violence Coalition he could trust to keep his identity secret, and take responsibility for getting the girls to permanent safety.

CHAPTER 49

G ordon Emerson placed his service Glock 22 on the kitchen table. He
pressed the release and slid out the magazine, then ejected the round
from the chamber.

He stood it on the table, a few inches from a laptop computer that was
booting up.

Next to the Glock he placed his credential case, a black wallet holding his
FBI identification card and badge.

He stared at it.

As a boy he watched Elliot Ness on television.

When he graduated with a law degree, he saw his buddies get recruited to
law firms, Fortune 500 companies, and their local governments to work as
prosecutors or public defenders. He loved the law, the idea that even as evil
preferred to fight in the dark, good dragged it into a sunlit arena with polished
marble and walnut. He loved that each side followed rules encoded by the very
people who agreed to live by them. And he believed if it wasn't for the good
guys standing up to darkness, there'd just be evil.

With that view he understood the quality of justice always came down to
the quality of the team wearing its colors.

He'd wanted to play first string. Prosecutors were indispensable, but the
lawyers on the front lines—the ones carrying badges and guns—were truly in
the battle.

Gordon Emerson joined the FBI.

His eyes on the FBI identification card, the shield, he sighed and was surprised by the rattle in his throat, like an old chest cold that wouldn't break up.

After so long, at war with himself ... the end was a relief.

He'd visited the nightclub shortly after it went into business. The Butcher Shop. When it opened, it was *the place*. He wasn't a drinker. Didn't go to bars or especially nightclubs, but when everybody talks about the same joint, eventually you want to check it out. He'd stopped in with some friends and when they wanted to leave, he didn't.

A girl had connected eyes with him a few times. She was small and dark. Latina.

Coy.

Her body moved with the music, and he couldn't resist imagining her moving that body on top of him, keeping that same pelvic rhythm, that same intensity that kept pressing out her pubic triangle against her red silk dress, each time she thrust forward her hips. She'd seen him watching her, and now she danced for him. It was like watching a spinning ballerina; each time around, she snapped her head straight to him, and they shared strobe-like flashes of connection. All while her thrusting hips allowed him to read her outline through her dress.

He tried drinking up the gumption to talk to her, but each time he convinced himself to go to her, he couldn't imagine what the interchange would come to. He was older. She was younger. He had a gut. She was flawless. He'd say something to her, and she'd freak out. Scorn him. Or some unseen man would come up and claim her.

Gordon drank more that night than any occasion since his undergraduate days. He drank like he had no mission in life. No tomorrow worth his clear best.

He thought about it afterward, how seeing the girl in the red dress redirected his mission from law and order to lust.

Since law school, Gordon had dated, but never married. He tried to connect with women, but never made a connection deeper than dinner, a movie, and a fish-lipped goodnight kiss.

He dropped his leg from his James Dean wallflower pose and walked to her. She took his hands and he bounced to the beat, drunk-awkward, drunk-not-caring. She spun and he pulled her, she backed and he followed, she pressed her body to his and he felt the sheerness, the places she was firm, the others where she was soft. She retreated but held his hand. Led him past a short haired Nordic looking man standing with arms crossed by a pair of doors. She opened the one on the left. They were in a storage room. Again, more doors. Now they were in a hallway.

"Your name?"

"Amy."

"You are beautiful Amy."

Keeping his hand in hers, she led down a hall to an elevator. The doors closed on them and she dropped to her knees before him, opened her mouth wide like to consume a tennis ball, and pressed her lips to his pants. She blew steamy breath, heating his organ. He dropped his hands to his zipper but the chime rang and the door opened.

Amy pulled him by a belt loop.

The hallway light was better on this floor. Exotic paintings. Brass fixtures. She wore no underwear. No lines. In a moment she opened a door to a room. He sat on the bed. She crawled across it, shedding her dress like a snake slides out of its skin, until she was over him, on all fours. She planted her mouth on him and he tasted her.

When he felt a second set of hands on him, a second mouth, he froze.

It was dangerous... a second woman coming from nowhere, maybe already hidden in the room. Something fired in his brain, a warning. But the girls' mouths were persistent and he'd never been with two. He felt along the back of one. Then the front of the other. Sampled four breasts. He shook and moaned and quivered until his head ached from the blood pressure and stress.

When it was over she smiled at him, and the other girl disappeared before he could see her face.

Amy walked him to the elevator, then to the ground floor, and left him at the double door with the Nordic man, who smiled and said, "Good night, Gordon."

And Gordon Emerson knew one day, he would have to make the impossible decision.

A few days later, a packet of photos arrived at his home. He didn't need to open them, but did. Didn't need to read the letter, but read it anyway.

The girls were thirteen and seventeen years old.

After that, when Wayman Graves wanted information, the decision always came down to the same question. Was he ready to die? Because otherwise, there was no way out. Only the constant deferral, one day to the next.

Gordon always gave Wayman what he wanted.

Gordon opened a browser window on his laptop and went to a news aggregator. He clicked a link.

MASSIVE PEDO RING BUST: HUNDREDS OF VIDEOS.

It always came down to the same question.

Gordon Emerson picked up the S & W .40 bullet from the table, fed the Glock, then his mouth, then the wall.

CHAPTER 50

Maggie Sandberg—no longer dressed for her undercover role as Wayman Graves's lover Claudia—stood on the driveway taking in Luke Graves's log mansion. She thought of the countless girls the Graves family had transported.

Sold, murdered, and made to vanish.

She rubbed fists to her eyes. Tried to blink them alert. The week had passed in a flurry.

First, Gordon Emerson had been found in his house, suicide. His laptop remained opened to a breaking story that felt like old news by the time his body was discovered the morning after his death.

It was a canary in the coal mine event, foreshadowing a seismic aftermath.

Video evidence had arrived by electronic means to more than a hundred law enforcement and press organizations. While the former scrambled to verify the videos, the press began quickly disseminating snippets showing various men in stages of undress before consummating their attacks on blurred—but apparently underage—girls. From these videos made freely accessible on the Internet, many men were quickly identified. In the last twenty-four hours, two US congressmen had committed suicide.

Dozens of news organizations broke stories about a pedo and snuff business—on the upper floors of the Butcher Shop nightclub—being the location of a mass murder.

Gruesome details, such as human flesh being found in the kitchen and an entire floor designed with easily sanitized "kill rooms," had not yet leaked to the press. But they would, and the furor would only grow.

Already three billionaires had been arrested for murder. The FBI rumor mill said many more—maybe dozens—would follow.

Who knew there were dozens of billionaires? When did that happen?

Each subsequent day brought reports of the arrests of powerful men. Social media blazed with speculation about who would be next. On television, everyone was an expert.

Whoever had released the videos to the press had done a great disservice to justice, because the only way to take down big money was to investigate until the case was unassailable. Any man worth a billion dollars who was also a criminal—she'd like to see the overlap on a Venn diagram—also had an escape hatch ready. So while the press directed heat on him, all it did was warn him to leave the country.

The surviving girls who had been victims of the Graves trafficking organization stayed at the Mexican embassy. They had not met with media, but as a show of good will, the Mexican government had allowed them to meet with a joint investigative task force made up of officers from the Mexican Federal Ministerial Police and the FBI.

It was destined to become a political clusterfuck. Another gift of the assholes who'd shot up the Butcher Shop and freed the girls.

About the same time as Gordon Emerson's body was discovered, Maggie's colleagues in Flagstaff—dispatched to investigate Luke Graves after she reported having seen Wayman's operation first hand—reported back that Luke, his wife Caroline, and an FBI agent named Lou Rivers were all found murdered at the Graves's house. Later that day Maggie received an update: Wayman Graves was also among the dead, apparently in an unrelated attack by a wild dog in the woods near his father's home.

Right.

Hours later came another jolt.

A Smith & Wesson 629, in a .44 magnum, was found in the grass in front of the Graves house, near the garage.

Expedited ballistics had taken three days. Fingerprints, one.

The firearm belonged to the North Carolina man now subject to a nationwide manhunt for the murder of two FBI agents—now possibly a third, Lou Rivers—four police officers—and more than a dozen civilians.

What was the tie-in with the human traffickers in Arizona and Salt Lake City? The North Carolina suspect was reported to have been a hermit who never left his small town. How could he be connected to Arizona?

Maggie Sandberg had never seen the FBI quite so frenetic to catch a killer, and confused on how to do it.

Ahead of her stood the deputy director of operations. Beside him, the sheriff of Coconino County. They walked slowly, heads down, plotting what would be the biggest, most coordinated manhunt the wild west had ever seen.

Maggie also noticed a white surveillance van and, next to it, two men in FBI jackets kneeling by a boulder. They were preparing to capture video of the area in the coming days and possibly months. It would be unlikely for a crowd to gather at a place this remote, especially after the bodies had been removed and the news crews had gone. But because killers so often return to the scene of their crimes, FBI cameras would monitor the Graves house.

Maggie thought it unlikely to bear fruit. From what she'd read, Baer Creighton was a vendetta killer, not a sicko who needed violence to get off, and who would return to a crime scene to relive it.

They'd also place cameras near the highway that passed a few hundred yards from the Graves house, in case the killer only sought a glimpse. They'd capture every face that passed and transmit it to a supercomputer in Virginia. Using facial recognition software developed in coordination with the NSA, they'd screen for not just Baer Creighton, but every other face on their list.

When an operation has a hysteria factor this high, you do everything with even a remote chance of working. You overwhelm the odds. Play the lottery a hundred billion times, you win.

Maggie learned that morning she would receive the FBI Shield of Bravery for her undercover part of the Graves investigation.

She wondered.

Was the FBI inserting a pretty face into the news cycle to deflect criticism they'd arrived late, after some vigilante solved the problem for them?

She didn't know how to feel about her commendation. She'd followed a hunch and through undercover investigation confirmed it was correct. Nothing more.

The whole thing had started when she agreed to meet some girlfriends to blow off steam at the Butcher Shop nightclub. By happenstance, she'd followed a portly gray-haired man of obvious wealth from his Mercedes to the entrance and, within minutes of arriving, noticed he was nowhere in the nightclub. Ever-curious about probably-unimportant things, she'd asked a man who'd made a pass at her to look in the restroom for her "date." The portly man wasn't there. She'd stepped outside, verified his car was still parked out front, and then she went into the Butcher Shop restaurant.

The man had disappeared.

She'd stood on the sidewalk, looking up and down the street, then skyward. Interesting ... Where was the entrance for the apartments on the fourth through sixth floors?

The next two days she observed six more well-dressed men entering the club and disappearing. Shortly after, from inside, she watched Wayman Graves meet a man on the balcony, and welcome him into his office.

When he emerged two hours later, it was through a pair of double doors on the dance floor level. There was always a bouncer near the doors.

She wanted closer to the action and scored when a guard looked her up and down and allowed her to dance with the girls on the upper balcony.

Then Wayman Graves approached her.

Thinking fast, she realized he probably was accustomed to having nearly any woman he wanted. She refused him, and within weeks he wanted to marry her.

For that, the FBI Shield of Bravery.

What she really wanted was something to take away the ache in her heart that came from knowing the Graves operation was only one in how many across the United States? A dozen? A hundred? More?

It was too early to make sense of anything. She needed facts. She needed a pile of evidence she could assemble into a picture. The involvement of the man wanted for murders across the country, Baer Creighton, seemed impossible. And yet his gun was on the property. More facts would explain it.

Maggie Sandberg released a deep breath that didn't relieve the tightness in her chest. She stepped toward the house. Because of the odd connection between the North Carolina murderer and the Graves operation, she'd been placed on the task force searching twenty-four hours a day with unrelenting focus on a single mandate.

Find Baer Creighton.

Okay. Let's find Baer Creighton.

CHAPTER 51

Doctor been good 'bout checking in each morning on the leg. He say today like to be his last for a handful; had a bout of summer weather come through but the storms is ready to push out the warm and leave six feet snow. Same thing every year, says the high school girl they got on the nightly news.

Leg better. Doc come back second day and put a rubber band up the hole. Puss drain constant. Doc says it'll do that a year two. No shit, says I. No shit, says he. All the dead meat up there got to drain out. But they's a good water seal, and take the antibiotic I be fine. Someday he'll take out the rubber band he stuck up there to hold the drain open, and maybe a few month later the hole 'll heal.

Pert near unbearable living with Mae.

Nat Cinder said ...

Give a man a powerful need for the spirit. Accourse ain't been able to walk fer shit and she won't get me a bottle, so it's nothin but screaming little Joseph, Morgan and Bree, and niggle naggle tongues'll waggle Ruth ...

I wonder what Nat would say.

Mae! Ease up on the bullshit!

One girl got the hormones clucking, the other got her old woman nurse polished up. "Here baby let me get that for you. Oh, by the way, I saw the strangest thing on television ..."

If I had Smith, I'd ask him one last kindness.

Whole time I been waiting the FBI to show up at the door. Left Smith at

Graves's place and they musta knowed it was mine that day. Had the news on every day since, and after I come off the pain drugs and could hear the women's voices instead of just looking at they boobs, turns out the whole world's looking Baer Creighton. Every time you part the curtain they's a man in a suit on the sidewalk. You know he's Fed 'cause local boys druther get dunked in a sewer than wear a suit.

So we sit here marveling we ain't been hauled off to jail. I's ready haul ass to Idaho, some shit, but noooo ...

I wonder what Nat Cinder thinks we should—

Ahhh, hell. Somebody shoot me. Somebody got a gun somewhere ...

Knock on the door.

Feeling spry this morning, like I could get out the hotel room and mebbe walk a mile if I was allowed. I check the peep hole. See black. Good enough.

"Feeling good Doc—"

It ain't Doc.

"Tat."

"Who is it?" Mae says from the other room.

"C'mon in. C'mon. How you been?"

I look in the hallway. Bring her in. Lock the door.

Tat clean up good. She don't look the vagrant wanderer like when she found me on the mountain.

She enters, stands stiff. Eyes search about like they never find what they seek. Her mouth is always flat and little come out it.

"Glad you come by. I never got to say my thanks. You coulda left me fer dead but didn't. I's grateful. 'Cept for now I live with these nags. Drive a man extreme."

She look like she ain't heard a word. Some folk don't know what to do with kindness, or gratitude.

She wear a black pistol holster on her hip—got a gun in it. Accourse in Arizona, you don't carry, people think you's touched.

"I found your dog."

"What?"

"Your dog. Stinky."

"Joe. Where?"

"Same place we were. He comes each night."

I been troubled on Joe. How I sniggered at him, he wished he was a bear. The hurtful things I said.

Living with women turned me to mush.

And now we got the snow set to come in and bury him. North Carolina dog, barely got enough fur to warm a house dog. I think on him snuggled in the sleeping bag, and how cold that ground get froze.

Time to fetch Stinky Joe.

I grab a jacket. A cane Ruth bought from the pawn. Holster and Judge.

"I want to go back fer Joe. How you get here?"

"I walked."

"Holy moly. Mae, I need them keys."

"What keys?"

"The car."

"Go ahead. You'll get caught, and all this shit'll come down on the rest of us. Right when things are starting to go good. You know Nat and me—he knows people who can make new identities for us. Change fingerprints, the whole deal. All we have to do is lay low a little while."

Find the keys in her purse.

"Lessgo."

Close the door. Hotel got a back exit, leads to the alley and parking lot off Main. Limp down the steps with the cane. Got the old man fedora, big ass plaid coat. Look civilized enough for Flagstaff. Fire the station wagon, blink a couple times to clear the eyes.

I think on Stinky Joe, that time he first found me in the cave where I was fittin' to slaughter men with poison, how he come up and woke me with dog slop kisses. And how I give him cheddar and eggs.

Make a man misty.

Tat climb in the front seat.

"Nat say you give him a helluva time up there, but you did real good."

I pull out the lot, slip on sunglasses resting in the cup holder. They's so many suits it appear God loosed a plague of yuppies. Ease down the street, no squealing tires, no failure to signal. Speed limit and all that.

Tat don't speak.

"Tat?"

She look at me.

"Got something on yer mind?"

"I didn't know about you. What you did before."

"You mean all the killin'?"

She nod.

"Well, suppose it's like all yer killin'. Somebody gotta do it, or it won't get done."

"Makes good sense."

"How long you figger to stay?"

"Here?"

"Uh-huh."

"Maybe."

Wait her out.

"Maybe a long time. I found something safe."

"Mmm. I had a cave. Couldn't wish a better hideout. Bad fellas come up, you got sixteen lanes of fire, all downhill. Get enough ammo in there, 'nough food, fuck 'em all. Fuckemall a good long time."

Tat don't speak, and I drive with just the wheels making noise.

"Do you get used to it?" Tat say.

"No. I ain't. But I ain't got a helluva lot of lead on ya. I did my first killin' a month ago, is all."

"I killed a priest. Last year."

I drive. Pass a camera, side the road. New way to catch speeders. Used to be, if you broke a law and no one saw it, it was like a bear shittin' in the woods and no one to hear it. Or a tree, the pope, something. Nowadays it ain't like that. They say you got to mind the law whether someone lookin' or not.

But they morals—that the kicker. Nobody got to mind a moral at all. Ever. You can't legislate the morals. So we can't fart without bustin' a law and they know, but lie like the devil, cheat yer neighbor—

I hit the brake.

"You see that? Fuckin' idiot. Didn't even look."

Nobody got to give a shit about nobody. Make a man want to live in a hole.

Take the exit I recall from last week when the whole funshow started.

"Every day or two people come back to the house," Tat say. "It's best to park here and walk."

I ease to the side. Got a good burst of dry weather and the dirt don't sink. Close the doors. Outside is quiet, save the eighteen-wheeler tires rollin' by.

Tat lead into the brush, follow a trail set by deer mebbe. I follow best I can, in no time barely touch cane to ground. Calf seeps with the work—feel it on the leg and I bet that sock about nasty—but the exercise is good and the lungs still fill deep with air, and with the sky turning gray and the simple wonderment of silence, I's so happy I could shit a diamond, and never civilize again.

And Stinky Joe out there.

We climb the hill and with elevation look down on all below. Head west, keep level, and if my right leg was three inch shorter that'd make it easy, on account the slope. Then Tat lead to a trail mebbe used for hauling logs and the going is easy.

"Oh shit."

Tat turn. See me look downhill.

One, two, six vehicles. Got the Coconino department Blazers, black sedans.

People jog back and forth, arms waving. They form a line and start forward, not like they's looking close, but like they wanna cover land fast.

"We's fucked."

"Hurry."

Tat trot ahead.

"I can't move like that."

"Hurry."

I hobble 'long.

"Hey, dammit! Where Stinky Joe? At least mebbe I see 'm 'fore they take me."

She disappear around a bend.

Cold on my nose. Snow. Mebbe she think to find a spruce with low branches, wait 'em out.

I follow 'round the bend and there she's stopped, eyes bold and smile on her face. If they saw us they can't now.

"Why you grinnin'?"

"You saved me. You saved my sister."

No sparks. No red. No juice or nothing.

She know it the end. This is where she's gonna leave me to fend fer myself. Pat my hip. Got the Judge.

"You go on. Got yer whole life ahead. And all that. We appreciate ya."

Snow fall like it come off the back a truck. In two second her hair is sparkled. Sound's muted. Air thick with it. Look out and hardly see a thing.

I nod, and she stand still as a planted post. Got the creepy feel, can't ken shit. Then like she decide something, she smile bigger. Turn around and face the rock behind her.

Dogs bark below, like a mile off, though it's a couple hundred yard at best. They got the hounds on us.

Tat put her hand on the rock.

It move.

She push.

Rock swing on a hinge.

Though I see, I don't believe. Look a fairy to fly out. But Tat say, "Come in, quick."

I follow. She push the rock back and it latch.

Swallow hard. Some kinda dungeon. Like mebbe they made it for World War Two ... 'cept the cement ain't old. They's a light down the way. Tat lead. I follow. She open a door, jog down some steps. Air get warmer and warmer.

Open into a room with sofas and chairs and smells like tacos. Big ass television on the wall, show the whole hillside below. The snow falling. Men running. Everywhere.

Light on in the other room. Another girl stand in the entry, wary.

I nod.

She dip.

"This is my sister," Tat say. "Corazon."

"Howdy."

"We have food," Corazon say.

Tat's brows is high and hopeful. Tears in the eyes. Chin puckered. "Thank you," she say.

I slap her arm.

"Shit."

Leg start to fuss and I want a seat so I take it. Sofa made out rubber, something. Firm. Lift a leg to the table and rest. Watch the television takes up half the wall, tuned to the hillside below.

Men below walk side by side, stumble and slip. See one already found hisself a punji pit. They's two others make a fireman's carry.

A blast of dirt and leaves pull the eye. Land mine.

A way off ... way off ... they's a mound snow look like a dog, look like a ghost. He bound off, mebbe got a place for the winter.

Stinky Joe, I hope you got a place to winter.

CHAPTER 52

S tinky Joe inhaled air sharp with cold. He saw the sky far off turn deep
silver and smelled the change in the air that meant snow.

It was time to leave.

He'd revisited this place daily since Stinky Baer disappeared in the
machine. He'd been bleeding, but not in the way of a dying creature. And
something had changed in his voice.

When Joe first found Baer in the cave they became fast friends. Baer's voice
was like cooing, and his hands scraped all over his back and belly, a divine
sensation impossible to reproduce on a tree.

But his voice had changed. His laughter found a new target.

Baer was injured and bleeding. The girl who'd caused him grief was back,
and when Baer passed out after shouting her away, Joe had followed,
untrusting her intent.

There was something wrong with her. She emitted coldness like a scent.
He crept up on her, and watched as she built a fire and cooked meat that Joe
recognized as forbidden. His heart recoiled at the smell.

She offered some to him and Joe recognized the scent as the woman in the
house. The girl spoke to him in a voice he distrusted, but the scent of roasted
meat confused him, and the girl had human authority. He allowed her to place
a thin green cord around his neck.

He watched her leave and waited for her to return. She never did, but she
left him the human meat, and when the fire died and night was fully upon

him, Joe ate the forbidden meat and, hearing coyotes, knew he must free himself of the green line. He chewed through it.

Although he explored the land for game and shelter, every day he returned to where he left his master bleeding in the snow. He smelled him near the dead man, and killed the other when he tried to wound him from afar.

Every day he looked for Baer, and at last saw him with the girl who tied him with the green string.

Joe watched a long while after they disappeared into the hill. Then he turned and bounded away.

THREE FOUR THINGS...

I hope you dug _Pretty Like an Ugly Girl_!

Next stop is widely regarded to be the most enjoyable of the Baer books so far. (The one you just completed is considered the most violent).

The first time I enjoyed reading I was in seventh grade. Somehow I discovered Jim Kjelgaard's _Big Red_. I read everything our library had by Jim, then I found Jack London's _Call of the Wild_ and _White Fang_.

It's fair to say after Jack London, I understood writing well to be the highest achievement possible to mortals, and the best subject: dogs.

I always wanted to write a dog-centered novel, and Stinky Joe's the perfect character. He's been through a few tight spots, but he's never proved his mettle.

Baer 4 also introduces Shirley Lyle, a character whose arc is worthy of a new genre: Chic Grit Lit. We'll revisit that after you're through with _Outlaw_.

A game dog is a dog that never quits, never gives up, toils to the end and whose example makes the human heart yearn for that kind of sincerity in all of life.

The Outlaw Stinky Joe is one dog's test. Whatever you think at the end, you'll have _no doubt_.

What's next in the Saga? Good question! The Short answer: The Outlaw Stinky Joe.

The Baer Creighton Universe currently includes six novels, with another on the way. Visit the series on Amazon here: Baer Creighton Series.

(https://www.amazon.com/gp/product/B07DYGBK6F)

Want a new ball cap?

T-shirt?

Sweatshirt?

Mug? Clock? Blanket? Pillow? Bath Mat? Shower Curtain?

Bikini?

Yeah, we got a Baer bikini and lots of other items at the Baer Creighton Shop. Always adding new products by reader demand, including t-shirts with some of Baer's snappiest lines...

If you don't see the shirt and phrase you want, use the form on the bottom of the front page to send in your suggestion and I'll build the item just for you.

Check out the Baer Creighton shop here: Baer Creighton Shop (https://claylindemuth.com) to see all the books and the best order to read them.

Do you have a moment to leave a review?

It is one of the most beneficial ways you can help an author. Please consider leaving a review on Amazon here:

https://www.amazon.com/review/create-review?asin=B07FR82VL5

Want to connect with other Baer fans and stay up to date on the series?

Help me pick covers, names for bad guys, etc? Get a couple free books? Access to beta-reader copies of new releases? Join my Facebook group, The Red Meat Lit Street Team:

Https://www.facebook.com/groups/855812391254215

ABOUT THE AUTHOR

Hello! I appreciate you reading my books—more than you can know. If you've read this far, you and I are fellow travelers. I suspect you sense something is not quite right with the world. It's not as good as it's supposed to be. We human beings aren't as good as our ideals. Yet, we prize and want to fight for them.

I do my absolute best to write stories that portray the human situation with brutal transparency, but also I strive to tell stories that are not as bleak as the human condition sometimes seems. There's no limit to the darkness. Light is rare. But it exists, and I hope when you complete one of my novels, you find your values validated.

I'm grateful you're out there. Thank you.

Remember, light wins in the end.

CPSIA information can be obtained
at www.ICGtesting.com
Printed in the USA
LVHW031926301220
675432LV00007B/717